The Militia Man's Lady

CW00616973

Copyright©Da

Digital publication February 2018.

Cover design by Rocking Covers.

Publisher, Dawn Bolton.

PUBLISHER'S NOTE.

The Militia Man's Lady.

Dreda's Men Book 2.

Chapter one

Denman, whistled to himself: Happy and relaxed he was riding to his sister's wedding. He was returning from a visit at his friend, Francis Dreda's villa. Dreda, recently married, was now Commander of the Taylian State Security Bureau, the secretive sister organisation to the state Militia.

The path climbed a high hill. From the top he could see his father's villa through the haze; it was set in a deep valley with vines and a river, giving it ample water for cattle grazing. He had always loved coming back to this peaceful haven, particularly after his energy had been dissipated in violent and destructive battles during his period in the Imperial Army. He was able to soothe his spirit which had been stirred by war and relax and rest.

He was about to carry on when he heard a cry and turned around. Urging his horse on, he galloped back down the track to where he saw a carriage. Some bandits were bludgeoning the groom with heavy sticks. One was climbing onto the roof of the carriage, rocking it and trying to climb through the window.

A gloved hand pushed the man away with a jewelled cane sword, slicing him in the gut, He howled and let go the window, sliding down the vehicle as he lost his grip, trying to stem the blood seeping from his wound. The hand belted him on the head rendering him dazed. Denman swiftly disposed of the others. One he sliced on his sword arm, leaving him useless to fight. The other he bashed in the mouth with his pistol, breaking his teeth. The fellow fell off his horse. The third scrambled for his friends and helped them get back on their horses with difficulty. Bleeding profusely, they made off as quickly as their steeds could carry them.

He pulled the groom up. The man had been hit hard on his head but looked fit and strong and would survive. He showed his badge with a bow and a smile.

'May I offer you my help Ma'am? I am Officer Denman Ma'am of the State Security Bureau.''

A pair of green-blue eyes assessed him cautiously. Calmly, not at all flustered, the young girl replied reluctantly, 'Thank you Officer. My name is Helena von Vagna and this is my maid. We are grateful for your kindness.' He bowed his head slightly. 'It is my duty Ma'am. I am paid to protect citizens of the state!'

'Where do you go to?'

'The next town.'

He went to inspect the carriage and found it was fit to use. 'I will help your groom into the carriage. I can guarantee your safety if you let me accompany you! It is on my way.' She nodded thanks in her quiet way.

He drove the carriage himself, his horse tied behind it. A first-rate whip, he made quick headway along the rutted track. He was amused. Although the girl was polite and grateful she clearly resented having to be rescued. Most women would have 'thrown themselves into his arms in gratitude', but she clearly hated being vulnerable. This girl was no milk and water miss.

The girl watched him warily. She seemed rather wary of his unusual English name. She asked herself, 'What was a man with such a name working for the Militia?' He did not have the olive complexion and dark hair of many native men of her state and was much taller than the average male she knew.

His eyes were brown with green flecks. He gave her direct looks, showing he liked what he saw. He was no dissembler or shyster. What you saw was what you got with him! His polished manner and fashionable and expensive clothes indicated he was a man of wealth and heralded from the top drawer, but he had worn his superfine wool jacket, lawn shirt and cravat with ease and gave himself no airs and graces. He had taken his jacket off and rolled his shirt sleeves up to lift the groom.

He was a well-made man; his shoulders and neck were thick and muscular, and his biceps bulged beneath his rolled-up sleeves. He had lifted the man with ease, his breathing steady, as if the man was a child. He was clearly as fit as a fiddle and in his prime; a man who enjoyed each day as it came, in his casual way.

He carried himself with a quiet assurance and his straight back and fine seat indicated he had spent time in the military service, possibly in the cavalry. She found him over-confident and the way he took over their guardianship irritating. It was as if he were used to taking control and leading from the front on all occasions; a natural leader and diplomat who charmed his way through life. A man whose charm hid an iron will, who was used to being obeyed, she suspected; accepting no arguments when someone dared to gainsay his words or actions.

Helena wanted no truck with smooth spoken charmers and domineering men. She had met too many of them in her short life. Her natural reserve and reticence with strangers made her hate having to accept his help but she knew it was a necessity. She gritted her teeth and tried to appear grateful although she would rather have driven the carriage herself.

Denman recognised her reluctance to accept his authority. 'The Militia officers in the next town and hotel will guarantee that I am bona fide Ma'am,' he reassured her. Having no other choice; not wanting to be left waiting as prey for other bandits, she had accepted his escort as a fait accompli, hoping her trust in him was justified and he was not a criminal himself.

He took a good look at her. She was tall with pale blond hair and good skin. Her eyes were her best feature, a clear green-blue like the sea. Her lashes were long and brown, and she had fine eyebrows. She was of slender build but with a good developed figure. All in all, if she didn't scowl she could be quite a beauty but she was clearly irritated, with the situation or with him; which he was not sure. He decided she was not a girl to cross or to be taken lightly. There was something about her; a defence and an icy reserve that made him think that despite her age she was mature beyond her years; not a girl to trifle with. What kind of woman would he find if he tried to melt that icy façade to reveal the real Helena von Vagna?

When the groom had recovered somewhat he sent him to the villa to warn them he would be late arriving and drove on to the nearest town. He found a very safe inn with staff who wouldn't cheat a young girl and booked them in.

'I would wait here Ma'am until your groom arrives before you go on ahead. It is not safe for ladies to travel unaccompanied.' Although clearly irritated by the delay the girl nodded. 'Thank you, Officer, I will do as you say and then we will go on to the next city tomorrow to complete my business.'

'Please wait until your groom comes back before you make more arrangements. He may not be ready to travel long distances for a few days.'

'Thank you, Officer. I must stay in this town as I have business to contract. I hope my groom will be well by the time I have to go to my next business appointment.'

She was totally self-assured although she could not be more than two and twenty. She still would not tell him her business, treating him with formal curtesy. Feeling redundant he made his way home.

He was greeted warmly by his mother and father and his extended family. His family were all like him, warm and open. Dreda had often spent his holidays and leave with them, enveloped in their love and warmth; a contrast to suffering the icy atmosphere in his unwelcoming home.

At the dining table Denman described the girl and her unnatural wariness. His father wrinkled his brow. 'I recognise the name from somewhere. A family scandal. Perhaps, that is why she mistrusts strangers.

'The father became sick and the brother took over the management of the farm, but he is a drunk and has let it go to rack and ruin and gambled a large part of the fortune away. Helena was engaged to a duke from a very noble family and he jilted her a month before the wedding. He was clearly interested in the family fortune and not her. Rumour says she is looking for a new rich suitor to save the family fortunes. Be careful, she might try to entrap you.'

'She was very independent and as cross as a cat at being delayed. I don't think she is a gold digger.'

Well he wasn't going to meet her again although her lack of interest in him had piqued his curiosity. Usually, once women had made his acquaintance they wanted to know his background and then competed for his attention. He was a flatterer, a ladies' man. Dreda had often sat in the background, more reserved while his gregarious friend had his arm around a wench.

Forgetting the girl, he concentrated on his lively family and thoroughly enjoyed the next two days. Food, wine and some good company were a relief after the political intrigue at the State Security Bureau, headquarters of the Militia and the tight secret division headed by his friend.

He set off two days later for the next town to do business for his father. Two days of heavy celebrating had left him feeling relaxed and hungover, but he needed to do something more energetic than sitting around. He reached the town and booked in at the inn. He was surprised to find the girl still there, this time arguing with the owners. She seemed to be getting her way as she nodded, satisfied and paid up.

She noticed him and nodded her head in acknowledgement but still made no effort to engage in any conversation with him. This was a unique situation for him. Most women threw themselves at him. He had been a prize on the matrimonial market for years but had avoided being leg-shackled, thoroughly enjoying his bachelor days.

The groom brought the carriage round and they also had an extra mule carrying lots of provisions. They had obviously come for goods they couldn't get in their village. There looked to be none of the fripperies; ribbons or lace which he expected when a lady went shopping. The goods were appropriate to solid hard farm work. The groom looked in poor health and the girl was offering him water. She looked serious, frowning and feeling his forehead as if to divine if he had a fever. He went over and thought he would ask if they needed help.

'Forgive me for interfering again Ma'am but your groom looks in poor shape. May I help in any way?' The girl again looked as if she resented his interference, but she thanked him.

'I am grateful for your concern Officer. We have had to stay a little longer than I expected as my groom has suffered a fever due to the attack on him.'

'He looks as if he needs a few days' rest.'

'We can't afford the time.'

'How far are you going?'

'One hundred leagues to the west. My family villa is just outside of the town of Kabletz.'

'You pass my family's villa. You can rest there the night and break the journey. If he is still not well, he can stay over, and I will drive you to your villa.'

'I am capable of driving the carriage myself. I am just wary of going without an outrider or groom given the problem with the bandits.' She hesitated, not wishing to be obligated to this man. He was too easy and charming. With a toss of her head she swallowed her pride and accepted his offer.

The landlord of the inn had verified who he was, although she was a bit perturbed to find he was a high-ranking militia officer. He seemed too relaxed and smooth to hold such an important and serious role. He in turn had asked the landlord a few things about her. She had struggled to find the money for the accommodation and had bargained the price down. He was surprised. She looked very well dressed, spoke in an educated way but he remembered the story about the scandal and the loss of the fortune.

The groom rested in the carriage and Denman drove it with the two animals by each side. The girl and her servant were invited to dinner and she slowly opened up to this kind family, but she was still aloof to Denman.

'Since my father fell ill I have managed our family farm and vineyard. My father let me help from when I was a child and taught me well.

'You have no brothers or sisters to help you?'

'One brother but he is unavailable,' she said quickly. They knew better than to ask any more details.

'I should have been back today to sort out the harvest.'

'I will take you tomorrow and your groom can follow when he is well.'

She agreed. He was used to taking the lead in situations. She was used to being her own mistress, so this didn't sit well with her.

They set off the next morning. His aim was to travel as far as possible even if it meant getting to the villa that evening. He had engaged in long and hard campaigns during a short career as a mercenary and fifty leagues were nothing to him. For the women, being jerked about on a rough track was unpleasant but they did not complain.

He sighed with relief when he saw the villa. Two women and one able bodied man could have been an easy target for bandits. He had noticed that the girl had a small pistol in her bag and wondered how good a shot she was. He suspected she would be very good.

The villa was designed in an old-fashioned way and old paintings and sculptures covered the corridors. The family had clearly been wealthy but had fallen on hard times. There was evidence of neglect, buildings not having been maintained for a few years. Helena showed him his room where he would stay the night and then went out to supervise the harvest.

Her mother greeted them warmly without her husband. 'I fear my husband is ill and will not recover Officer.'

He was invited to look around the farm and was surprised to find it organised and well managed. Helena was in old clothes, handkerchiefs around her neck and head helping collect the olives. She had grime on her nose but was still lovely.

He helped her lift a basket on to a cart and asked, 'Why are you doing this?' He could have bitten off his tongue when she replied, tossing her head with pride, 'There are no idle hands on this farm. Everyone works.' She picked up a basket. 'Please excuse me but I am busy.'

He was bored and so took off his jacket, tied a scarf over his head to prevent heat stroke and joined in. His clothes were dusty from the day before, so no harm was being done and he made short work of lifting the baskets on to the cart.

Later she brought him water and wine and some bread, cherries, cheese and ham. He patted the ground next to him where he shaded himself under a tree.

'Please sit down, Ma'am. You must be thirsty and hungry by now.' Hot and pestered she did so, for some reason trusting him. He had given her no reason to mistrust him and had only tried to help her.

'You seem to manage this farm as well as any man Ma'am. How long have you been managing it alone?'

'Three years Officer.'

'Your brother is here often?'

'Not at all! He has other pursuits to engage him.' It was as if a shutter had come down on her face making it impassive and expressionless. He tried to engage her in other conversation about herself, but she would give little away, so he talked about his family, the wedding and his job and life at court. When he was not trying to delve into her business she was happy to talk to him.

She could believe his was an ex-army officer by his bearing and ability to take control in emergencies. She felt he did not fit well into the role of a militia officer. He was clearly responsible and gallant by the way he had helped her but there was a lack of seriousness, a lightness and feeling that life was just one big joke to him which meant she could not take him seriously. He in turn thought she was too serious and needed more fun in her life.

'The wine will soon be harvested, Officer. It is a good harvest this year and I hope for a good price. We will reinvest the profits in new vines as this had not been done for a few years. We also hope to buy more cattle as we sold some a few years ago.' She sighed and then said, 'The farm is not prosperous yet, but it is improving.'

'Who taught you farm management?'

'I always helped my father. My brother was not interested. I was brought up to know when the vines needed replanting and the cattle taking to market. It came naturally to me to take over the management of the estate and I love it.'

'Didn't you want a season in the city?'

'I was to have one, but circumstances changed, and I stayed here instead with my family.' Her face shuttered again. She was a closed book. She did not invite any more questions.

She turned to him, wanting to stop his interrogation of her and to turn the tables on him. This man seemed too interested in her business. She was a private person, having found to her detriment in the past a loose tongue could lead to scandal being passed around about her. She rarely went to town or associated with people from 'polite society' preferring her own company and staying out of trouble.

She focused those clear green-blue eyes on him challenging him to explain himself. 'And yourself. Why did you leave the army?'

'I got as far as I could without having to be involved in the politics and court life of a senior officer. That would have bored me to death. My friend and I travelled Europe as mercenaries fighting Napoleon but we both wanted to have a more stable life, a change, so we joined the Militia. He is now Commander after the assassination of the former Emperor and I am third in command. I don't particularly want to go any farther in that organisation.' He did not elaborate any further. He clearly had itchy feet again but didn't know what he wanted.

She pondered over his answer. Her life was mapped out for her. She knew she was stuck here on the farm until she could turn its fortunes around. Her family and servants depended on her. She had accepted her fate but resented this lightweight coming in to her life and inferring that she had the choice to do other things.

She got up and started carting baskets again. *Thank God, this harvest is good.* Her brother's largest gambling debts had been paid off by selling some land and paintings and she could now start thinking about reinvesting in the future. The chances of a marriage were limited because of her lack of fortune and the scandal attached to the family name but it mattered not. She cared little for men.

They worked until dinner, but she entered the dining room in a smart dress and played the hostess with an elegance and charm he had not seen before in her. He could see her in a duke's household, managing the household to perfection. Her mother recounted stories about the old days when her father was healthy and made them laugh at the antics of the Emperor's household when they had come to visit.

The Emperor's grandmother had been a kleptomaniac and items of silver were likely to disappear with her. Another of the Emperor's aunts had always been in debt being an avid gambler on the horses and had spent months there and expected the best alcohol to be at her disposal. They always outstayed their welcome, but these stories showed how grand the von Vagna household had once been.

The groom did not arrive. Denman had a few days to spare and needed to work off the effects of hard living. He would stay two more days. Helena was not pleased but with his charm and sunny personality he won her mother over, so she agreed with bad grace. She felt she was being coerced again in a gentle but forceful way.

Helen regarded his figure when he was not looking; he was strong, muscular and appeared not to carry any spare flesh. He got up surprisingly early and she suggested he supervised the collecting of the olive baskets while she sorted the vineyard out. They would be separated which suited her. He was too nosy. He did his work in record time and she realised he was an asset and gave him more work to do. All day and the next day they worked in the baking sun until the harvest was brought in. She was truly grateful to him. She appreciated how hard he had worked without complaint or promise of reward.

At dinner that night she started mellowing toward him. She had suffered the company of too many weak lightweights but now realised he was not one of these. Her mother feeling ill, had excused herself from dinner and had left them on their own. Denman made a toast to the success of the farm and her management. As they ate on the terrace they were at peace with the world

He found out she had studied music at the city conservatoire and gave public concerts until the farm started to suffer and then she had given this practice up. Denman enjoyed her company, her stillness and calmness in the face of her problems. He wanted to extend the evening with her.

'Will you play something for me?' he asked. She smiled. What harm could it do to spend more time with this charming man who had helped her, expecting nothing in return?

She took her violin out and played some Mozart. When she played she was lost in another world and became a different girl, eyes tight with concentration, totally focussed on her notes. *No wonder she was serious,* he thought; *having given so much up for this farm.* She could have played professionally if she had wanted. She certainly shouldn't be holed up in this rural backwater. She deserved better, to be married into a wealthy noble family where her skills could be displayed at musicals and applauded, and she cherished; not being forced to work like a farmhand or peasant girl for a few coins.

They wondered down to the pool and the fountain and the dark set, in casting shadows on the walls. He took her arm and they looked by lantern light at the carp playing there.

'I have enjoyed these two days, 'I feel I have done something useful.' She recognised in him a man who needed to be active; he was too energetic and forceful to be a pen pusher.

She sat on the wall and dangled her hands in the water. In the moonlight she was an ethereal figure, long blond hair flowing around her shoulders and down her back and a blue loose gown trailing behind. With any other girl Denman might have taken the opportunity to hold her in his arms and kiss her but something was different here. He felt he would break the easy friendship developing between them. So, he inwardly shook himself, told himself to act like a gentleman and led her inside. She in turn was surprised he had not taken advantage of the situation. She was beginning to like him a little.

He was packing his saddle bag when he heard a shout and a lone horseman appeared. Helena looked dismayed and did not welcome the visitor. Like her, he was tall, very blond but sturdily built. He had the same blue eyes, but his face was red and puffy. He carried too much weight, the sign of a heavy drinker. His eyes shifted toward Denman and she introduced them.

'This is Angelo,' she said. *Anything less like an angel it was more difficult to think of,* thought Denman. Unlike his sister, he looked as if hadn't done any work in his life and had fallen out of bed straight on to his horse. Angelo frowned, *Denman, where had he heard that name before?*

'Militia,' volunteered Denman, reluctantly and there was instant recognition on the part of the other man. He had lead the militia when they broke up drunken fights in the inns between the customers vying for the attention of the ladies there, before they became too violent. His reputation for fairness had gone before him but some people had a chip on their shoulders and hated any militia man. This one clearly fell into the last category.

'And my lovely, hardworking, industrious sister,' he said, smiling, putting his arm around her and giving her a bear hug. She stiffened and wrinkled her nose, pulling away from him. Denman could smell the wine on him from where he stood.

'What has brought you here?' she demanded, unwelcomingly.

'I heard you are restoring the fortunes of the farm and vineyard. I thought you might want some help.'

'Everything is done. We just have the marketing to do.'

'I'll take the produce to market for you.'

'Thank you but no.' She knew the money would be directed to the nearest wine cellar. She didn't trust him for a minute and wondered how she could get rid of him.

Denman had a change of plan. 'I am escorting your sister to the market. I'll be here for a few more days anyway.' His look dared Helena to contradict him but she didn't. She was too grateful for an excuse to keep her brother from the proceeds of the harvest.

Denman took his saddlebags off and changed back into working clothes. He started chopping trees for logs. She brought him lunch, a light wine and bread and chicken and a fruit torte. He was bare chested, brown as a nut and his muscles rippled as he chopped the logs. He looked like a Greek god, an Adonis and her opinion of him had rocketed. She passed the wine to him as he lazed against a tree.

'Thank you for intervening; he is bad news for this estate. I must get rid of him.'

'How long has he been like this?'

'Five years and he upset my father so much he suffered an apoplexy, but he will inherit the estate one day unless he drinks himself to death first,' she said bitterly.

'Well he won't get his hands on the income from this harvest. I will help you take it to market and then buy and put the vines in and bring the cattle home. How is your groom?'

He is recovered and can plant the vines for me. The grapes are already fermenting. We take the olives to market tomorrow and buy the cattle.'

She wondered why he was helping her. In fact, he had always worked hard to get to the top of his profession instead of using his family name to buy his way there. Patronage was the normal way to get progress in the army but like Dreda, after purchasing his colours he had rejected this mode and had earned his promotion by merit and had gained respect from his men. He saw in her a worker; someone who rose to a challenge and like himself, one who would not easily give in to bad circumstances. He would not allow a drunken spoilt layabout to ruin her plans for her if he could help it.

When he went back this evening Angelo was already drinking in the kitchen. His sister looked contemptuously at him and was surprised when Denman got a jug and started drinking himself. She raised her brows and was going to intervene, but he shook his head as if warning her to back off. Later when her brother's head was on the table and he was in a drunken stupor Denman explained they would go early to sell the olives and be back with the cattle before Angelo woke up.

He didn't tell her what else Angelo said. Denman had a very hard head, used to heavy army drinking and Angelo had a loose tongue. Denman had sat listening to Angelo's explanation of his plans.

'Need her to get the estate back into the black and then I can take over. Will put a steward in and live off the proceeds. My income isn't enough to support my lifestyle. But I need to find someone to who will marry her with a small dowry and take her off my hands. I have a few friends who want her. They are coming in a few days.'

'What does she want?'

'I don't care what the bitch wants. She has never considered or liked me. These men will know how to deal with her.'

Denman felt like tipping him into the fishpond but then it wasn't deep enough to dispose of him permanently. He knew what this sort of man Angelo's friend would be like, 'persuading' women with black eyes and threats. He wouldn't leave the farm until Helena was protected fully.

He wondered how ill her father really was. By all accounts he was at death's door. He needed to put Helena's fortune and her custody into the hands of a guardian and trustees. Ordinarily the brother became the guardian, but that sot was clearly unsuitable. He spoke to her mother, but she admitted that the father couldn't show the capacity to make the decisions for his daughter's future.

The next morning, they were up at dawn, he 'nursing' a mild headache. At the olive market she bargained with a ferocity he could not have imagined and got more cattle than he had hoped. They drove them up to the far field away from the eyes of cattle bandits and afterwards collapsed, exhausted, with a good meal in front of them. The wine would take longer to deal with and Denman hoped he would get her brother out of the way before that could be sold.

Angelo had come down like a bear with a sore head. He had looked for the olives and realised he had been duped. He approached his sister silently on her home-coming and held her to him violently, shaking her until her teeth rattled. Fear was in her eyes and he was about to slap her when a voice from the doorway said very quietly, 'Let her go or I will break your neck!' Denman touched his pistol gently and his hand was on his sword, a silent warning.

'She is my sister and while my father is ill I have the authority to look after her. It is the law.'

'To hell with the law! Are you going to do what I say, or do I break every bone in your body?'

He moved menacingly toward the man and Angelo moved his hand to his pistol. With a flash Denman's sword hand had moved and he had whisked the gun out of his opponent's hand. The next minute the sword was at Angelo's throat.

Denman nodded to Helena and then to the door. 'Out,' he said in a voice that broached no argument. She went quickly, knowing she was only in the way. Denman then pushed Angelo slowly against the wall at sword point and whispered, 'If you ever touch her in that way again you will regret you have ever been born. Now get to your room and stay there.'

He went to find Helena who was unnerved but defiant. 'His friends are coming, and he intends to marry you off to one of them. We need help. How many of the servants could fight for you?'

'Very few, most are old. We have the groom and one other of fighting age.'

'Right!' He sent the groom to Dreda who luckily was near in his summer villa. He would bring some of his men if they could get here on time. The alternative were the militia officers in the next town but there were some unsavoury characters there that Angelo could bribe to help him. He would have to hope luck would be on his side. Helena rang for dinner and they sat quietly over it neither feeling cheerful.

'I want you to go,' she said decisively. 'This is not your battle, we have already exploited your kindness and you could get hurt.'

'No, I have been in worst fixes than this,' he said, thinking of the times he and Dreda had been ambushed and captured.

'I am staying whether you like it or not.'

She was torn, angry that he had disobeyed her wishes but grateful that he was not going to leave her unguarded with her vengeful brother on the loose. He observed her, the conflicting emotions showing on her expressive face. She was a quiet, secretive girl but her emotions had risen to the surface; the thought of losing her independence and income making her angry.

The desire to tell him to leave and the need to accept his help warred within her but common sense won out and she said reluctantly, 'Thank you Officer. I would be grateful for your help, but you must not put yourself in any danger for us.'

He rose and took her chin in his hand and looked directly into her sea green-blue eyes and said, 'I am not scared of a few untrained villains Ma'am. I have sent for help from my friend Officer Dreda, Head of the Security Bureau. With luck he will bring others with him and we will dish these men what they deserve.

'It is a pleasure helping you Ma'am. I have enjoyed the work on the farm these past few days.'

She pulled away from him. He could see how she hated taking help from him. She was distancing herself again from him. He did not know if she behaved like this to all unfamiliar men or just him. She seemed not to want any intimacy with him. He wondered if her attitude stemmed from a bad love affair. She was a mystery he wanted to solve.

She shook his hand as if wanting to establish formal relations between them again. 'Thank you, Officer. We will always be deeply grateful to you.' She was trying to ignore the fact he had held her chin gently in his hands and stroked her cheek as if trying to comfort her. He was treating her like a sister or old friend.

She did not understand this man. One minute he was the easy-going help-mate on the farm, the charming aristocrat who put her mother at ease at the dining table. Then later, he became the domineering militiaman, taking charge of her life and making decisions for her. His change into a severe ex-army officer threatening her brother showed her the hidden steel behind his easy-going exterior, the aggression under tight control. He was not a man to be taken lightly. Her brother had better watch out!

She also wondered about his ease with women. His eyes had travelled over her, from top to toe, assessing her, making her feel as if he was mentally stripping her, enjoying surveying her. He had not tried to toy with her, had behaved the gentleman; yet under those polite manners and courteous exterior was a man who enjoyed women and played with them, easily gaining from them what he wanted. His wealth, his looks, his title, gave an impression of power; a man who would take a woman, use her and then drop her when he became fickle and tired of her.

She had met men like that before; her own fiancé had been such a man and had dropped her like a hot cake when her fortune had gone. She had no desire to become the pawn of any powerful and rich man again! Her independence was more important to her. The farm was her future if she could stop her brother from taking it over.

Chapter two

Two days later her brother's friends arrived, three of them, all smelling of drink and tobacco. There was no sign of Dreda. There was no indication that the groom had even got to his villa. He could have been killed by bandits. The men swaggered in travel stained. Their horses looked in worse shape. Denman had no respect for a man who didn't look after his horseflesh. In the army they were too important to neglect. He made sure they were fed and watered and bedded for the night.

Helena was ordered by Angelo to find them food and wine. Denman noticed that one man's eyes were all over Helena. When she served him food he put his arm round her and thanked her by hugging her tightly.

'This is your beautiful unwedded sister, Angelo?' She wriggled away but his intentions were clear. He was the one who would gain the control over the inheritance for Angelo.

Denman stood lazily by the door. He had no intention of intervening until Dreda was there unless they attacked Helena. She was strong enough to cope with a bit of groping. She kept herself in the kitchen except when serving them and when they started drinking heavily she escaped. Denman had armed the servants and told them what to do if he called for help, but he had misgivings about using them.

He watched the men drink themselves into stupors and then sent Helena to bed telling her to lock her door. He was in two minds whether to sleep in her room that night but for his own peace of mind he decided against that. That dolt mauling her had made him realise how desirable she was to other men. It made him feel uncomfortable, so he pushed that to the back of his mind. He preferred to see her as a friend and have a clear mind for the forthcoming fight.

She in turn had mixed emotions. She had seen him fight before but this new cold, menacing Denman was a new man to her and she didn't look forward to him hurting her brother even if she could willingly smother him herself. The officer was one of the most intelligent and attractive men she had met, and she was beginning to trust him. When he had stood with her by the pond she had wanted him to kiss her. She had had a fiancé and had been kissed before and was not a prudish young miss, but she was glad he had not taken advantage of the situation. She was totally confused!

She admitted to herself that damned officer was growing on her. His easy smile, his gentlemanly manners were gradually seducing her into accepting his help and she enjoyed his company. If he did not try to dominate her and order her about she could like him. She had to accept his orders while she was in danger from her brother but after that he could take his commands and leave her farm. She would try to ignore his good qualities and concentrate on his irritating habits, even if in her dreams his face appeared, and she found herself wanting him to hold her tight and comfort her and kiss her.

Dreda had got the message and was on his way. They had covered each other's backs many times before and he knew Denman wouldn't ask him to come unless the situation was critical. He had sworn two friends in as temporary militiamen as he didn't know in what capacity he was entering the villa.

He had heard of the household and knew Angelo as a bad sort so expected the worst. Having only recently honeymooned with his new wife he wanted to get back to her as soon as possible. He only had ten leagues to go. From the top of the hill he could see smoke the other side of the valley where the villa must be and pressed on.

In the villa the men had got up with sore heads and were grumpy and antagonistic, looking for a fight. The one who fancied himself as Helena's groom was pestering her. Denman kept himself on a tight rein; trying to restrain himself from punching the bastard's daylights out. His tight control was being stretched to the limit as that ape pawed her and tried to corner her. He sent her servant in with a message that she was wanted in the salon and she escaped, thankfully!

Unfortunately, her brother was there, looking through her father's papers. When she challenged him about them he grabbed her arm and said, 'You were not very friendly to Henri last night. Be nice to him if you want to be treated well. He is to marry you very soon.'

'Will he indeed?' she retorted pulling away.

'You will do as you are told, you ignorant, disobedient wretch. He flung her across the room. As he approached her she took a knife out of the drawer and threatened him with it.

'If you try to beat me again I will use this on you.'

She was truly scared of getting a violent beating from him, the way he had dealt with her disobedience in the past. She had the knife at his throat when Denman walked in and ordered, 'Put that down. I will deal with this,' and motioned her to leave the room. From the doorway, he said, 'I warned you,' and then moving like lightning he knocked the man flat out and carried him to his room and locked him in.

Dreda arrived that evening. Denman saw him coming and rode out to explain the situation. Dreda was interested. He rarely saw his friend so serious about anything and this girl seemed to have captured his interest. He was looking forward to seeing this lady.

'The brother has been locked in his room, last night, after threatening his sister. The others are already sampling the wine in the cellar and will soon be in no condition to fight.

'Let's go and frighten the brother then,' suggested Dreda.

As they entered the villa they heard a shot and a cry sounding from upstairs. Taking the stairs two at a time they came to the landing. The bedroom door was now open, and they saw Angelo on the floor, his brains shot out and Helena standing over him with a gun in her hand.

Denman went quietly to her and took the gun away. She was shaking. She said wide eyed, 'The door was open, and I found him like this. I picked up the gun and you came in. I wanted him dead many times, but I didn't shoot him.' Denman replied automatically, 'I believe you,' but he really didn't know what to believe. Instinctively, he knew her not to be a liar, but she had been frightened and had threatened Angelo with a knife before. The militiaman in him told him that she could have reacted violently if she had thought he would hurt her and she could be in shock.

He led her downstairs and asked her abigail to sit with her. He then returned to Dreda who was examining the body.

'A bullet hole in the back of the neck, definitely murder and no suicide.'

'You will take charge of this one won't you Danitz? I am too involved and too close to Helena to make rational decisions. I want to believe her.'

'Certainly!' He was pleased his friend was acting as professionally as was possible given the difficult circumstances. They rounded up the men and arrested them and arranged for them to be taken to the jail for questioning in the next town. They didn't believe they had killed him, but they wanted them out of the way.

One of them had broken away from his captors and entered the room where Helena was sitting, her head in her hands.

'He is dead because of you. You killed him! He said you wanted him dead and I heard you and your maid threaten to kill him if he hurt you.'

Dreda dragged him back to his horse as roughly as he could before Denman could intervene. He had seen the dark look on his friend's face when the man accused the girl of her brother's murder. Clearly, she meant more to Denman than a mere acquaintance he was helping.

He looked as if he would have shoved the man's teeth down his filthy mouth without a second thought. Tightly under control, Denman walked away from the temptation, not giving the man a second glance. Only his fists clenched tightly beside him gave Dreda an idea of his feelings and what he would like to do with the other man.

'Shut your mouth! She has suffered enough,' warned Dreda. 'Denman, I am relieving you of all of your duties relating to this case until it is settled.'

Dreda went to Helena. She was still sitting looking at the wall and then at her brother's portrait, trying to make some sense of the situation. Her skin had the pallor of the dead.

'Get her something strong to drink, she is shaking. I need her to make a statement.'

He then started to question her. She stuck to her story. She had not seen anyone in the room and had not killed her brother. No matter how many times he tried to trick her she was absolute. At the end of it he said, 'I have no alternative but to arrest you until I find other evidence to prove you didn't do it.'

He then had the unenviable task of telling his friend. 'She is sticking to her story. I believe she is telling the truth and is suffering from shock. She needs a friend or her mother to comfort her.'

'Can I go to her?'

'Of course, but after that you must only communicate with her when I am present, i.e. at meals. I will let you follow the investigation alongside of me.'

Denman found her and when she rushed over to him, without thinking he held her in his arms and comforted her. 'You had best go about your normal business; you will feel better than milling around here with nothing to do. I will send your mother to sit with you. She is the best person to be around you now.'

He went out and took his anger and frustration on a pile of logs that needed cutting. Dreda was not sure whether Denman saw the girl as a good friend to be protected or as a potential lover. He had never been serious about any woman and loved and left his women easily.

This girl was different from the ones Denman usually associated with; neither being the bits of fluff and feather-heads he mounted for payment or the more intelligent widows he shared a fling with. This girl wanted nothing from him and was fiercely independent. From the little he knew of her she did not flirt or try to attract his friend's attention and saw him merely as a person who was trying to help her get out of trouble. His friend had admitted wryly over a bottle of wine she had treated him like an older cousin she wanted out of her hair; although she appreciated him rescuing from her brother's clutches.

Dreda did not presume to give his friend any advice but privately he thought Denman was misreading the situation. The girl seemed to rely on him and had willingly entered his arms when he had hugged and comforted her after the loss of her brother. He suspected she felt more affection for Denman than she was willing to admit. His friend would have to wait until the murder case was solved and then he could decide if he held a tendre for her and if he wanted to pursue a romance with her.

Dreda would be delighted if he had found a woman he loved. He wanted his friend to have the same happy home-life he enjoyed with the love of his life. This girl seemed to be made from the same mould as Felea; hard-working, intelligent and honest and independent.

She would make a good militiaman's wife and keep Denman on his toes. She was also beautiful and spirited enough to keep him out of other women's beds. For the moment Dreda kept his thoughts to himself. Denman was not the sort of man one pushed. He would have to find out what he wanted himself.

'We will have to move to the city and question the arrested men. She will have to come as well.' Over dinner they explained this to Helena who was worried about the farm. 'I will leave one man and you must give him a list of instructions to follow,' Dreda reassured her. The old servant asked, 'Why is my mistress leaving? She has not done anything.'

'She has been arrested for the murder? How do you know she didn't do it?'

'She couldn't do it. She didn't have a gun.'

Denman knew otherwise. The gun that had killed Angelo was the one he had seen in her bag. The old woman was trying very badly to protect her mistress.

'Who else may have wanted Angelo dead?'

'He had upset most people and owed gambling debts to people in the city. But he was worth more to them alive than dead.' It was obvious the one who would benefit most from his death was Helena. The outlook was looking bleak for her.'

'She couldn't have done it. She wasn't there when it happened. She was with me in the kitchen.' Dreda thought he would check that out. The other servants said no, neither of them was in the kitchen when the shot was heard. The old woman was clearly lying.

Dinner time arrived, and Helena came in well-dressed again but in black. She hadn't bought new clothes in years but working hard on the farm meant she could still get in the clothes she had bought years before. She looked at herself in the mirror and was disgusted. Unfashionably brown skin, hair grown and shoved into a long braid, her hands rough and chapped with short nails; she looked like one of her servants. How she longed to be treated like a lady just for one night instead of a farm hand.

To Dreda and Denman she looked lovely and calm but sad. The old woman was hovering about during the meal looking agitated. She kept whispering to herself and shaking her head in contrast to her mistress's dignified persona.

Dreda told her to stay in the kitchen as she was clearly upsetting Helena who could not understand the reason for her agitation. He decided to keep an eye on her; she could know more than she was letting on. He calmly proceeded to explain to Helena how he was going to carry on the investigation. She needed to be informed so she could get legal advice and he didn't want her to worry more than was necessary.

Something smelt fishy around here. He couldn't put his finger on it, but he felt in his bones that she wasn't the killer; someone had framed her or there had been an accident and she was getting the blame for it. Her father passed away that night. Luckily, he had not been aware of the death of his son or he would have been heartbroken. Her mother carried on as usual, trying to support her daughter as Denman did.

The body had already been taken to the town for a medical examination although this was a formality, it was obvious what had killed him, and the type of gun used. The two women packed their bags and the party started the journey to the city. Arriving at the city gaol, Dreda left her in an interviewing room before being formally charging her. He had no intention of letting anyone say she was getting preferential treatment and she would not have wanted any.

Denman was curious, Helena was very quiet and subdued, as if she had something on her mind. While they were working together on the farm he had found that under her quiet exterior there was a lively, mischievous sense of humour and a love of travelling and animals. They had chuckled together at the antics of the farm cats and dogs vying for the attention of the humans and he was missing her cheerful companionship

This girl intrigued him; the more he spoke with her the more he wanted to know what made her tick. She sat reading quietly, frowning.

'What is it you are reading?' She started nervously, as if she had been deep in thought. 'Oh nothing. I was just thinking.'

'My brother, why he turned out like he did! He had everything. My father spoilt him and gave him what he wanted. He had the best tutors and education, but he could not settle at anything. Lucia warned my mother and father he needed discipline but neither listened.'

'Your servant seems to care for your interests.'

'She brought me up when my mother had to give a lot of attention to my brother. He was jealous of me, attention seeking and demanding Mother's attention.'

Denman wished he had been there to give the boy the sharp lesson he had needed early enough to make an impact and avoid his death. He had dealt with many spoilt boys in the army, turning them into good solid officers.

He persisted. 'How did Lucia get on with your brother?' Helena sighed and said, 'She told him he was a fool,' but then she changed her tone. 'But they rubbed along well enough.'

Denman was not so sure. She had spoken too sharply as if she was trying to convince herself. He would ask Dreda to investigate the behaviour of this strange old woman who still walked around whispering to herself. Her odd behaviour had attracted the interest of others in the inn.

The landlord said she could be mad or a witch. Denman didn't want a witch hunt. He had seen women driven out of primitive rural villages while campaigning because of rumour and gossip. He also didn't want to upset Helena. He found the urge to protect her was growing stronger and stronger.

Helena was withdrawing into her shell. Denman, damn the man, was making her want to open up to him and trust him with her secret. With his gentle and comforting manner, he was gradually breaking down her reserve; those high walls she had constructed against men since her fiancé had jilted her.

Why did the first man she liked in years have to be a militiaman who could be responsible for collecting the evidence that could imprison her? She pretended she was not attracted to him but when he came close to her and hugged her she had felt secure and warm for the first time in years and yearned for the intimacy with him that she knew he wanted as well.

She could talk with Dreda without any fear of betraying her secret. Dreda, the cold detached militiaman was equally as handsome as Denman, but she had no desire to open up to him or rest her head on his shoulder for comfort. She was not attracted to him in any way. He was just a militiaman doing his job in his own formal manner. She was at ease with him.

Dreda knew she been watching her servant, trying to find out what was upsetting her, and he was letting her hang herself with her own rope. Either she was the killer and she would betray herself soon with her actions or she would lead them to the real killer as she was clearly hiding something, protecting someone. The key to this murder was undeniably the old woman. He felt it in his bones.

Dreda interviewed Helena. After hours of questioning he could not convince her to change her story but he felt she knew or suspected something.

The two officers were drinking in a bar in a quiet corner. Dreda had left Helena to stew in the cold clinical room.

'I think you should talk to her and try to find out what she suspects.'

'I don't think she will tell me anything.'

'I think you have a better chance than anyone else of getting the truth out of her. She has come to rely on you.' He didn't know how strong his friend's feelings were for this girl but there was a connection between them, if not an attachment. He had never seen Denman show so much concern for a woman before.

Denman sighed, finished his drink and sat opposite Helena. 'Dreda and I think you may suspect someone but are not telling us. You have got to tell us, or you could be in serious trouble. Everything points to you; he will have to formally charge you.'

'I know nothing and suspect no-one,' she said dully.

'Where was Lucia on the night your brother was murdered? She says she was with you but neither of you were in the kitchen.'

'She was in the study with me all evening and we both heard the shooting and I went to investigate.'

He knew she was now lying. A servant had verified she was on her own in the study until fifteen minutes before the shooting and those minutes could not be accounted for. She had no alibi, neither had Lucia who would not say anything intelligible.

'I am sorry, but we have checked out those facts and your version of the events is inaccurate.' He didn't want to accuse her directly of lying but he felt sick she had to lie to him.

'Start again and tell me the truth. Why are you protecting Lucia?'

She said nothing. Her obduracy angered him. He took her by the shoulders and would have shaken her if she had not looked so startled and he remembered her brother attacking her. He let her go and took her hand instead.

'If you do not answer me to my satisfaction then Officer Dreda will charge you.' Still she gave no answer, so he got up and left the room frustrated and angry.

He stalked into Dreda's office, forgetting to knock. Dreda looked up, brows raised inquiringly. 'I assume you got nowhere.'

'That damned girl is so obstinate I could strangle her.'

'My money is now on the old woman. She had the opportunity, we only need the motive.'

'She told me that the old woman had torn the boy off a strip. He was a sullen wretch so probably bore a grudge against her and they may have argued again when he was in his cups. But why would she have gone to his room?'

Dreda stood up, snapped the file shut on his desk and said, 'I don't know but we have given her enough time. Give the order to make out the charge. A night in a police cell may frighten her and change her mind.'

Denman shrugged his shoulders and went to fetch her, admitting to himself reluctantly, the girl by not cooperating had given Dreda no other choice. Dreda was the most reasonable person he knew if he felt a person was innocent and needed help. He had no desire to put an innocent girl behind bars.

He felt like throttling her! Stubborn, awkward, her own worst enemy; she was leading herself into a prison cell. Why the devil didn't she help herself? And why did he care? He asked himself why he was looking out for her when she had recently ignored most of what he had said to her.

He had no answer to his question. He could not explain why he wanted to protect her and rescue her from the mire she had trapped herself in. Calling himself a soft fool taken in by a pretty face he decided to treat her as coolly as she was treating him.

Helena was charged and put in a cell. She shared this with thieves, common prostitutes and debtors and stood out like a sore thumb. Denman thought it might shake her up but the next morning was informed by the warden that some of the women had tried to bully her. The altercation had started when Lucia had brought her a basket of food and one woman tried to muscle in and steal some of it. If she had asked Helena would have shared her food but her arm had been wrenched behind her back and her face slapped.

Having been brought up with a spoilt aggressive brother she had learnt to defend herself and they picked on the wrong girl. When they released her arm, she had turned on the intimidating woman and punched her on the nose and in the stomach. Others joined in the fight and she was hauled from the woman and put into a cell on her own, nursing a black eye.

Denman came to see her and smiled. 'You don't look good.'

'You should see the other woman. She tried to steal my food!' she replied indignantly.

'Well has this shown to you what prison life will be like if you are lucky enough to have a death sentence commuted to life. Have you changed your mind about telling the truth?'

'I am sticking to my story.'

'Which in court will be torn to shreds.'

There was no answer. She merely stared back at him, meeting his eyes directly, arrogantly, as if she didn't have to answer to him. This time he did erupt in anger, his promise to himself to stay detached forgotten. He pushed her against the wall. He lifted her head, his hand under her chin until he had eye contact. Spearing her with his eyes, he said quietly and deliberately, 'I will not allow you to perjure yourself and be executed or rot in a place like this.'

She stared defiantly at him. 'Keep your nose out of my affairs. You are not my father.'

'If I were your father I would put you over my knee. You are a barefaced liar!' He was trying to provoke her, break down her barriers but merely inflamed her pride further. As quick as a flash she slapped him as hard as she could, but he was not a man to take that lightly. He took both of her wrists firmly and held them by her side and holding her against the wall he kissed her. All his militia training could not help him now. He was fearful of losing her and raw emotion took over. She resisted for a moment but recognising it was futile she sank into the kiss which seemed to go on forever.

A head came around the door and Dreda appeared, raising his eyebrows at Denman who shrugged, uncaring. He had seen Dreda behave irrationally when he was in love. Both parties to the kiss were breathless and their eyes clouded. The emotions that had gone through them had rocked them both. It was as if they had suffered a shock.

Breaking the silence, Dreda said to Helena, 'Your defence advocate wants to talk with you.'

'I haven't got one. I can't afford one.'

'It has been arranged and paid for. Don't argue if you value your neck. I have arranged for you to see him this afternoon.' They left her to mull this over.

Denman said, 'She won't change her mind.'

'And you were trying to make her?'

'I know I behaved unprofessionally but she makes me so mad.'

That confirms it; he is definitely in love, thought Dreda, remembering himself how Felea's defiance could enrage him when she endangered herself and she would not listen to reason.

Helena sat in the cell on the lumpy bunk, her head in her hands. She was confused, a maelstrom of emotions overwhelming her. She had thought she was doing the right thing. There was no evidence to prove she had killed her brother. No-one had witnessed the shooting and none of the servants, but Lucia knew where she and her brother were the night he was killed. Except for the actual murderer all others could merely speculate as to who killed him. She believed if she kept quiet she could be released once the militia found they had no evidence to support her arrest.

Now Denman had put doubts into her mind. That bloody man, twisting her emotions until she didn't know how to think. First, he had behaved like a friend, gradually earning her trust and then he had turned on her; accusing her of being a barefaced liar, kissing her and threatening her with a life sentence or hanging if she did not change her story. She had thought she could treat him like a friend; act with detachment like she treated his friend Officer Dreda. That kiss had proven otherwise.

That kiss had shown his feelings for her had passed the bounds of friendship. Possessive, passionate, it was the kiss of a man who was claiming his mate for his own; a man who wanted to dominate and impose his personality on hers, to dictate to her! He would try to make her change her statement no matter what the consequences for her and others. The easy-going gentle man was turning into the man of steel she feared; who expected obedience from women when he clicked his fingers.

Kissing him had turned her insides into knots. She had fought him at first, denying him, refusing to return his kisses but his passion had overwhelmed her. Her common sense had been demolished by the emotions he raised within her. She hated him interfering in her life and wanted to push him away from her but a little voice in her head said, "You want this man, you need him; he is the first man who has made you feel alive in years."

She had been living like a dead person for years, in a zombie like existence, all emotions drained from her, living from day to day, fighting the poverty that threatened to overtake them while her brother wasted their money. She had fought with bankers and money-lenders, facing them with a ferocity they little expected from a young girl barely out of school after her father had suffered his apoplexy when her brother had presented him with the total of his gambling debts.

When her fiancé had rejected her that had been the final straw! The turning of the shoulders by the local noble ladies when he had jilted her had made her withdraw into herself, to lick her wounds. She had come out a stronger person, but her personal needs had been subsumed under the role of looking after her father and mother and the necessity to pull her family out of the River Tick.

Fighting with creditors and working the farm, she had devoted every hour in the day to saving her family and had cared nothing for her own desires. She had succeeded financially but to what avail? She had no chance of a good marriage, had lost all of her school friends and had no-one to turn to now she was in trouble. Her relatives had washed their hands of her family after her brother had turned ne're do well.

She was alone and now Denman, that odious, provoking man had threatened her with prison. She hated him dictating to her and yet, she could not resist him when he kissed her. She had felt secure for the first time in years in his arms. She was a simple-minded romantic fool letting him take advantage of her when he was the sort of man who groped and tumbled the maids he met.

He had not said what he wanted of her, but she had no dowry to offer a man and what else would he offer than a quick fling or a carte blanche if she attracted him for a little longer. He was better forgotten if she could get out of this jail. This advocate she was meeting would help her return home and she would forget she even had met Denman.

Her advocate met her that afternoon with grave news. Her brother's friend had told the militia he had overheard her threatening to kill her sibling. Dreda had tried to make light of this accusation, saying it was done as an act of revenge for Helena rejecting the man as a suitor for her hand but it was to no good. The senior militiaman there said there was now enough evidence to make a case against her and he would send her to the acting judge in a week's time to assess her guilt.

Denman took her back to her cell. She was quiet and subdued. 'Will you change your story? It is your only chance to escape a long sentence. It is likely the judge will find against you. You have no alibi and the statement made by your brother's friend has cooked your goose unless we can force him to admit he has lied.'

'I have no intention of changing my statement,' she replied dully, 'and I don't know what business it is of yours. I thought you were off the case anyway.'

'I don't know why I am helping a stubborn, ungrateful wench like you but for my sins I care what happens to you,' he said shaking his head. 'I must be going soft!' He left the cell, slamming the door with force, cursing awkward, impossible females who would not listen to sound advice.

He had told her the truth. He cared for her and wished no harm to come to her. He had been as astonished and affected by that kiss as she had been. An experienced seducer and lover he was moved by the feelings it had uncovered in him. He had no idea yet how deep his feelings ran for her. He was certainly not interested in matrimony, but this young girl was slowly worming herself into his heart without wanting or trying. Pushing him away made him even more attracted to her. She intrigued him, and he would try to help her.

He spent the next day in the militia station with Dreda, trying to make her brother's friend change his statement. He lost patience and Dreda had to stop him when he pushed the man against a wall and threatened to break his teeth if he didn't tell the truth.

'Denman!' cried Dreda pulling him off by his collar. 'That is not the way to handle this situation.' He pushed him out of the cell. 'He has a friend in this station who will report you. I can only hush so much up. We have to be seen to be lily white in this case. Your interest in the girl has already been noted by others.'

'What interest?' retorted Denman. 'We can barely talk to each other without her cursing me and telling me to go to the devil. She dislikes me heartily.'

'It is plain as the nose on your face you more than like the girl. Try to keep a clear head or I will not let you listen to the interrogations in future.'

Denman sat down his head in his hand, rubbing his forehead. He was developing the headache out of frustration with this case.

'What am I supposed to do when that girl will go to jail if that liar is allowed to give evidence in court?'

'We can only hope the judge can tell from Helena's dignified quiet manner that she is not the type who would kill her brother.'

'Would bribing the man help? He clearly wants something from this case.'

'He would have gained half an estate if he had married Helena. You cannot give him that much. It would be too obviously be a bribe, and if found out questions would be asked about the Bureau's practices. Anyway, it is revenge he wants, on Helena! It was his best friend who died. He said he wants her neck or liberty taken at the least.'

Denman swore in exasperation. For once being full of blunt and coming from one of the most powerful families in the city wouldn't help him. He felt angry and powerless.

'She will have to stand trial and if convicted I will ask the judge for leniency. A crime passionel.'

'Fifteen years at the least,' said Denman. 'She will be eaten alive by those beauties in that place. Tough she may be, but she doesn't stand a chance against the gang-leaders who run that place. They will wear her spirit down.'

'Then we will have to change her mind in the next few days,' said Dreda. 'I will have a try with her as you seem to have rubbed her up the wrong way.' He watched his friend leave and smiled. Denman had fallen hard for a woman for the very first time in his life and it was an interesting thing to observe. No longer merely looking after his own interests, he was becoming a more serious, caring person.

Dreda was still not convinced by Denman's belief that Helena disliked him. The girl had relied on him until they had put her into prison and she now resented his interfering. She was raising her barriers against him and pushing him away, pretending she had no tender feelings for him.

Dreda saw through that façade. She wanted Denman to hug and kiss her and help her solve her troubles, but she could only help herself by admitting who she thought had killed her brother if it was not her. She was frustrated and angry and losing his temper with her only upset her and put her backup. Denman in love was not thinking clearly. The most even-tempered man usually, his friend was acting out of character, laying into her and chastising her like a father. He would have to make him stay away from the girl until he could control his feelings.

Chapter three.

The next day Helena received a visitor who passed a message on. There was an opportunity to escape the prison and go to the next city state. She would be a fugitive, but she and Lucia would be unharmed. Lucia had taken enough family jewels to pawn to keep them out of poverty for a few weeks until they found jobs or she a husband. When Denman looked in the cell two days later she looked different and turning her around he found an imposter had taken her place, bribed to do so by Lucia.

Damn the girl! If this was not an admission of guilt nothing was. He dreaded telling Dreda this but did so immediately after sending scouts out to find out when her visitor had arrived the night before. Dreda issued pamphlets for posting around the city walls identifying her. Then with the aid of John von Thomatz, the scout, they started looking for her.

Lucia had found lodgings for her in the worst part of the city. She would stay there until they could find someone who could be trusted to take them out of the state. Whores lined the streets after dark, displaying their wares and pickpockets mingled amongst the crowds. Drunks were physically ejected from the bars. They often lost their monies to the crooks who waited for them to sleep their stupor off in the dark shadowed streets.

Helena was dressed in a man's clothing and with shorn hair dyed brown, hidden under a hat. She only had to lengthen her stride to appear convincing. She was desperate. Her advocate had come again to update her about her court appearance and said she was likely to be pronounced guilty. Lucia had found her gun and a small sword which she could handle should she need it.

They slid into an alley and through a narrow entrance. They climbed stairs to what was to be their room until they could bribe someone to take them through or under the city gates. The room was littered with rubbish and the smell of cabbage soup permeated the air. The beds were alive, and Helena heaved when she smelt the effluent heaped in the gutter under her window. Life had been more hygienic on the farm with running water from the river. Here there was a privy outside, shared with a dozen families and no running water.

Prison seemed preferable, but she shook herself and thought death wasn't and pulled herself together. The room was cheap, and they could afford it until she could find paid work. She told Lucia what she needed to do and sent her away.

An icy chill penetrated her body as she considered her future. Lucia was becoming less lucid every day. She seemed to lack understanding of what was going on around her most of the time. When she did seem clear minded she was a good companion, but she rarely had these moments and soon she Helena would have to find someone to look after her. With little money, no place to go to and no skills to sell where could she work?

She would have to skivvy to keep them both in food and shelter. Hard work didn't frighten her; she had done enough of that on the farm, but she had no-one to give a reference about herself to an employer and what could an employer offer her but hard manual work. She might have to work in one of the inns if she was lucky.

The idea of working in one of the bars terrified the life out of her. Passing by one of them she had looked in through the open door and had seen the men opportuning the women working there. She would have little chance of retaining her virtue if she ended up in a place like that.

She put her head in her hands, trying to get rid of the headache she had been suffering all day. Lucia had been repeating all day, 'He would have killed you my Lady,' until Helena wanted to smother her although she knew the poor women had little control over her actions or statements now.

She now knew Denman was right damn him! She was hoist by her own petard. Escaping had made her look guilty, but she could not let Lucia end up in jail or on the end of a rope. She had always been loyal to her family and protected her from the beatings threatened to her by her aggressive and jealous brother. It was time for her to remain tolerant of the old woman and to protect her faithful servant.

Little did Helena know, that her entrance had been watched by one of the whores who had been dallying in the street. A sharp pair of eyes had observed the slightness of the boy's figure; the rounded bosom which had been bound and attempted to be disguised by the long jacket. The hair was too fine to be that of a boy and the eyes were delicately framed by soft lashes that clearly belonged to a young girl.

The woman's minder would be interested in the tall willowy young girl who was pretending to be a man. What's more she had no protector. She would be easy game for any man who wanted to take her. She must be desperate to end up in this street, home to only those who had no other place to go and who could sink no lower. She described the girl and gave him her address.

'You are sure she has no male friends?'

'No friends nor a protector; only an old woman to look after her and she has little mind left. She is addlepated!'

'Do we know where she comes from? Or what she is doing here?'

'No, she appeared from nowhere, disguised as a young man and has remained hidden while the older woman has gone to get provisions. She seems to be of noble birth and the old woman referred to her as 'my Lady,' when she didn't think we were listening.'

He gave her a coin and set a watcher on the building to see if she had any protectors. He smiled to himself smugly, anticipating making a good trade. If she was innocent and from noble birth, he could sell her at a good price to one of the choosier and expensive brothels where looks and birth and culture in a woman were important to the clients. She was too good for the customers around here; the dregs of humanity who barely scraped a living and generally lived by the rule, dog eat dog, scrambling over each other to survive.

Dreda and Denman had questioned the girl who was not all right in the head and had been duped by Lucia into her role of imposter. She suggested places where they may have gone and Thomatz found their trail. Dreda's worst fears were proven correct when he heard which district she was in.

Denman looked white and said, 'If I find her safe I will throttle her for causing us this worry. She is more trouble than she is worth!' Dreda smiled at his friend's indignation and anger borne out of worry. He suspected Denman would more likely to want to kiss her if he found her safe rather than throttling her. He had personally supervised the search for her and been up all night looking for her.

They arrived in the street where she could be located and went to the bar. Both were dressed in their old army uniforms and they pushed each other along the bar, appearing to be in their cups. Denman had had no time to shave having been up all night. A day-old stubble was darkening his chin. He looked far removed from his usual urbane and suave self, filling the role of a man down on his luck to perfection.

'Where is the nearest whore house, not too expensive mind,' demanded Dreda. A black toothed but reasonably clean and well-dressed man offered to find them some company.

'I know of a new girl in town, pretty as a picture, likely a virgin who is looking for a night out with men.' By the girl's description it appeared to be Helena. Denman wondered who else he had offered her to and hoped they were not too late. His heart sank, and he felt a burning anger at the thought Helena could already be violated. He pulled himself together. He had never felt such anger about a girl being ill-treated before. He was taking this far too personally, unlike the detached militiaman he should be.

He must retain his self-control and save his anger for when and if he found Helena; to direct it to anyone who had harmed her.

The man said he would sort their business out while they had some ales. He stomped up the bare stairs and listened at the door to try to hear if Helena had anyone with her. Like most bullies and cowards who preyed upon women he did not want to face the woman's protector without his own men to support him in taking her away from him.

He opened the door but there was no female there. A fire iron was on the floor and the chair and washstand was overturned, signs of a struggle. He swore; someone had got to the girl first and he had lost a good commission. He would have to tell his clients he could not satisfy them this time.

Chapter four.

Helena was washing and half-dressed when the door handle started to open, and a man's face peered around the door. Satisfied with what he saw he came in.

'Who are you? What do you want?' she cried, trying to cover herself up.

'You my dear.'

He grabbed at her and she hit him with a fire iron on the shoulder. He screamed in pain, but he still lunged at her and held her round the waist. He punched her and gave her another black eye, making her head spin and she saw stars. She would not give in, screaming and shouting but she was lifted over his shoulder and he moved quickly to the landing and down the stairs going by the back route.

He tumbled her into a hackney cab, holding her down as he gagged her with a filthy handkerchief, tying her hands. Her journey lasted only a few minutes and he pulled her out and pushed her over his shoulder again. Entering through an open door he made his way to a salon and deposited her on a chaise longue.

She pushed herself up by her hands. 'Where am I?' She faced him appearing fearless although she was trembling inside. She was not going to show fear or give in easily to this scum who had kidnapped her.

'You are at a place where your beauty will be appreciated my dear. There are many gentlemen who appreciate a cultured voice and good manners.'

Her blood ran cold at this appreciation of her attributes. She knew many men would pay a high price for a girl of culture and would enjoy boasting about taking a girl of noble blood. She wondered if she could make him talk longer to give her more opportunity to escape this place.

'Who owns this place?' she said. 'Surely I should talk to the lady who will responsible for my future if I am going to be forced to work here.'

'You are a forward piece aren't you,' said the man taking her hair and pulling her head back making her wince. 'We will soon knock the cheek out of you. A few of our clients get great satisfaction from taming women like you.'

'Are you the owner of this establishment then?' she said, amazed he would run such a luxurious looking villa. It was richly furnished, and alcohol was plentiful in the cabinets. Any man who frequented this place had to be 'full of blunt' as the saying went.

She knew young aristocratic men often went to 'rough it', in the 'old town' brothels and spent their money on the young virgins and experienced whores who worked there. This was clearly a typical example of one of those establishments; the type she suspected where Dreda and Denman had gained their experience of light-skirts whilst in their youth.

'No, my dear but my lady, Antonia runs it,' he said. 'I merely come her when she entertains me.'

Helena thought, he had a good figure and handsome face although his face was scarred, and his manners were rough. He might attract a certain type of woman who was not too fussy given her line of work where she met even worse looking and poorly behaved men every day.

'Wait here and I will find my lady,' he said as if she had a choice. When he left she went to the window and tried to look behind the drawn curtains to see where she was and if she could escape. It was a dark and badly lit street with more whores and tramps hanging outside and soldiers with injured limbs who had nowhere else to sleep. She heard someone coming and jumped back on the chaise longue and waited for the newcomer to come in.

A tall but very buxom red head stood at the door looking at her. 'You did well Michael. She is a beauty and has a good figure to boot. She will gain a good price when I put her description around our more discriminating clients.'

Helena noted her cultured voice and manner. She had clearly fallen beneath her station; probably seduced by a libertine and forced to make her own way in the world with the only attributes she had left, her body and her wit. She almost felt sorry for the woman until Antonia lifted her chin and opened her mouth to inspect her teeth.

'She looks after herself as well although her hands show signs of manual work. How did you end up here my dear?'

'That is my business. What are you going to do with me?' asked Helena. 'He assaulted me and kidnapped me from my lodgings. My servant will be looking for me and will tell the militia.'

'If you are hiding in those lodgings in this mean part of town I suspect you are hiding from the militia,' said the woman sagely. She saw she was right when Helena's face went white and a hooded expression came over her eyes. Helena thought a long prison sentence might be preferable to living under this woman's roof. She saw no mercy in this woman's eyes. She was merely a piece of merchandise to be traded for the right price.

'I guessed right then, my dear. Did you murder your lover?'

Helena gave no answer and the woman said coldly, 'Strip her! We will soon see if she has had a lover.'

'No!' said Helena. 'I am still a virgin. I killed no-one.'

'We will ask at the prison. Our sources will find out what you have done and where you come from. For the present you can stay in a room with Marie, one of our best ladies and she will explain the ropes to you. In two days we will have negotiated a price for you with one of our nicest gentleman.

Helena glared at her, but the woman pulled her hair cruelly and said, 'Just be careful my Lady. Any attempt to escape and we will give you to the first gentleman who will pay the highest price for taming you and you will regret it.

'Understand?' she said giving an extra tug of the hair. 'Do you understand?'

'Yes,' said Helena through gritted teeth.

The man roughly pushed her up three flights of stairs and face forward on to a bed in a very plush room. He left her there and a petite blond with a warm smile cut her bonds and helped her sit up.

'You are going to have some shiners tomorrow. 'I have some salve that will take the bruises away and mend your cut lip. Michael doesn't know his strength.

'He is a brute,' complained Helena.

'Oh, he isn't as bad as some pimps I have met,' said the young girl considering her minder.

'He doesn't hit out unless there is a reason. Others hit out when they are in a bad mood or have had too much booze. Michael has some common sense.'

She soothed Helena's bruises and cuts and said, 'He will be kicking himself for marking you. They can't sell you until your face is clear of bruises.'

Helena bit back an acerbic remark. This kind girl was trying to reassure her and she privately thanked Lady Fortune she might get a reprieve from being sold for a few days to the highest bidder.

'I need to get a message to the militia. If you help me I will give you twenty sovereigns if I am rescued.'

'Where would you get that blunt?' asked the girl, assessing her clothes and lack of jewellery.

'I promise you I have more than that at home. If you talk to the militia, ask for Officers Dreda and Denman. They will pay you the monies, I promise you.'

The girl wrinkled her nose trying to make up her mind about this new girl. She had heard of Dreda, a man to be feared by any criminal. His reputation for his ruthless treatment of the rebels had even reached her ears.

Helena needed to convince the girl of her sincerity. Deciding to take a risk she drew a necklace from a pocket sewn in the inside of her breeches. 'This is worth more than a hundred sovereigns. I could pawn this to pay you if you help me.' The girl in looked at her in awe and said, 'You were rich then?' Helena nodded, 'Many years ago, but I am like you now, needing to work for my living. All I want is an opportunity to work in safety and live a peaceful life. If I can't have my freedom and do that then my next best bet is to ask the militia to rescue me.'

'Are you in trouble with the militia?' asked the girl warily, not wanting trouble with the law. Helena nodded. She might be a fool for trusting this girl but what alternative did she have now. 'I was arrested on suspicion of murdering my brother, but I didn't do it and escaped. I cannot prove my innocence without hurting another person who I care for.'

'A man?'

'No, a vulnerable person who needs looking after! Please help me. I may get you a better position in a household although I make no promises. I will struggle to find a household who will accept me without references.'

'I don't mind this life too much,' said the girl philosophically. 'Antonia picks nice gentlemen out for me.'

Helena thought of the girl's future; the disease, the violence that might come when she was no longer so pretty and decided she would still help her if she escaped. This girl was too kind to be enmeshed in this sordid type of life at the mercy of other more exploitative criminals.

'If you pass a message on to the militia they will reward you well.' Lucia had seen posters offering a large reward for her re-arrest. 'That and my sovereigns could set you up for life; get you in safety to another town or even another quarter if you do not want to leave this city.'

She could see the girl turning the idea over in her mind. *Please say yes?* She prayed. She prayed the saints were on her side. If she were rescued she would attend church every week and not curse as often or think malicious thoughts about those who had ignored her when she had been jilted. She would make up for the unchristian thoughts and behaviour of her past.

The girl chewed Helena's words over in her head and then said, 'You don't fit in a place like this. I know this area, but you would shrivel and suffocate here. I will help you whether you help me or not.'

'What about your safety?' asked Helena. 'You could be hurt if they find you helped me.'

'They won't,' said the girl full of self-assurance. 'I know how to cover my back. If you pretend to try to escape, we can cover my leaving while they are trying to find you. It is risky but safer in the long run although they may clobber you for trying to leave.' Helena thought this was jumping from the frying pan into the fire, but she had no choice.

'What do I do?'

'We sleep tonight but tomorrow morning I will find some clothes for you and show you how a professional whore behaves before she sleeps with the gentlemen. How to look after him and find out what he wants.' Helena's mind boggled. Her education was going to be broadened by this young girl!

'If we are downstairs there are more opportunities to escape. There are tunnels under this villa that lead to outside of the gates of the city. You can hide in those until Michael or the militia find you.'

Helena slept well that night believing the girl Marie would try to help her. The reward was enticement enough. The bed was soft although she had carried a few fleas with her from her former lodgings and her hair itched a little. Waking up, she washed in hot water and was told a hot tub would be available later.

'Antonia believes our gentleman like their ladies to smell clean. Come now, we will find some clothes for you.'

Marie led her down to a room off the salon where some clothes were laid out for inspection.

'Virginal white will not suit you,' said Marie. 'Blue or green are your colours.' She picked out a sea green and turquoise blue and necklaces and shoes to match. Helena noted all the dresses had deep necklines and were made of the thinnest silk, designed to be worn without petticoats, showing one's shape beneath their fabric.

'We will dampen the dresses a little to exaggerate your shape,' said Marie when Antonia came in and watched.

'Is she cooperating Marie?' asked Antonia.

'Of course. I told her what Michael would do to her if she doesn't, but I think her face will not be ready for two more days.'

'Damn Michael! He is too heavy handed. He will have to watch his step in future. I already have two men bidding for her and wanted to show her to them tonight.'

'Make them wait a little. The anticipation is worth the wait and may drive the price up a little,' advised the world-wise girl. Antonia, with an impatient swish of her skirts, left them and Helena breathed a sigh of relief.

'I think you have given me an extra day's grace,' she said. 'I cannot thank you enough for what you are doing for me.'

'It is a pleasure,' said the girl. 'I was brought up for a life like this, but you weren't.' Helena felt like slapping her for her acceptance of this life, but she hadn't been brought up in these mean streets and had to sell herself just to survive as Marie had. Marie had described her own story the night before.

Beaten and sexually abused by her step-father, he had tired of her and sold her to the brothel when she was fourteen. Antonia was a gentle woman, compared with her mother, who had turned a blind eye to her husband's violation and brutalisation of his step-daughter. Anything was now better than the life she had come from.

She smiled and waited for Marie to finish picking clothes and accessories for her. 'Now we are going to go to the cellars and you are going to leave by the tunnels. See how far you get but I think they will catch up with you. You will say you vanished while I was in the water closet. Antonia and Michael will be out for hours and no-one will be looking for you.'

'Here is enough coin to pay for a cab to take you to the militia headquarters,' said Helena, giving her last coins.

'I won't take a cab until I am a long way aways from here,' said the girl wisely. 'I don't want them tracing a cab to here. I won't be back for a few hours so don't worry about me. She put her pelisse on and a pretty hat and pushed Helena through a door which led to a tunnel.

A candle in her hand, Helena started down the tunnel, screaming when a rat ran over her feet. *Sweet Jesus, I will be grey by the time I have finished here,* she thought. *Please let Marie get to Dreda.* She was taking a great risk trusting her, but she had no other choice. She felt a claw grab at her neck. She dragged a shrieking rat off it and thudded it against the wall and stamped on it with her foot. Gagging, she ran as fast as she could, hoping the candle would stay alight. She had some tapers and a tinderbox but dreaded what would happen if the light went out and she had to light the candle in the dark.

She pushed on, banging her head when the roof of the tunnel lowered and at one point it was so narrow she had to step sideways to get through. Her timepiece had said she had been in the tunnel for an hour, but she knew the tunnels stretched three miles to outside of the gates. She had managed only about a mile and had another two miles to go. She had to slow down as the ground was rough and she had nearly toppled over. Her skirts had caught on the jagged rocks and she made slow progress but was determined to go on.

Another mile and a half and she was almost certain she was going to make it, but she heard a noise in front of her. Heavy footsteps stalked her. She heard Michael call her name. Marie had warned her that there were other tunnels he could use to cut her off and meet her from a different direction. She had no place to hide. This tunnel only led in one direction as far as she could tell. She saw lights in front of her and out of the darkness loomed a big figure who held a lighted torch in front of her.

Michael had found her. He grabbed her by the arm and without speaking turned her around and pushed her in front of him, speeding her up; holding her if she nearly fell over the rough surface. Half an hour later she was in the brothel again, sitting on the chaise longue, waiting to meet her tormentor. He left her in silence again and she waited, wondering what was going to happen to her. At least she had bought some time.

Chapter five.

Dreda had waited with Denman but the man did not come back. Thomatz had followed him and traced the man to a mean street with narrow alleyways and tall terraced houses, many of the windows boarded. The man went upstairs and came down alone.

Thomatz grabbed him by his arm and said, 'Militia! Come with me quietly if you don't want anybody here thinking you are an informant.' Fear was in the man's eyes. Thomatz knew he had hit on the right threat. A police informant could lose his tongue, eyes or ears if found out by the gang-masters who ran this quarter.

He pushed the man into a doorway and through into a shop. The shopkeeper was an informant of his and went into an inner room as soon as he saw Thomatz enter. Thomatz grasped the man by his throat and snarled at him. 'It is safe to talk here but if I hear you have mentioned me coming here to anyone you will end up in a prison cell for the rest of your natural life. I will tell the other prisoners you are an informer. Help me and I will give you something for your information. Got it?' He released the man who started coughing but nodded.

'Good, now tell me where the girl could have been taken. I gather someone got to her first before you could drive a bargain.'

'I was going to sell her to those officers you saw me with, but the room was empty when I got there. The man you are looking for is Michael Ranitz and his lady Antonia Grine runs a brothel in Allez Romana, Villa Dramatyi. If you are quick, you may get to her in time. She will propose men bid for a cultured virgin of noble birth. That girl had quality written all over her and it was obvious she was a lady to any trained eye.'

'She had better not be harmed or Francis Dreda will have your liver for dinner,' warned Thomatz.

'I thought he had had more women than hot dinners,' said the man contemptuously.

'Not unwilling women,' replied Thomatz, taking his hands off him, wanting to wash his filthy presence off them. He tossed him some coins and left him there gasping, wishing he could finish the job properly.

He hated men who bullied women. Women came easily to him. He had difficulty fighting them off. Money and a title meant he could have most women he wanted provided he bought them from the demi-monde; ladies who traded their virtue for the appropriate payment of jewels or houses. Rarely did he dally with ladies of his own class, although he had the occasional liaison with a compliant widow who missed the touch of a man or a married woman whose complacent husband ignored her behaviour if she cuckolded him.

He had used these brothels when he was a young man and had worked with Dreda to bust gangs when their leaders became too strong and engaged in gang wars. Vice was tolerated by the militia until it crossed the boundaries where important figures were blackmailed because of their peccadillos. Dreda was too busy containing the advancement of the rebel army to intimidate the madams or the pimps who organised the brothels. They were a necessary evil one became accustomed to in this city dominated by vice and crime.

He sent a message to Dreda to meet him at the brothel and went there to keep an eye on it. He wanted to help his friend Denman. Dreda had intimated Denman had a personal interest in saving the wench and he had seen how anxious his normally happy go lucky friend was when he had told him where she had taken lodgings. Denman had sworn violently and had been impatient to start out to find her. This girl seemed to mean a lot to him.

He waited until it was very dark and then he climbed some trees. A few street urchins said a tall girl dressed in breeches had been taken into the villa. Reaching the top of the third tree he heard a voice more cultured than the rest, asking another to go to the militia. This sounded like the girl. Another voice suggested she try to escape the next morning through the tunnels. He climbed down. It was one o'clock in the morning. He would send a message to Dreda and meet him here the next day. He would stay here in case they moved her, or she tried to escape.

Dreda received his first message and waited for the next which would confirm where Helena had been taken. They played cards, he wanting to distract his friend from his black thoughts. Denman was clearly worrying about Helena's safety. At four o'clock in the morning a note arrived and Dreda said, 'We have her at last. Thomatz is there waiting for us to meet him but he suggests we go in the morning. She is safe and asleep now. She has a friend who is helping her try to escape.'

'She could be in a worse position if she tries to escape and gets lost. Or they may hurt her if she is found trying to escape.' Denman looked more worried, thinking about that eventuality.'

'She is going to escape tomorrow morning according to this note from Thomatz. He must have overheard her conversing with a lady of the house.'

'We need to get to her before she becomes another lady of the house.

'Thomatz said, 'They are not going to sell her for two more days.' The price is being bid up. He has eavesdropped under several windows in the brothel.'

'Well he is certainly familiar with how they work with his reputation,' said Denman wryly. 'He was no saint when he was a lad.'

'Hark whose talking,' said Dreda smiling. 'Kettles calling the pot black I think.'

'You can hardly speak either,' said Denman. 'You just hid your peccadillos more carefully than the rest of us.'

'Well I have no need of any distractions with Felea warming my bed. She is more than enough for any man,' he replied happily, thinking of his young wife waiting for him back at his villa. He still thanked Lady Fortune for sending him to her house where he had met her, and she had intrigued him. He had wanted her for his lover but later he decided he could not offer her a carte blanche and made her his wife. He was still enjoying the first few months of his marriage, a contented man for the first time in his life.

'When we finish here we must solve the other crime,' said Denman. 'Where is the servant by the way?'

'She went back to the lodgings. We will pick her up from there after we have found the elusive Helena. I thought this was going to be a simple case of protecting her monies; not investigating a murder, rescuing a kidnap victim and shutting down a brothel,' said Dreda wryly. 'Felea will never forgive you Denman for separating us.' Denman looked even angrier.

'Don't blame her too much Denman.'

'She deserves her arse kicking,' said Denman.

'And you intend to do it for her,' asked Thomatz, enjoying roasting his friend.

'It will be opportune to raid the brothel in the morning,' said Dreda, deflecting his attention away from the angry Denman. He felt he had suffered their tormenting enough.

'I am going to try to get some sleep now and I suggest you do so.' He kept several bunks in his offices made up for the men to use when waiting for information.

Denman woke up at the crack of dawn and moved quickly, washing, eating and meeting with Dreda for a briefing. They would go to the brothel and find out from Thomatz if Helena was still there and where she was being kept. Then they would demand entrance and get her out. Dreda intended to make sure this madam and her pimp were prosecuted.

The business of brothel keeping was dirty but a necessity but when he found out women were being kidnapped off the streets and sold to the brothel he had to step in. He knew it went on but turning a blind eye was not the same as ignoring clear evidence. Shutting it down merely meant the girls would turn to other houses of ill repute but it would be seen as a clear warning to the other brothel keepers to keep their houses clean and only recruit volunteers in the future.

They set off at nine o'clock knowing the occupants of the house would sleep until about eleven o'clock or midday due to their nocturnal activities. Thomatz met them around the corner of the street. He had been waiting for them. To Denman's impatient query he said reassuringly, 'She is safe and untouched. We can move in now. The madam and the pimp have gone out somewhere.'

'She deserves a hiding putting us through this,' said Denman. 'I wish I was her father. I would make her arse so sore she couldn't sit down.' Thomatz raised his eyebrows but Dreda merely smiled at him. 'Let us go and find her. You can then decide what you would like to do with her.'

Arriving at the villa they heard a crash. Looking through the salon window they saw a big man approach Helena who was sitting on a chaise longue. She had picked up a lamp and threw it at him, narrowly missing his head when he lunged at her. Dreda banged on the door with his cane and a footman came to answer his summons.

'Militia! Open up and let us pass.' He showed his badge. 'There was a tall blue-eyed girl brought here yesterday. She is in the salon. I want to talk with her immediately or your head will be on a platter. Understood?'

The young man noted the severe man's piercing eyes and menacing expression. He said stuttering, 'Yes Officer, immediately Sir,' and led them to the salon.

The man had pinned Helena down on the chaise longue, her dress torn and was about to punch her in the face.

'Let me,' said Denman dragging the man off her and hitting him so hard he fell unconscious against the wall. Dreda manacled him to a desk. Denman took off his jacket and his shirt and giving Helena the latter he said curtly, 'Put it on.' Shaking, she obeyed him, and they motioned her out of the door into the hall and into a cab.

She was taken to her former lodgings and waited for her servant to come back. Denman had barely spoken to her. She thought he would have been pleased they had rescued her. He just stared stonily at her and she waited to hear her fate. They had given up hoping the old woman would return and were going to usher Helena out when a dark figure entered the room holding a pistol. She motioned them silently to move back and told her mistress to come with her.

Dreda delayed her by saying, 'Your mistress needs to sleep and eat. We can get her some food.'

'I will look after my mistress as I have always done. No man will hurt her,' muttered the old woman. Her eyes looked vacant and bleak and she kept muttering to herself as she pushed the girl to the door.

Denman said, 'Did Angelo try to hurt your mistress Lucia? Did he wish her harm?' She turned around angrily. 'He was never any good, that boy. He hated her. He was always jealous of her.'

'Did you go to him?'

'Lucia, don't say anything!' begged Helena but the old woman clearly wanted to clear her conscience.

Lucia carried on. 'I heard him threatening Lady Helena and went to tell him to leave her alone. My Master wanted her to go to the city and find a suitor who would look after her, but he was too ill to organise it. That sot laughed in my face and told me to go to bed. He said he was going to take her to the priest the next day.'

Her eyes glazed again as if she had difficulty remembering the course of events, but they waited patiently and slowly she came back to reality and carried on. 'I warned him I would stop him, but he would not believe me and tried to take the gun from me. I resisted, and I shot him.'

Dreda thought, *I can make a case of self-defence if she plays her cards right and does what I say.*

Helena cried out, 'If you arrest her I will say I did it.'

'No, you will not,' interjected Denman. The old woman panicked and turned to her mistress, taking her eyes off the men for a second. It was a split second but Dreda acted like lightning. He grabbed her wrist and pushed the gun toward the ceiling where the fired bullet lodged. He gently took the gun and led her away. He had no intention of letting an old woman, clearly confused and possibly going senile, go to the gallows for killing that sot. Helena turned angrily on Denman, 'I want to make a statement admitting my guilt.'

'You will not be believed once we have given evidence and told what we have just heard. Don't worry, Officer Dreda will get her off! She needs looking after anyway. Has she any relatives?'

'No, I will make sure she is looked after on the farm. It is all she has known.'

She breathed a sigh of relief, knowing that she would be freed and allowed to go back to her villa. Dreda left them, feeling de trop. Denman now relieved and calm again walked over to her. Taking her chin in his hand he backed her against the wall holding her there with his body.

'You were a bloody fool you know. You made everyone believe you killed your brother and escaping confirmed your guilt. What was totally stupid was moving into that quarter. You needed your head examined living there. What got into that pretty head of yours? Were you trying to shock us?'

'Don't be so stupid,' she said pulling her chin away. 'Put yourself in my position for a change. I had little money and that is all we could find that I could afford. I had no references, no family nor friends to turn to in the city. What else could I do?'

'You could have trusted me and told me the truth. We thought it was your servant and wouldn't have let an old woman suffer if she was ill in the head.'

'How did I know I could trust you? You work for one of the most severe and bloody organisations in Europe which executes people every day. I barely know you. All I know is the severe militiaman, the fierce fighter who fought and defeated my brother and the kind man who helped me on my farm. I don't know the real Denman.'

'And you don't wish to find out,' he accused her. Angered, he carried on. 'You could have been violated in that brothel. We only rescued you just in time. You are a feather-head who acts first and thinks later and cares not for the consequences. If I were your father, I would have put you over my knee, years ago. You deserved to be treated like a whore, escaping in man's clothing; in tight breeches which allow men to ogle your body.'

'Well you are not, so keep your hands off me,' she snapped back. Her eyes flashed at him, challenging him to do his worst. He tipped up her chin and ran his finger over her lips.

'Be careful Ma'am! Else, I might be tempted to tame you once and for all. You are ripe for picking and need a strong man to master you.'

'Touch me improperly again and I will kill you!' she spat out. 'I do not behave the whore. I was merely trying to escape prison.'

He pressed on, angry again at her defiance, although he knew he had provoked her ungallantly. The temptation to rile her was irresistible after she had put such fear in him. 'You do not behave as a lady should. You should go back to the farm where your hoydenish tricks will be appreciated.'

She would have slapped him, but he caught her hands and held her arms above her head, reminding her of that day in the prison where he had punished her with a kiss. He held her imprisoned by his body against the wall, not letting her move a muscle. She was his to do with what he wished! He could feel her heartbeat rise and saw a pulse move in her neck. She was as aroused as he, waiting to see what he would do next; fear and anticipation in her widened eyes, her pupils darkening to a turquoise blue-green.

God, he wanted to kiss her and tame her! She brought out the worst in him, made him forget he was a gentleman. Remembering that kiss himself he pushed himself away from her and tried to retain some self-control.

'I will take you back to headquarters Ma'am. You can rot away on your farm to your heart's content. I have washed my hands of you!'

She nodded, withdrawing mentally from him and followed him silently. She needed a bath and she itched. She had calmed down but had mixed feelings about Denman. She was confused, feeling he had interfered in her business too much and he could have got her servant into serious trouble.

She knew her actions had been rash, but she had been backed into a corner by her loyalty to her servant and had been forced to escape the prison. She had not known anyone well enough to trust them. Denman had shown his loyalty was to his job and the state. She had had no-one else to turn to.

She had apologised to all the officers and admitted she had caused them trouble by her actions. What more did he want from her? He seemed to want her to grovel to him and he had insulted her and said she dressed and behaved like a whore. He was an easy-going man with others, but she seemed to ignite his temper.

He held her arm tightly and threatened to put her in manacles if she resisted. Denman then drove her back to the gaol.

After she made her statement he signed the release papers and took her to a luxurious inn.

'A large chamber if you please, for this lady, not in the attic and with a view of the gardens and the lake.'

In the morning she would see the gardens where a proud peacock flaunted himself across the lawn and carp were lazing on the top of the water in the lake. The sun would pour through the balcony windows, a different sight from the barred windows and the sound of the cries of women squabbling in prison.

'I will send your clothes over and try to engage a maid for you. We may have to keep Lucia for a few days.'

'Not in the prison.'

'Dreda is a sensitive soul. He will find her somewhere suitable. I will arrange for you to go to the farm as soon as is possible.'

He did not want to leave her. He came closer and twisted a straying wisp of her brown hair around his finger. 'Such pretty hair, a shame to cut and dye it. You make a better wench than a man, my Lady,' he murmured; still wanting to stay closer to her. He gently brushed her lips with his fingers, a delicate butterfly touch then moved back, distancing himself from her. She was addictive but not his, he reminded himself. He must retain self-control.

He had cooled off and regretted his harsh words to her but now he felt her coldness toward him and backed off. He had been put in an invidious situation and felt she was now treating him unfairly. He took his leave and went back to the jail to make the arrangements and then to his quarters. Little sleep and worry had tired him out after days of hard manual work and he now slept like a log. He overslept and Dreda told him when he arrived at the Bureau she had left for the farm with the promise that Lucia would be treated very leniently.

'Do you want some leave to go to see her?'

'No, I don't think I would be welcome.'

'It is not like you to give up so easily. I thought you were made for each other.'

'She hasn't given me much encouragement recently.'

'She was in an impossible position; you must recognise that.'

'She told me barefaced lies.'

'And you would have done the same for a loyal friend,' suggested Dreda.

'Anyway, the episode is finished now. She has returned to her domestic life and I am now ready to return to work after my working vacation.'

Dreda gave up. He knew not to pursue the subject. Denman could be as stubborn as a mule.

Helena arrived home safely. She loved her farm and only the poverty and hardship made her want to leave it for the city. She wrapped herself around her mother and gave her a hug. Her mother was the real sufferer here. She had had to try to manage the farm whilst she herself was in poor health. Helena could relieve her of that burden now. She intended to bury herself in work and forget the events that had occurred in the city and that infuriating man Denman. During the journey his face still kept popping into her head, his smiling countenance jogging her memory, reminding her of his jokes and teasing before he started scolding and admonishing her for hiding the truth.

Denman would have forgotten her by now. She had heard of his reputation whilst in her common prison cell. Some of the women had enjoyed maliciously explaining to her his exploits in and outside the bedroom. They warned her she might have to exchange sexual favours for his help in securing her release.

In fact, apart from that kiss he had behaved the perfect gentleman the whole time she had known him. For some peculiar reason he had not flirted with her nor tried to charm her into his bed although he knew how impecunious her financial situation was. He could easily have been tempted to offer her a carte blanche and ease her family's financial worries with a stroke of his pen if she had agreed to be his mistress. Rather than trying to charm her he had dictated to her and argued with her, behaving more like a brother or father than a lover. He had treated her as if she were a child, forgetting she had run her family's farm and was slowly pulling it out of the river Tick.

Then again, he had said she dressed and deserved to be treated like a light-skirt. She could not forgive him for calling her a harlot. He was a typical nobleman who had never suffered financial hardship in his life and couldn't empathise with her, a girl who had been given few choices. It had been run or rot in a gaol for years. He had not understood her loyalty to her servant who had protected her from the wrath of her brother in her adolescent years when her father had spoiled him and turned a blind eye to his cruel taunts and bullying ways. No! Officer Denman had had his life presented on a silver platter.

He had enjoyed a career he had chosen and now split his time between working as a militiaman and enjoying the delights of 'polite society.' He admitted to her he had not a care in the world while his father was still alive, and he did not have to carry the burden of managing his family estate. He had no understanding of the burdens she faced each day.

A small voice interrupted her thoughts, irritatingly reminding her of the good points of Officer Denman. He was generous with both his time and his money. He was not frightened of hard work. He had given his time on the farm for nothing. He had worked hard in the army for his promotion and was now Dreda's right hand man. He might be light-hearted but Dreda had acknowledged when he had a crime to solve, the joker and ladies' man turned into a goal-oriented machine. He was the man Dreda would trust above all others to get a job done thoroughly, but with charm and a light touch which other men lacked in dealing with a sometimes-difficult public.

She found it difficult to reconcile the two aspects of this man's personality. Gentle and caring, he became a ruthless brutal fighter when faced with her brother's friends. Those warm hazel brown eyes had turned to cold dark pebbles focused on the men he intended to defeat and eliminate. That determined chin spelt danger for anyone who crossed him. He was a man to be wary of if one was on the opposite side of his. She disliked this cold, hard, merciless side of Denman. It scared her and made her wonder what he would do to her if she was in his power.

Despite her dislike of him and his contempt for her he was sadly still the most handsome and charismatic man she had met. And he could certainly kiss. She scolded herself for remembering that kiss. He had caused her head to spin when he had held her tight and forced her against the wall. She had been unable to resist him. She had been more stimulated by that one kiss in prison than by all the kisses her fiancé had given to her.

She must be a wanton as he had suggested. She had wanted another kiss, to be comforted after her ordeal. She had wanted him to kiss her but not to want to tame her. She could never love a man who treated her like a featherhead and ignored her feelings and opinions. She admitted to herself, if the circumstances had been different and Denman hadn't been full of blunt and a womaniser she might have been interested in him. Without money, she would now be regarded as a gold-digger and his family would only see her as good enough to be his mistress now her family's reputation was as black as mud.

She cursed her dead brother for pauperising their estate but told herself to grow a backbone and stop being self-pitying. She still had the farm and had to put her head down and start to make plans to make her estate more valuable. Officer Denman had to be forgotten. He was in the past.

Chapter six.

Six months passed. The city lit up at Christmas. Dreda and Felea were going to the Emperor's ball in two days. Denman usually attended this but was having second thoughts. For the last six months he had attended ball after ball, dancing with gay abandon with the young girls who had been presented that season. He was regarded as a great prize by most matching making mamas. He arrived at the opera with a newly widowed woman who after her mourning period was enjoying the freedom her newly found status had given her.

She had wed at seventeen to a man old enough to be her father and twenty years later with four boys ranging from fourteen to eighteen she now considered it was her turn to enjoy herself. An affair with this handsome militiaman who wanted only a casual attachment suited her very well. She still had her beauty and a fortune and didn't need a husband to order her about.

Denman handed her out of the carriage looking devastatingly handsome in his uniform. They made a handsome couple, she a diminutive but lively brunette and he a tall gregarious charmer. Both were social butterflies, engaging conversation with everyone but developing no serious relations with anyone.

He spent more time in gaming hells coming back often half cut. He had always been a keen card player and could handle his drinking but the men he was playing with now were libertines; men who lived on the boundaries of society, barely tolerated by the haut ton. Dreda feared he might become one of those men, continually looking for excitement in a new card game or a bottle. He was pleased his friend had found this new mistress.

Civilised and intelligent, at least she kept him away from the hells some nights. She was wearing a red dress with a ruby necklace lying between voluptuous breasts. She wanted him to take her to the ball and after much persuasion he agreed as he didn't have any real reason for not going.

One ball was the same as another he thought, but there was little else to do with himself. He had exhausted all the gaming hells that week and wanted to lay off the cards and brandy for a few nights and give his head and body a rest from the heavy drinking he had become used to recently.

He could not understand the lethargy that had overtaken him. He usually enjoyed the gaiety, but he suffered the megrims recently. He was blue devilled constantly and didn't know how to lift his spirits. His militia work satisfied him less these days. Dreda was comfortable with the intrigue but sometimes Denman felt he was in the wrong job. He had enjoyed being a soldier and was a good leader of men, but the militia was still full of back stabbers. He was a more open character than Dreda and did not enjoy watching his back all of the time.

Dreda was filling the Militia with new recruits; loyal-ex-army men he had known when he was a Colonel in the Imperial army, but the older officers were friends of the former Emperor, sycophants, of limited intellect, having gained their jobs by patronage. Often second sons, they were there for the status and a secure income, wanting an easy ride until they secured a bountiful pension at an early age.

Dreda vowed to get rid of these parasites but had to tread a careful path between easing them out and upsetting their older powerful friends in the Cabinet Office who still maintained some influence over the new Emperor. The new Emperor was a much wiser ruler than the former one and there were fewer rebellions now, so the work was less hazardous and less interesting. Having itchy feet, Denman was looking for something else to occupy himself, wanting to help Dreda only a few days each week with the difficult cases that would stretch his brain.

He had even distanced himself from Dreda who worried for him. He seemed distant and preoccupied most of the time but if Dreda asked him a question about anything other than work he politely but dismissively changed the subject. It was as if throwing himself into whirl of dances, soirees and balls might keep his mind occupied and off other things.

Only his mistress seemed to light his days now. She was a cheerful woman with an infectious laugh who gained the most out of life like him. Some people thought they were so alike he might marry her but neither of them wanted marriage and despite enjoying her company and her delightful attentions to him in her bed there was something lacking in their relations which made him hold back from offering for her.

Dreda, once the confirmed bachelor now advocated the merits of the married state. Denman did not love his mistress and after recognising the happiness Dreda enjoyed with Felea, his soul-mate, he didn't want to make a marriage of convenience. His parents had made a marriage of convenience and love had developed but that was a rarity. His father had said he would not want such an arrangement for his son. Denman was not as cold and detached as him. He would not stay loyal to a wife he did not love and would take lovers. He needed to marry for love and that was unlikely given the simpering vacuous girls paraded for him each year at the debutantes' ball. He would stick with flings with his widows instead.

He picked his lady up the next night and she looked vivacious and elegant. The colour enhanced her dark, heavily lashed eyes. He thought she looked so enticing, so edible and looked forward to spending part of the evening in her arms. She was a generous lover, undemanding, allowing him freedom to gamble and drink and he had spent many a pleasant afternoon in her apartment. He was always discreet, and he tried to protect both their reputations.

They danced the first dance and then mingled separately with their friends. He was drinking champagne with Felea and Dreda when Felea enquired, 'Who is that divine creature coming in? She wears her dress beautifully. I have not seen her at court before.'

All eyes were on the newcomer, not a young debutante but clearly used to mingling with noblemen and ladies. She was willowy tall, blond and had a good figure. Her hair was quite unusually short and dressed in waves around her slim face. Her major asset was her green-blue eyes which seemed to dominate her face. She wore a sapphire and turquoise blue dress with tiny flowers embroidered over it and the colour enhanced her eyes.

'It is the girl we recently investigated,' said Dreda and Denman only half listening turned around on his heel and stared at her, not believing his eyes. Denman realised she was being reintroduced into court again. She was accompanied by a dragon who was the friend of his mother, so he could find out more details later. She looked divine, cool and elegant and detached. She must have reconciled herself to the fact that she needed a rich husband to help restore the family fortunes. He believed any husband would need to be able to help her sort the farm and vineyard out first before his own issues. She had been solely focussed on those when she had been at the farm.

He had hoped he had rid himself of her memory in his heavy nights of drinking and gambling but now he admitted to himself his repeated dreams had focused on a pair of green-blue eyes defying him. Imbedded in his psyche, she haunted him and reminded him of pleasant memories of the farm and contentment he had never experienced before with a woman.

He caught her eyes and nodded to her, bowing slightly, assessing her reaction to him. Her eyes had widened like a deer caught in the fire of a hunter, fearful and wary of a stronger predator who had her in his eye.

Interesting! *What has disturbed her?* He looked behind him but nothing else could have caused that reaction. He was the one who had disturbed her equilibrium! She looked at him as if she wanted to flee from him.

Helena had felt him there before she had looked at him. Her heart pounded; the colour draining out of her face. He had recognised her despite her mask. She thought he rarely attended court functions and hoped that she would be able to face him easily on the few occasions they met. She steeled her heart and willed the colour to return to her face. She bit her lips to make them red again; for she was sure she resembled a phantom and plastered a beauteous smile on her face and nodded her head to him, acknowledging him with her own small bow.

He watched her eyes turn like ice as she maintained a cold indifferent smile in his direction. He understood her comportment now; her attempt to deny how his presence affected her. Her rejection stung, and his predatory instincts rose to the fore. He wanted to warm those icy eyes up and kiss that false smile off her face; to make her admit she had missed him as much as he had missed her.

'Please don't come over and ask for a dance,' she pleaded silently with him. She could talk with him in her aunt's small circle without giving herself away, but a tight seductive waltz was much too intimate.

Her pleas were unanswered. Denman felt her unease, something he intended to explore. Why did his presence make her uncomfortable? Did she still feel the chemistry he sensed between them sparking across the room despite her frigid attempts to deny her awareness of him? Despite their separation he was still fascinated by her and could not resist the urge to remake his acquaintance with her.

Most of the debutants were shallow, boring him in minutes with their coquettish glances behind their fans and their superficial small-talk. Helena made no effort to entrance him nor did she try to renew their friendship. Only her unease and pallor suggested anything other than she was disinterested in him. She was a mystery worth unravelling and a quarry worth pursuing.

When her dance card came out he made sure he got a waltz. Looking up at him coming over she wished she had filled the slow dances in with the names of men who posed no threat to her peace of mind. He bowed, took the card from her very deliberately and put his name in with a flourish. He smiled, made his leave and left her agitated, although she did not show it, having for years kept her temper when Angelo was aggravating her.

His mistress thought he was just playing the part of a man about town and was not jealous. 'You know the girl?' she asked Denman, noting his eyes kept focusing on her.

'Yes, I helped her when her brother was murdered. She must have come back to catch a husband,' he said dismissively, not wanting his mistress to think he was interested in this woman.

'Has she a fortune?

'Regrettably no. She has a run-down farm she is trying to improve. Her brother gambled most of the family fortune away.'

'She is beautiful,' said his lady. 'But a trifle glacial. She probably thinks her beauty will catch her a rich husband if she plays her cards right.' She eyed Helena up again. 'She is a bit long in the tooth despite her looks, almost an ape leader. Her chances are small if she is a fortune hunter. There are too many like her.' Denman began to see her in a new light and passing her on to a new partner to dance he began to think about detaching himself from this lady.

Felea had had severe treatment from the ladies of a foreign court when she had been engaged to a duke. Whilst an unmarried girl she had suffered poisonous barbs hurled at her by jealous rivals for Dreda's attention. She had been insulted, called a 'spoiled dove'.

Only the influence of the powerful Dreda had stopped her from being accused of being a spy and hung. He had protected her from the barbs and insults and their marriage had cloaked her with status and respectability. She was slowly becoming accepted.

She took pity on new debutantes and was friendly to them. She went to the woman and swiftly engaged her in conversation.

Dreda had whispered in her ear that this was the girl Denman may have formed an attachment to. He had watched his friend freeze when Helena walked in, unable to take his eyes off her. The girl had also looked as if she had been struck by lightning when she saw him. Even across the room the attraction between them was evident; each trying to pretend they were politely indifferent to the other and yet drawn to each other.

Then Denman's expression had changed. Her look of disinterest had changed his mind. Dreda recognised a look in his friend's eye he had not seen before with any woman. He had seen that look on the hunting field when his friend had sought out his quarry and chased it without mercy until he had nailed it.

This girl had piqued his interest again and he intended to net her; to prove she wasn't indifferent to him. God help the girl when Denman wanted her. He would have a word with him. His friend was a gentleman who shared his own moral boundaries and didn't chase innocents and Dreda wouldn't encourage him now.

Felea couldn't resist the temptation to find out if this young girl held a tendre for their dearest friend who had looked so despondent and lost recently. She took her arm in hers and said, 'I hear you were helped by Dreda and Denman. They thought you were wasted on your farm. I am so glad you decided to enter society again. Are you here for the whole season?'

'Yes, I am here for the whole season Lady Felea. My uncle is sponsoring me.' She spoke honestly to Felea. Her reputation abroad proclaimed her as fair and un-judgemental. She was her own person, fiercely independent of her powerful husband and making her own mind up about any person she met.

'Now my brother is dead and will not bring scandal on his house he and my aunt will recognise me. He has been very generous and my aunt kindness herself. With several daughters already married she has the experience to ensure I meet the right people and do not incur the disapproval of the patronesses.'

Felea knew it would not take much for this girl with a tainted family reputation to incur the wrath of the powerful and judgemental patronesses who ruled the balls and soirees as fiercely as the army generals ruled their troops. One false step and a debutante could have her vouchers removed and be ostracised by polite society. Helena had to walk a tightrope until she was accepted by those severe ladies who dominated 'polite society.'

'I will send you vouchers for my next ball and would love you to play at one of my musicals. I hear from Denman you are an accomplished musician.' Helena coloured, unused to compliments. She wondered what else Denman had told this gracious lady.

'I have some skill and studied and performed at the Conservatoire in my town. I am out of practise but if you are prepared to accept my limitations I would gladly play for you at one of your evenings.'

Felea instantly liked this modest young girl. She noted she avoided discussing Denman. Most debutantes gushed about the man if he gave them the slightest attention. This one pretended he did not exist.

How interesting! thought Felea, her clever mind quickly summing up the situation. She noted the couple kept passing swift glances at each other when they thought the other wasn't looking. Then Denman had fixed her stare on Helena and she had been the first to break eye contact. She was nervous of Denman's attention. When he took her dance card from her she pulled her hand away from him quickly as if she didn't want to acknowledge the contact between them.

Felea knew Denman. She had seen him chase women time after time until he had snared them, enjoying the chase as much as the capture. This girl was too inexperienced for him. She could get hurt if he fixed his attentions on her and flirted with her, toying with her. She was no experienced courtesan or widow or bored wife, ready to play the delightful game of illicit liaison until Denman or she became bored. She did not understand the rules of the game. She was not like the bits of fluff or hoydens Denman usually associated with. Serious and intelligent, she bore the scars of a broken engagement. She was not a girl to be trifled with.

Felea, a woman whose heart had held secrets recognised a kindred spirit. Only since she had married Dreda and trusted him with her life had she opened up to him; her icy reserve dissipating as she was sheltered and protected by his love. She would warn Denman off. He was too strong meat for this young girl. Allowing him to pursue her would be like tossing her to the wolves.

Helena confided in her. Her Uncle and Aunt were ambitious for her. It was not the first time a beautiful woman had had her dowry gambled away by a dissolute brother. They hoped to find a wealthy suitor who would want to marry into an old lineage and have a graceful and beautiful wife to reign over and manage his household to perfection. Her aunt entering into the conversation said she was an excellent organiser and hostess and she talked with ease to all types of guests.

She was inundated with young men wanting to dance and had a pleasant evening but when the first waltz came, and Denman walked over her heart sank. She took his arm and they proceeded to dance. She was tall, but her head only came up to his shoulder and at first, she didn't look into his eyes. This was clearly rude and when he engaged her in conversation she put up a polite front and pretended to be light-hearted.

'When did you arrive?' asked Denman.

'A week ago, but my aunt made me visit dressmakers and milliners before she would allow anyone to see me. She described me as a brown faced country bumpkin.'

'Is Lucia at the farm?'

'No, she deteriorated so badly we had to put her into a convent hospital and the nuns are nursing her. They think she will not last more than a month. She does not recognise me.

'Mother persuaded me that life alone on a farm was not pleasant. She might not be here for many years as her health is poor, so I am come here to broaden my horizons.'

'Do you find it very different after your busy farm life?'

'Very, Officer Denman, but I have been so very busy I have had not had time to miss my former life, although I miss my mother and the farm-hands.' To herself, she wondered how she would avoid boredom given the feminine conversation was about men, clothes and balls and getting a rich husband. People in the haut ton were so much more superficial than those at home.

He was not surprised she had fitted in so well. She would be at home in any noble home. She carried herself like a queen with a natural quiet dignity that many other girls tried without success to emulate. He still thought she could be bored without any useful duties to perform. She had always been so busy and focussed on the farm.

'If it is not impertinent might I suggest that you attend the music concerts at the Palace? Your aunt may permit you to give some performances yourself in her house.'

'Thank you for your suggestions, Officer. My aunt has decided she will organise some musical soirees and I shall perform some music. I was used to playing in concerts before our family's misfortune meant I stopped attending these functions.

As the waltz grew faster he twirled her off her feet and for balance she leaned against him. He looked down at her and the look in his eyes made her heart beat faster. The beat slowed down and he led her back to her aunt. He had a determined and satisfied expression on his face which she would have given anything to be able to read.

Her aunt quizzed her about what he had said to her, saying he would be a good catch. She was intrigued to know he was the militia officer who had helped her niece and she would invite him to one of her soirees. Helena did not welcome that idea. He was too sure of himself and she was sure he knew the affect he had on her. She had known he was a flirt before but now she heard his terrible reputation had not been exaggerated and was sure he had been toying with her at the farm; she an innocent virgin he could laugh about later with his friends. He had behaved ungentlemanly, kissing her at the prison, taking advantage of her vulnerable situation and he had insulted her.

She had not told her aunt what he had done but she had just explained he was not interested in her in any romantic way and would make a terrible husband. Her aunt was unconvinced. Denman rarely danced with a debutante and had made a beeline for her niece insisting on the waltzes and making it clear he admired her. She would watch them carefully.

Helena had not read Denman correctly. For once he was unsure of what he wanted from life. He was no longer blue-devilled. For the first time in months he felt stimulated and there was something worth getting out of bed for. That young wench had re-entered his life and had turned it upside down again without any intention of doing so. He realised he had missed her sorely.

They may have squabbled but there was that spark between them that could not be extinguished. She was still the most intriguing girl he had met. Most of the other women he knew were full of fashion and the latest balls and bored him in minutes. His lively mistress paled into insignificance by her side.

He had thought he wanted a woman who would laugh with him, comfort him and warm his bed but now he needed more, stronger meat; a woman who would challenge him if he got too big for his boots. Helena was like Felea. He had seen the diminutive Felea, hands on her hips, remonstrating with Dreda, a man nearly double her age and a severe disciplinarian who made grown men quake when he threatened them. The two women were cut from the same cloth.

Helena would not stay quiet if she believed he Denman had made the wrong decision or treated someone badly. She would fight him tooth and nail to defend her principles or her friends. He realised he loved it when he made her angry, her eyes sparkling with green-blue fire. The ice maiden disappeared, to be replaced by a young girl who was alive and passionate and made his blood heat.

He longed to have her in his arms again, not merely to hold in a dance but to kiss her and persuade her to give herself to him. He was certain she was attracted to him. He had felt her heart race when he had pulled her tight. In prison she had melted in his arms when he had kissed her passionately, her arms moving around his neck, pulling him to her to deepen the kiss. Yet she had seemed angry at herself for showing she was attracted to him. He told himself sternly attraction was not the same as liking or loving a man though. She behaved as if he irritated her all the time, as if she only tolerated him. She exhibited self-disgust for giving in to her attraction for him.

Denman still balked at marriage, but he recognised Helena was not like his 'light-skirts.' He could not offer her a carte blanche or indulge in a fling with her. Her reputation was too fragile since her brother had gambled away his money and she had been arrested for killing him.

Mud stuck unfortunately. Some doors had been closed to her by the redoubtable patrons who led society. She was trying to restore her family's reputation. She was not the sort who would accept anything less than marriage and he was not ready to become a tenant for life. For the moment he would simply enjoy her company.

Chapter seven.

Helena's next month was to be a month of balls and soirees. After Helena practised her pieces her aunt realised how talented she was and arranged some musicals. Her niece was an instant hit and she was invited to perform at many functions. Denman came to the musicals and surprised her by moving her music sheets for her and singing duets with her in his strong tenor. Her aunt gave her friends knowing looks. He was much more interested in her niece than she had led her to believe.

He always asked for the waltzes with her and unsettled her further although he never made any romantic gestures toward her. Helena felt like a mouse waiting for a cat to pounce. Her aunt asked her what they talked about but all she said was music and dancing and the theatre. Like Dreda he had a fine brain although it was well hidden under his preoccupation with horseracing, women and dancing. He had had good tutors and could now extend it with a dancing companion who had as sharp a mind as he had.

Helena' aunt was satisfied. Her niece was becoming one of the most popular debutantes that season. Surely, such a beautiful and accomplished and genuinely pleasant young girl could catch a husband and not be forced to go home to her miserable impoverished life on the farm.

Unfortunately, disaster struck. Helena's mother had caught a fever and was not recovering. Her heart was weak, and she needed careful nursing. Helena immediately packed and was escorted home. Her mother had taken to her bed and the farm showed signs of neglect. The labourers had taken advantage of her weakness and absence and had become lazy.

She feared her mother would die but careful nursing day and night brought the fever down although her mother's heart was weakened even more. A physic suggested she could live several years if she was careful and did not try to manage the farm. Helena was furious her mother's good-nature and weakness had been abused. She dismissed the two lazy labourers and took on some of their work herself. She found two hard-working and very submissive young men who would do as they were told.

Tired but pleased the farm was improving under her firm direction she tried not to yearn for the city life. Letters from Felea reminded of her happy musicals and outings with her new friend. After the varied city life, she now felt suffocated on the farm. She had not been restricted in the city to the superficial conversation of the haut ton. Felea had introduced her to a group of intellectuals who stretched her mind at their meetings and soirees.

Her only visits outside of this farm were to market where she made little conversation with the other farmers' wives there who were suspicious of this formerly wealthy girl who had deserted her rural life for the city and thought herself too good for them. The noble people in the region still ignored her after hearing rumours about her brother's traitorous behaviour. She was not one of them any longer, nor would they risk their neck to help the sister of a traitor.

Lonely and bored she worked hard to make herself sleep. Her uncle at last wrote to her, telling her he could put a steward in the farm if she wanted to return to his household again. For the first time in two months she felt alive again. She might be able to visit the city again and get away from this hardship for a while, a breathing space to give her time to decide her future. She missed the musicals; the playing before an audience which lifted her soul when she played her beloved instruments to those who appreciated good music. A natural artist, she enjoyed giving pleasure to her audience. She would write back to her uncle asking for an escort.

A hammering and then a thundering on the door woke Helena up from an uneasy fitful sleep. She had been worrying about money again. The persistent thumping made her drag herself out of bed and pulling on a warm and thick wrap she ran downstairs to where her groom, her faithful retainer was waiting at the door, pistol in hand waiting for his instruction from her.

Wearily she nodded to him to open the door a crack. She should be pleased the man took orders so readily from her but sometimes she had wished the new men on her farm had more energy and would act manlier; more willing to shoulder responsibility and take charge. Too often they ran to her to settle every little dispute and could not act alone to make decisions which should not come to her. Very young, they lacked the ability to lead when situations became dire.

Two men pulled a young boy, bloody and caked with mud into her kitchen. Ragged and thin to the point of emaciation they dragged their friend to an empty chair and held him there.

'Water quick, warm to bathe his wounds and cool to drink, he loses blood,' the older demanded, pulling a coat around the injured boy who was shivering, his face pale and creasing with intensity as he closed his eyes as if to shut the pain out.

Helena recognised the boy, still not sixteen. His family, tenants, had been kicked off a neighbouring farm when the yields fell, and they could no longer feed themselves. His father, brothers and he had vanished, presumably to join the rebel forces. The mother and younger siblings had been sent to the workhouse. The family had worked casually on her farm when her family had more money. She could no more turn this boy away than she could her own kin if they came demanding aid. They were bonded together by the land, a bond that crossed classes and political boundaries.

Her father, while a patriot had still aided any injured rebels who had come to the farm to seek help. Too often the rebels were men desperate when the harvest failed, and their children starved. They had asked to buy the stocks of grain the landowners kept but their requests had been rejected, the militia hunting them down when they had stolen to keep their families alive.

The officers of the militia often resented the job of guarding the grain until it could be sent to the towns and exported at a much higher price to neighbouring states where the harvest had also failed. Some officers had turned a blind eye to thefts but when their fellow officers were court martialled for this offence they enforced their superiors' orders and hung the ringleaders.

Angry and wanting retribution and revenge, hot-blooded and hot tempered young men had joined the rebel forces in droves. A new leader stirred their blood and promised vengeance. He promised them enough grain, lower taxes, a greater share of the land and decent livings if the rebels won. He motivated them to make raids on the militia and grain wagons being taken to the large towns.

Helena was in two minds. Her brother's behaviour had put her in grave danger. She could not condone theft nor violence, but she sympathised with men who only wanted to save their families. This boy would die if she didn't help him. She also had been forced before into a hard place without any choices and decided to help him.

'Fetch water, towels, blankets and salve,' she ordered to her doubtful servants. 'Put him on the couch in the salon.' Muttering grimly, her groom left. His mistress had gone too far this time; her kind heart risking their necks if the militia found they were helping a rebel.

Helena follow the man and tore his shirt off his chest. The wound was far worse, a jagged opening in his stomach. She doubted he would survive the night even with her care. The younger of the two men watched her closely and then said, 'We need food if you have some to spare. Bread and cheese will do. We haven't eaten in two days.'

She nodded, and her groom told the servants, 'Bring food and ale for these three.' He held the man down while the fellow wriggled and jumped whilst she poked a knife in his wound trying to pull the bullet out.

'Sit down you two.' He still held his pistol at them. There was a look in the older man's eyes he didn't like. He had seen that look before when serving in the Imperial Army with Helena's father. It was the way the man's eyes searched the room, eying the locked cabinets, assessing the value of the worn carpets and wall hangings and the ring and necklace Helena wore. It was the look of man who couldn't be trusted, who took what he wanted. He prayed they could patch the injured man up and send these three on their way before they took all the food and anything else of value they could pawn or sell.

'That is all I can do,' she said tightening the bandages over the man's torso. 'He needs rest now.' She got up.

'You can all sleep in a cottage until he is well enough to travel.

'We'll need your cart to take him.'

'You can forget that. We need it to transport goods to market.'

'Our need is greater than yours. You can collect it when we have finished. We will leave it with an inn-keeper in Hedri.'

'No, if my groom collects it he will be deemed to have helped you. The man goes on his horse. I must protect my servants. They cannot be associated with rebels.'

She looked him in the eye. 'You are rebel soldiers, aren't you?'

'Yes, Mistress. We thought you would want to help us as we worked with your brother. He supported the cause.' That was the last thing she wanted to hear. Any cause her brother supported was bad news. He had only ever brought trouble on their house. She made up her mind quickly. No dissembling here.

'We will give you shelter and food but that is all.' Johann reinforced her words with a rifle aimed at them. The man looked angry but agreed. The able-bodied men from the farm helped them carry the man to the cart and he was transported to the cottage where a stove and blankets would keep them warm.

'We haven't seen the back of them, my Lady,' grumbled Johann.

For pity's sake. Do I really need to be reminded of the danger? When would he look on the bright side? They had got rid of them for a while. They might be back but at least they had left the villa.

'Lock the villa up and take it in turns to guard the window. If you hear anything untoward wake me up,' she ordered and went back to grab a few hours' sleep. The men were back the next morning, hammering on the door again.

'What do you want this time?' demanded Helena aggressively. Being nice would get her nowhere. These men were out for trouble. She could now feel it in her bones, the way they assessed her and found her wanting. She was just a pathetic weak young girl in their eyes. She could only hope she could satisfy them with some food to take away.

'Our friend is dead. His wounds were too bad. He lasted only an hour. We need to get away. New clothes, food and monies. Your brother said we could come to you for help.'

'Well he was wrong. He over-estimated our earnings. I am still paying back his debts from the income of the farm. I can give you some food and clothes but that is all.'

'There are militia men in the village. They are hunting rebel escapees from the battle at Villia. They are searching all the cottages on the estates in this area. We only just missed being captured yesterday. We need to hide here a few more days, but in the villa. They won't believe you are hiding us, your father having been an Imperial soldier once.'

'No, I won't have you in the villa. It is too risky. We will find you somewhere else.'

'You have no choice Mistress. There is no other way,' said the younger man called Balatz, putting a pistol to her head. 'We must get back to our leader. He has work for us. We cannot let him down now he is so close to winning this battle.'

Unlike his older colleague who was more pragmatic, his fervent speech and burning eyes betrayed his fanaticism. He was a true believer in the rebel's cause; willing to sacrifice himself and her.

'Lead us to a spare chamber we can rest in and get us some more food.' Helena agreed reluctantly and led them to a chamber in the attic. The older man Gremetz fell on to the bed.

'Soft! I'll be asleep in minutes.'

'You stay here,' he ordered Helena. 'You're our security if the militia comes.'

'I promise you I will tell them you have not been near here. My servants have burnt your dead man's clothes. They said there is no blood on the bed. If you are quiet, they may go away.'

'No, you are our insurance. Sit.' He looked her up and down sending a shiver down her back. His eyes were hungry. He clearly had not tasted a woman in a while. He withdrew his eyes and gave himself a little shake, obviously pulling himself together.

'You need not fear us Mistress. We have wives at home. Under these rough clothes we are gentlemen unless you betray us. We have no desires upon your virtue. But betray us and you will die with us.' Satisfied she was safe for the present Helena sat down and read one of the books that were by the bed. Poorly written and childlike, it was the book of a servant but kept her mind occupied. Agile and acute, she would otherwise have worried about her servants. They took turns, one man sleeping whilst the other guarded her.

Interrupted sleep the night before made her drowsy and she was woken up by a downstairs door being opened and a familiar voice. 'I seek Lady Helena,' said the unwelcome voice.

'I am afraid she is not here,' said Johann. 'She is visiting a friend.'

'She went last night. She should be back in four days, Sir.'

Oh, please let him go away. Is he leading the militia troop searching for these men?

Trust Denman always to be around when she was in trouble. He must have a sixth sense for danger, the dratted man. She had hoped if these men had hid in the attics they might have escaped in a few days. If Denman was searching for them they would stand little chance of escaping. She had seen how thorough and observant he was when he had searched the farm before and interrogated her servants. She believed the men when they said they would kill her if they thought she had betrayed them.

Denman bowed and left the house. His hairs were rising on the back of his neck. The groom Johann seemed perfectly relaxed although he had come to the door armed with a rifle early in the morning. Helena rarely left the farm for more than a day. She said she had no time to spare for idle gossip. She had denied having any close friends after her family had lost their money and her fiancé had dumped her.

He walked around to the stables. The carriage and her horse were there. Who had taken her in their carriage? There were horses, badly fed thin things, as if they had lived in the rough hills for weeks. They probably didn't belong to anyone on the farm. Helena had visitors and poorly fed ones it seemed if these fellows were like their horseflesh.

Johann came out. Denman pulled him into a stable holding him by the throat. He did not know who a traitor was and who was a rebel supporter.

'Where is Lady Helena?' he demanded. Johann blubbered as he coughed and spluttered, unable to speak clearly. Denman released him a little giving him the opportunity to make out a few words

'She is in the attic. She helped an injured rebel soldier who died last night, and his fellows are with her.'

'Damn the woman. She has a nose for seeking trouble.'

'They came here seeking help. She did not invite them here,' cried Johann defending his mistress.

'It matters not, she still has helped them. Are they fit to leave?'

'Yes Sir. They have been sleeping and eating. They are in poor condition.'

'They are probably the escapees my fellow officers and I seek. I took a few hours out to ensure Lady Helena was safe with these escapees on the loose. It seems I was right to check.'

How the devil am I going to get her out of this fix this time? Her bleeding heart will get her hung one day. He cursed her liberally. He did not believe she was a traitor, just a soft-hearted girl who would let her heart lead her brain.

'How many are there and what sort of men are they?'

'One of honour, gently spoken if roughly clothed, the other less trustworthy and too interested in the belongings of this household for my liking, but Sir, they said they will kill her if they think she has betrayed them. I think they will not violate her, but they said it behoved her to help them as her brother had supported their cause and helped them personally. He had told them to come here for help if they were in trouble.'

Shit! It was worse than he had thought. They would not merely take her hostage but would kill her in cold blood if he tried to take them back. They were clearly fanatics, not the ordinary poor peasant lads encouraged to join a cause for bread and ale.

'We need to clear this farm of this vermin. How many men do you have available?'

'Two others who are young like me.'

'Have them armed and ready to serve me. Bring the rebels doped wine and we will pounce later. I will stay in here until you call me.'

He sat down on a bundle of hay. *Wait till I get hold of you my girl. You won't know what has befallen you?* he threatened an imaginary Helena.

Johann woke Helena up from her snooze. 'My Lady I brought you and the gentlemen some food and wine. Your medicine is there at your feet. The men stirred and gratefully ate the food and drunk the wine, clearly a luxury they had not experienced in months.

Helena blinked. *Medicine! What medicine?* She was as healthy as a horse and her mother was recovering well.

Johann continued. 'I know you want to drink the wine, but your doctor forbade you in your condition. He sent a message saying he wants to talk with you soon.'

Helena now understood. The wine was doped. Someone was trying to help her. Was it Denman? This was just the type of jape he would appreciate if it were not such a serious situation. She drunk her medicine, some foul concoction made to look genuine to her observers.

'How soon will you be able to leave?' she asked the soldiers.

'Are the militia still searching the area?' He pointed his pistol at Helena. 'The truth now. I can tell if you are lying. We can ask the other servants. Their loyalty won't stretch to losing their lives to protect their mistress.'

Johann shrugged. 'They are still around but have searched our out-buildings. They seemed satisfied and are leaving the area tomorrow if the rumours at the inn can be believed.'

'We still need another night to be sure. We leave the day after tomorrow.' He settled down again in his bed, a luxury he was enjoying after a bedroll on cold hard earth.

'Damn the men,' swore Helena under her breath. Why couldn't they just go? If Denman came they would be caught and taken back but there would be a fight and bloodshed. He would not let them go again to fight the Emperor's troops. He was too much of a patriot and Emperor's man like Dreda to allow that. He might be hurt. She couldn't contemplate that. He might be irritating and dominating but he was a decent kind man who had tried to help her. She had to stop him.

She got up, the men aroused and immediately anxious. One laid his hand on her arm in a tight grip, stopping from moving.

'What do you intend Mistress?

'I need to try to send a message to the doctor saying I feel better or he will turn up here asking to see me.'

Denman was waiting for the summons from Johann to rescue Helena. He had told Johann to send for his men. They were to arrive under the cover of darkness. The rebels should be drowsy by then and easily taken for prisoners. If only Helena cooperated with them and remained safe all would be well. He had misgivings. She was woman enough to make her own mind up and try to escape her captors.

Johann peered around the stable. 'My lady is demanding she leaves the chamber, but the men won't let her.'

'She is better out of there than in. They may hostage her if we try to enter the chamber.'

'I think that was in her mind Sir, but they see her as their insurance.'

'Your mistress should not have let them in. She has brought this on the household.'

'She knew the lad who died personally, Sir. It nearly broke her heart to see him dying.'

'It will break her neck if she ends up on the scaffold for helping traitors,' muttered Denman. 'Or perhaps she prefers a bullet through the head for betraying the rebels.'

Dusk fell early, and the officers arrived. Denman gave his orders quickly. 'Johann will show you to the secret passage which leads into the attic room. You come in behind the beds where the men are lying. I will distract them from the main door. When you hear one come to the door and unlock it enter. Blow their brains out of necessity; just ensure Lady Helena is safe and out of the way as quickly as possible.'

He crossed himself and set up the stairs. The door to the attic was thick but he could hear an argument taking place. Helena was imperiously demanding to go downstairs. It was now or never while they were being distracted by her vehement complaining.

He knocked loudly on the door making the inhabitants jump and turn around hastily. The man holding Helena pulled her to him and said, 'Open the door,' but Denman shot the latch and pushed it open surprising him as Helena stabbed him in the gut as hard as she could with a letter opener. He doubled over, and Denman kicked his pistol out of his hand. Grabbing him by the collar, Denman pushed him on the bed and manacled his hands behind his back.

Johann and his officers crept through the secret door. The rebel felt cold steel prick his neck, the bayonet of a rifle and dropped his pistol.

'You are safe my Lady and unharmed?'

'Yes, they are rebels but gentleman at heart. They only wanted to escape not violate me.'

'You bitch, you betrayed us,' cried Gremetz. 'We should have killed you when we had the chance.'

'Not so,' said Denman. You betrayed yourself when you came here. Your tracks were easy to follow. You should have left the cottage and tried to make your way to the mountains.'

We can still take her with us,' said Gremetz maliciously. 'We will say she aided us rebels. The court will thank us for serving a traitor to the Emperor's militia. She will be trialled with us as a traitor, the rebel's accomplice. Who will believe she isn't a traitor after her brother's traitorous activities.'

'I didn't betray you. I was going to try to stop this officer from coming here until you after you had left to give you time to escape. I wanted no bloodshed.'

'You murdered your brother, why not betray us?'

'My servant killed my brother and she is dead now. I took the blame to protect her.'

Denman watched this argument, his face turning darker and harder like stone. These men were consumed by hatred now. They believed the rumours about her brother now they were captured. Nothing would change their minds. She would be sacrificed for their revenge.

Making his mind up quickly, he took out his two pistols. 'There will be no trial,' he said softly and pulled the triggers. The two men looked shocked as they crumpled to the floor, two holes appearing in the foreheads as their brains were splashed across the walls. Helena knelt on the floor and checked their pulses. Dead as doornails, the both of them.

'Don't look at me like that Woman. It was you or them,' he snapped, looking at her shocked countenance. 'They would have taken you to the gallows with them. You cannot rationalize with fanatics like those. They were not like your brother, out for money. They believed in their cause.'

He turned to Johann. 'Get the youngest and strongest men and dig some graves in the most isolated place, somewhere the graves will be covered by undergrowth soon. Take these men and bury them. I will pay ten gold sovereigns each to the men and women in the household to keep your mouths shut about this but if any of you blab I will report you as traitors to the militia. You understand!'

Johann nodded. Colonel Denman was not to be messed with. He had earned his reputation for ruthlessness under Dreda's command and had proved it true in this room. He moved swiftly to carry out the officer's command.

Helena still felt sick as he helped her up. He led her down the stairs to the salon and poured out a brandy for her.

'Drink! You look faint. It is the shock.' She drank it and the colour came back into her cheeks. She had to thank him. She cursed herself. Two men had died because she was soft-hearted and had let them in the house. She should have let them take their chances and try to outrun the militia. They were fools and fanatics and she believed they would have given evidence against her in court. Her story wouldn't have been believed. Denman had saved her life. She knew he could be ruthless but killing men in cold blood showed her the type of man he really was.

'I am grateful to you officer,' she uttered carefully, not wanting him to guess her misgivings. His eyebrows rose, the scepticism written on his face. 'I realise you saved me from the gallows. These were not reasonable men and I shouldn't have let them in the house. Their deaths are on my conscience.'

'Forget your conscience,' he said scathingly. 'They would have sacrificed you in an instant, be sure about that. Your bleeding heart nearly got you hung again.'

Cursing her inwardly, he changed the subject. 'Your uncle asked me to find out if you needed an escort back to town. You are missed dreadfully. Your mother is recovered now?'

'Yes, and she wants me to return to Aunt and Uncle, but the farm fell into disorganisation when I left, and Mother was sick. I have restored order but what do I do while I am away? No-one is strong enough to take charge.'

'Your uncle is sending his agent to select a man to take on the stewardship of the farm while you are in the city.

Helena acquiesced. 'Then I will be ready in two days. When will you have finished rounding up the escapees?'

'Two days is enough. I will collect you at ten in the morning Lady Helena.' He picked up his cloak and hat.

'You must break your fast with us.'

'No thank you my Lady. I have work to do if I am to complete my task in time.' He bowed and left swiftly. He had felt her coldness and withdrawal and wanted out of her company if she found his presence distasteful. Cursing delicate and oversensitive females he would succour his wounded feelings with a bottle of brandy that night and the welcome attentions of the female at the hostelry he lodged in.

Helena did not hear from him until he turned up with a militia escort at ten o'clock sharp. *Damn the man.* He still looked stern and unfriendly, wearing his disapproving Friday face. Gone was the jovial flirting man about town she remembered.

'We leave in ten minutes sharp my Lady,' was all he said after politely asking about her mother's heath. *This was to be a wearing journey,* she thought. He still hadn't forgiven her for aiding the rebels. Did he think she condoned the behaviour of the rebels? She empathized with their need to feed their families, but she did not condone the ambushing and killing of the Emperor's troops particularly when it brought retribution on the villages.

She knew Dreda was trying to change the Emperor's policy. He tried to get the Emperor to demand his landowners sell more grain to his own people instead of inflated prices abroad, but his ruler relied on these rich landlords for men to supplement the army and militia when there was a threat of invasion by one of the city states that surrounded Taylia. So far, he had not succeeded in changing the Emperor's mind, but the tactics of the rebels held back his cause.

Half way-through the day she could not stand the icy tension between them any longer. In the private parlour of the inn where they made their luncheon, she ventured, 'I would have words with you Officer Denman, in private please?' Denman raised his eyebrows in that imperious way of his and replied, 'Of course, I am at your service.'

Her maid left. Gathering her courage, she asked, 'Do you consider I am a patriot Officer Denman or do you believe I condone the actions of the rebels against the Emperor's officers and his property?'

Denman considered her words. She was brave making this direct request to him. What had got into that sharp brain of hers? She may act featherheaded at times but despite her reckless actions she was still one of the most intelligent females he had met. In the army she would have made a good officer if her recklessness had been tamed and directed in the right way. On the farm it just led her into trouble.

'I do not think you are a traitor nor a rebel sympathiser. You are like Felea, too soft-hearted and your bleeding heart will earn you a noose round your neck if you are not careful.'

She was grateful he did not think she had traitorous leanings. *Why the devil is he so disapproving of me then?*

In fact, Denman was sore she had treated him like a leper when he had saved her neck. Most other ladies deferred to him or tried to attract him, treating him like a war hero; flattering him and asking him to recount some of his hairier experiences in the civil war.

What more could he do to make this girl respect him? She was attracted to him, but he felt she did not like him or award him the respect a senior militia officer deserved. He did not know what he had done to deserve the way she behaved toward him; always ready to challenge him and point out when she thought he was in the wrong.

'I'm so pleased you do not think I am a traitor, but I am sad you resent my womanly leanings. I shall endeavour to keep out of trouble and save you the task of helping me in the future.'

So saying, she swept out to the carriage and slammed the door shut, burying her head in a journal. *Bloody man! If the Emperor was more sensitive and caring, then perhaps this civil war would not have been prolonged, and we might have peace.* It was pig-headed advisers in the cabinet who encouraged the Emperor to hold a hard line when Dreda was asking him to soften his approach and negotiate with the rebels and change his policies to make life for the peasants easier, so they were not forced to leave their rural life.

Damned girl, always wanting the last word. Denman climbed on to his horse and the journey proceeded, the protagonists maintaining a polite and frosty silence until Helena was delivered to her aunt's house safely and he made his adieus.

He made no effort to visit her at her aunt's. She only saw him at balls where he was very formal and aloof.

Felea asked Helena what had caused this coolness. Helena frowned. Only Denman, Johann, his officers and Dreda knew what had occurred at the farm. They were sworn to secrecy. She decided she could trust Felea. When she remembered that night she felt ashamed of her stupidity.

Denman may be an odious manipulative man, but he saved my life again. She had been repelled by his ruthlessness but in retrospect she had recognised it was necessary. Harsh times required harsh methods to stay safe.

'You do not know what happened at the farm. I was foolish. Two rebel soldiers knocked on our door asking for help for their injured colleague. I knew the boy and could not turn them away. The next day they told me he had died but insisted I gave them refuge in my house. They were to hide in my attic until militia officers in the area had left and they could leave safely.

'Denman was leading the search for these men and had come to the farm to offer an escort back to the city for me. The men insisted I slept in the attic with them as their insurance.' Felea's eyebrows rose.

'Oh no, Felea. They behaved gentlemanly. They did not touch me, except to make me sit in a hard chair. Denman was sent away but came back. Johann drugged the men and Denman and his officers forced their way into the chamber and captured them. Sadly, they blamed me for their capture, accusing me of betraying them. They had warned me that they would kill me if I betrayed them to the militia. They accused me of killing my brother and said they would say at their trial I was a traitor and had aided them willingly.

'They were fanatics, absolutely dedicated to their cause and I would have been hung as a traitor. Denman said there would be no trial and shot them dead. I was shocked at his brutality and ruthlessness and later asked him if he thought I was a traitor. He replied, 'No, but my bleeding heart would get me hung one day.' He was contemptuous of me and clearly thought I should have been more grateful. He has been acting cool to me ever since.'

'Francis acted the same way to me when I was investigated and accused of financing arms for the rebels. He was just as ruthless. I heard he would have tortured a man who tried to frame me until he told the truth. They are two of a kind, kind to their friends and family but there is a dark side they contain and let out when they confront even harsher and more sinister men than themselves.' She shivered. 'I am just glad I am not their enemies.

'I would have done the same as you in that situation. I could not let the poor boy die. Many boys join the rebel army because they are impoverished and have no homes nor employment. Their choices are almost non-existent.

'Denman will come around in time. He rarely holds a grudge. I will ask him to escort us to the Zoological gardens.' Felea was determined to end this stand-off by her two best friends. Dreda was out of the city and she demanded his escort. Denman came reluctantly. Dreda had told Felea that Denman considered Helena treated him like a leper.

'You are wrong. She feels guilty and thinks you hold her in contempt. She was just shocked you had to take such drastic action to save her and is grateful to you.'

'I don't hold her in contempt. I just wish she was not so reckless. She endangers herself by her courageousness.'

'Don't bring the subject up. Just admit you missed her and charm her out of her sullenness.'

She explained to her friend, 'He is not contemptuous of you Helena. He was merely feared you would be harmed. Francis was the same when he feared I would be hung by uttering unwise words. Just ignore the incident and make him welcome.'

Helena feared another tongue-lashing but despite her misgivings she wanted to be friends with Denman again. Under that devil may care personality was a caring man. He would always joke her out of her black moods when her future looked bleak. Her life without his attention had felt as dull as a winter sky.

Denman, now mollified, took Helena's arm and walked her around the enclosures where they could get some privacy. He had missed her acerbic company and sharp wit. He had overreacted and was sharp with her instead of making her feel comfortable with him. She was not one of his militia officers, used to making split second life or death decisions.

'Look how elegant this lady is,' he said to Helena as they watched a leopard slink along the branch of a tree.

The animal stared at them unblinking from its resting post.

'Stunning!' replied Helena.

'And cunning. Look how silently she watches.'

The cat saw a keeper throw her dinner on the ground and sprung on to it, taking it and devouring it at the back of the cage. Helena shivered. 'I would not like to be her prey. Her instincts and reactions are too good.'

'Come,' said Denman. 'Let's go to the tea room for an ice, a treat after that unpleasant scene.' Pleased he was in a good mood, she smiled that brilliant smile of hers, which always made him feel sunny inside; good relations having been restored between them at last.

Chapter eight.

Felea felt sick at times. At first, she worried she was enceinte, but her courses came, and headaches accompanied the sickness. The sickness often preceded a vision. Marriage to Francis Dreda had brought her security and safety. Her telepathic powers were growing with their intimacy. Trusting her he had relaxed, and they were much closer; so close she could frequently read his mind and what he was thinking. Her visions were clearer, usually warning her of danger but when she was near a person she could absorb the vibrations emanating from their bodies and read their emotions and sometimes their thoughts.

Felea instantly gelled with Helena and took her under her wing. They closeted themselves in her salon to talk of men and other feminine topics. Helena felt like she had a sister in her friend. Warmth and kindness vibrated from Felea. She hated deceit and spoke frankly like Helena to those she could trust.

They both had strong social consciences and Helena helped Felea organise her charity balls. She mentioned if she had sufficient funds she would help young women like the young whore who had been abused and sold to the brothel by her father. She had found her work in her household and the girl was engaged to be married to one of the farmworkers.

Over a year ago Felea had visited the rebel women's makeshift camps. Their houses had been burnt down by Imperial troops and Felea had raised money for these women's needs. Dreda had anonymously organised the provisions for these women. They would have refused his help if they knew the money came from him, the Emperor's right-hand man.

Felea had visited the camp with a male friend without Dreda's permission. He had prohibited her from doing so, being afraid of her catching the fever which flew around the unhygienic camps. She still heard horror tales of hardship and women selling themselves to the Imperial troops for food and grain. Helena's blood ran cold, also sickened, remembering how close she came to becoming one of a pimp's whores; nearly being sold for the highest price a virgin could gain and then to be passed on to less discriminating men.

'We should visit the camps Felea,' said Helena emphatically. 'They might tell us how we could help them, perhaps find them housing and work in the city.' She thought the provisions may not be getting through although some women would always prefer lying on their backs to gain money rather than working for their living if their men were absent. It was the way of the world and some women liked this work. *Not I,* she decided, remembering being pawed by one strange man. She would only want intimacy with one man who loved her.

'There is something else Helena.' Felea hesitated, unsure how much she could trust Helena. She had only been a friend for such a short time. She cast that doubt out of her mind, usually a good judge of character. Once or twice she had been duped and her more experienced wiser husband, always waiting in the background, a shadowy but reliable presence, had stepped in with a few quiet menacing words and she had been left alone. She now knew who she could trust and felt in her bones Helena was honest and decent and trustworthy.

Helena gave her that serious look as if waiting for her friend to state something important. Felea took a deep breath and smiled at her and started her explanation. 'You have probably heard I have visions.' Her friend nodded puzzled. *What was it to do with me?*

'I saw a vision a few days ago of women starving but worse! Of a man holding a woman down and violating her and others parading themselves in front of men as if on sale at market. The men looked as if they were eyeing meat on a butcher's slab, choosing the right piece for their delectation. Usually the vision is hazy, but I cannot forget the look on that girl's face; the look of terror and hopelessness.'

'If we can we must help,' said Helena remembering her own terror when the pimp had grabbed her. She had hidden it well under a show of bravado but even now she felt cold, as if her blood was freezing in her body. No woman should know that fear. No woman would if she had her way.

'We will go together. No-one can mistake our good intentions for traitorous activities when we are only trying to help women in the control of more powerful lustful men,' said Felea. 'I will arrange it. Francis is away for three days soon and will never guess. What he doesn't know won't harm him.'

'Are you sure you want to hide this from him?' she asked Felea. 'You are so close to him he might resent your attempt to hoodwink him if he finds out.'

'He fusses so Helena! He would say it is unhealthy and dangerous. No, we will go alone,' she replied, her natural stubbornness kicking in.

Helena smiled. Her friend was more than the polite sophisticated hostess, drifting through her husband's social engagements, charming everyone. Under that beautiful face there was a steel-trap mind and will of iron. Few men would challenge Dreda's instructions, but his wife, just aged twenty years, insisted on making up her own mind and pursuing her own direction when she pleased.

They set out on horses with two grooms armed to the teeth. The women neither came out to greet her nor to acknowledge her. She approached the Officer in Charge and introduced herself. He was shocked to find her identity.

'My husband doesn't know of this visit. He worries about me unnecessarily,' she confided to the man. 'I am sure you will keep me safe,' she said, her hand on his arm, her charming smile melting his resistance. 'We will only stay an hour and keep away from any infection.

'I want to talk to the women's leaders please. Pray, send them to me,' she demanded and went to stand by the food tents where two women were bent over pots peeling vegetables for a meagre stew. 'Do you have enough provisions to feed your families?'

'Food gets here in enough quantities, but the quality is poor and is often thrown away.'

'I will try to ensure the logistics are looked at,' said Felea. 'Perhaps the food could be bought locally and be fresher.'

She looked at the women. Some seemed dressed rather too elaborately for a camp, wearing low necked dresses and dampened gowns outlining their shapes, more suitable for a night in town. Where did the women get the money from for such elaborate gowns and why would the women waste their little money on such outfits, useful to attract the attention of lewd men?

'How do the women get food if they don't have enough?' she asked the women.

Eyes narrowed, and one woman tossed her head as if the question asked was stupid. 'The way all women get what they need when they are desperate.'

Felea took out a purse and said, 'There is no longer any need for women to sell their bodies.' She called, 'Officer. This purse should buy more fresh food. I want you to ensure all the women get enough to sustain their families. There should be no need for these women to resort to immoral means to suffice their needs.' The officer shrugged indifferently. *His men had needs as well.*

Helena was watching this discussion but felt another pair of eyes on her back, boring into her. Uncomfortable, she put on her icy mantle that had protected her so well in the past and turned on her heel and stared back. An officer stared as rudely back to her, rolling his eyes down over her from the top of her feathered hat to the tips of her riding boots; insolently, a look that stripped her mentally and made her feel unclean. The same feeling, she had experienced when the pimp had eyed her up assessing her value.

This man might be an officer, but he was no man of honour! Women were merely playthings to him and his audacious look spelt danger for any woman in his presence without a protector. Coming alone with only grooms, mere servants to protect them, had made them vulnerable; laid them out as easy pickings for this loathsome man. His hooded brown almost black eyes narrowed as they rested on her bosom. She felt like slapping his face.

He stood watching them for a moment as if assessing whether he should make a move toward them. Then he turned and strode to where the inappropriately dressed women were standing, arrogance emanating from him. They stood back when he approached them and fell silent.

He clearly inspires respect or fear in them, thought Helena. He was not a man to cross. She had felt the same about Dreda. His reputation preceded him. A gentleman and kind husband and friend, he was nevertheless a bastard when carrying out his Imperial duties. He never let his darker side escape outside his official work role though.

This man was different. He did not contain his darkness; restrict it to dealing with rebels or other criminals. Darkness and evil emanated from him, enveloping those in his path.

The women looked wary now. He gave instructions Helena couldn't hear but they rushed to do his bidding. He pointed a finger at a young girl wearing an indecently low-cut dress sheltering from the hot sun under a tree. Crooking his finger, he nodded to her and she came quickly to him. He ran his finger over her bosom, close to the neckline and under the cloth.

Felea had turned and was watching the man carefully. Her instincts for danger had not deserted her. She had felt uneasy, as if someone malevolent was near. Even from a distance with her back to her she had empathised with the young girl, feeling her tremble.

This was not the tremble of a young girl feeling awareness for a handsome man. This was trembling caused by pure unadulterated fear. There was something here more than a mere whore selling her wares to the officer. There was a much more uneven powerful relationship between the man and this fearful girl.

The man spoke quietly to the girl and grasping her arm he took her to the far side of the camp where the officers' tents were raised. Helena could not ignore the terrified look in the girl's eyes when he ushered her away. She turned to Felea who looked faint.

'It is as it was in the vision Helena. A tall dark man pushing a reluctant woman in to the dark somewhere. She fears he will hurt her badly.'

She and Helena approached the women who stared at them. Their manner was unfriendly, unwelcoming their interference. Given their high status this man must wield enormous power over these women.

'Why is she so afraid of him?' asked Felea bluntly. 'Tell me or it will be the worst for you when my husband finds out an officer is abusing women.'

'Your husband has little power here,' retorted one woman scornfully. 'When you go he rules this camp.'

'He is only a junior officer, isn't he?' Inquired Felea, thinking of his stripes on his shoulders.

'Rank means little here. It is who wields the power that matters. The power over life and death.'

Felea was beginning to understand. 'Does he control the distribution of the food?' she asked. A woman nodded. 'And if a woman doesn't cooperate she gets less for her family?'

'Yes, my Lady.'

'Why is she so scared?' She had met whores before and unless the men were rough they did not have this naked fear of the men they serviced.

At first the women didn't answer, turning away from her as if scared. Helena grasped the least reticent one by the shoulder.

'Answer the Countess! We can help rid you of this monster if we have the evidence to tell her husband.' Reinforcing her argument, she said, 'Francis Dreda is Commander of the Security Bureau and has a position in the Cabinet office. He has influence far greater than the Militia and can have this man moved far away from you. He will not be able to harm you again.'

'He has friends in high places,' warned the woman.

'Francis Dreda has a network of spies throughout the country and in nearby states. He will route out anyone who will aid this man if they are a danger to you. The charity who supplies the provisions to you is also under the patronage of the Empress. By stealing from the charity, the man has stolen from the Emperor and that could be construed as treason, a capital offence. If her husband threatened the man with that he would vanish from your vicinity. Trust her!'

The bravest woman said, 'We have little to lose. Four children died of starvation and fever last week. They couldn't fight the malady; they were too weak.'

'Before he can hurt her badly, tell me!' urged Felea. She admitted reluctantly to the woman. 'I saw a vision with a man like him hurting a redhead like her. He nearly killed her in the vision, disabled her for life. We may prevent it.'

'He is a vicious cur,' said the woman. 'He likes his women to fear him and selects them young and naïve to mould them to his needs. You promise he will be dealt with?'

'Yes,' said Felea 'but you will have to look after yourselves until I get the word to my husband. I will tell the Officer in Charge if one of you are touched in anger or hurt his head will be on a platter!'

She stormed off in the direction of the officers' tents with Helena trying to catch up, a little angry whirlwind. Helena had never seen her angry although she had heard Felea was as nearly as ruthless as her husband when her ire was raised.

They reached the tent and they heard sobbing. 'Oh, stop your whimpering girl! You begin to bore me,' said a curt voice. 'It is only a scratch!'

'It hurts Sir,' whimpered the small voice. 'I bleed!'

'Well don't bloody bleed over my uniform! Clean yourself up!' ordered the unsympathetic voice, 'and pass me the brandy will you. Soon I will tire of you and what will you do then. I could pass you on to Batiz if you want?'

'Oh, please Sir, don't let him touch me,' begged the girl, fear in her voice. *What monster must this Batiz be?* thought Helena, *if she preferred this brute to him.*

'Come here then,' said the voice, now starting to slur a little as the brandy took him over. 'I need feminine distraction after seeing those pretty pieces over there. It is years since I have seen asses like that, both being ladies as well. Shame they are protected by Dreda and untouchable.' Helena felt the contempt for them and wanted to cut his contemptuous tongue out. Let her near him with a whip and he would know how she felt. He was a misogynist and worst a sadist.

Felea thought Dreda would want to know about this cur. He would lose his stripes after Francis had finished with him and be lucky to join the ranks. Her husband hated men who hurt women and was trying to rid the Imperial Army and Militia of its dubious reputation for abusing unwilling women. Despite his reputation in the bedroom he had never taken an unwilling woman and expected the same attitude of his men.

They heard a rustle and then a gasping and choking sound. Looking through the open door of the tent Helena saw the girl was being shaken about by the man like a rag doll. His hands around her throat, her eyes were bulging. She had cuts on her arms and blood was streaming from them. He let her go roughly and took his crop in his hand. It was tainted with blood already, but he pulled the girl up, ignoring her glazed expression in her eyes. She was trying to detach herself from the awful reality she was faced with.

'Bend over the chair,' he said and started to hit her as she started crying again.'

'Not there, Sir,' the girl begged. Helena saw he was hitting her dangerously near her waist at the vulnerable part of her spine. She launched herself into the tent and catching him unawares she shoved him as hard as she could, making him stumble and fall onto the makeshift bed.

'You will disable her hitting there,' she said. 'She will be an invalid.' Felea also pushed herself in. She pulled a pistol from her reticule. 'Out!' she said to the girl, 'I will deal with this bastard.'

Relieved, the girl scrambled out of the tent still gasping, her throat mottled and black with the bruises now developing.

'Go to my groom and ask him to guard you,' ordered Helena.

Felea faced the man who now stood up and he recognised the murderous look in her eyes. She was not the pretty young featherhead he had thought when she had arrived in the camp, a bored noblewoman wanting to ease her conscious. This was a mature calculating woman out to do damage to his crown jewels if he moved unwisely.

Felea assessed him carefully. 'If you want to be able to father any children in the future don't move and listen very carefully. I will tell my husband, Officer Dreda, Commander of the State Security Bureau what you have been up to.' She let her words sink in very slowly.

His face drained of blood. He now knew her power. It was the first time in years a woman had had power over him and he hated the feeling; felt sickened by his impotence. It was an alien feeling for him, recently having the power of pain and life and death over women in this camp. He had not asked for this move and disliked the work but enjoyed the perks of the available women. He had been given the boring job of organising the provisions and with another man had guessed the potential for fraud and money making and the women were a plus. All was now in vain.

This little strumpet pointing the gun at him would destroy him. He assessed her. She was totally confident holding the weapon. He could see in her eyes she knew how to use it. Her friend took her own out. He had moved forward a little and she had guessed he was assessing how easy it would be to disarm her.

'Don't think of it!' snapped Helena. 'If you took the gun from her I would shoot you.'

Another bloody virago! Where did Dreda find them? He was cooked!

'My husband will take your stripes away from you and move you to somewhere where you cannot harm these women. That is if you are lucky and cooperate with him.'

His eyes narrowed again. She carried on, a smile that did not reach her eyes governing her face. She hated bullying men and intended to make his skin crawl for hurting that young girl.

'If you do not cooperate with him, a charge of stealing the Emperor's provisions and corrupting officials is the start of the actions my husband will take against you. Theft of Imperial provisions makes you a traitor. Think on that Officer.' She left him to think about her threats. She had done enough to inspire fear in him.

Helena took over. 'You will leave the women alone. You will be restricted to your quarters and another man will take your place organising the distribution of the provisions.'

She pointed to the bed. 'Lie on it and wait there until your Officer in Charge comes to you. Now!' she ordered, menace in her voice.

'I would love to shoot you where it hurts you most!' she spat out as he hesitated for a moment to do as she bid. She backed out into the safety of the fresh air. Felea had brought the Officer in Charge over and was now explaining the situation.

'None of the women would admit their fear my Lady,' he admitted. 'One woman said something to us but disappeared the next day and then there was silence.'

Gutless coward! thought Felea, wondering if he was taking a stake in the proceeds of the stolen goods.

'My husband will start investigations when I speak with him. For the moment another officer will organise the distribution of the provisions in his place. I am taking that girl away and if my husband hears any sanctions have been taken against the other women he will have the perpetrator's ears nailed to a stake,' she threatened. 'Do you understand?'

'Yes, my Lady,' muttered the officer. 'Of course, my Lady!' His indifference had vanished replaced by a gut-wrenching obsequiousness she hated. He had underestimated her.

Turning a blind eye to the inadequacies of the system had gained him privileges and advantages in the short term but he knew his career was now damaged. He must try to put the situation right and show himself in a good light with her husband. Felea read his mind. Francis would not forgive him for turning a blind eye to the corruption. He was no saint with women but would not accept women being victimised and abused while the man was supposed to be carrying out his duty. This man's career was ended as far as she was concerned.

'I want to inspect the food now,' she said. She looked at the women gathered, now watching her with awe in their eyes. They had heard the row in the tent and now believed their position would change for the better.

An officer brought the women's leaders over. 'I have given the officer a purse of twenty sovereigns for provisions for you. I expect them to be used wisely. Your ladies no longer need to service the officers for food,' she said bluntly. 'I will ask my husband to check on the transport of provisions in the future.'

The women nodded but one said, 'You will not change the behaviour of all of these women my Lady.'

'I do not expect to. I merely offer them choices they did not have before.' She hesitated for a moment and then decided to tell them the blunt truth. 'We both nearly suffered being violated. We want no other woman to be put in that position. It is a hateful situation that no man can understand.'

She turned to look at a corner where women sat holding children who coughed and looked emaciated and thin. 'What do those children suffer from?'

'We know not my Lady,' said the women.

'Send a physic to these women immediately,' she ordered the officer. She tried to stay a distance from the sick people but the woman holding the child started coughing badly and vomiting, barely able to hold herself up, let alone a child. Without thinking Felea ran to the woman and gently took the child away from her and held it while another woman took the woman to her makeshift bed under the trees.

'Let someone else take the child, my Lady,' suggested the officer, worried for her health. 'You must Felea!' said Helena seeing the child's feverish red face and glazed eyes. Nodding, Felea allowed another woman to approach and they moved reluctantly away.

'We must send more warm clothes and milk and grain immediately,' said Felea. 'You are to tell Francis of our visit then?' asked Helena

'I must if we are to have help quickly,' admitted Felea reluctantly. Her husband would be as mad as fire when he found out. He was slow to anger but vastly unpleasant when furious as she had found out once or twice to her cost.

She did not look forward to explaining the circumstances of their visit to him. He would not understand. He believed in looking after his and her own health before that of others. A fair but hard man; that was how he had survived in war and in the murky world of army and cabinet politics when many were ready to stab his back.

They went to look at the supplies themselves. Opening a sack, Helena felt the flour. It seemed dusty and tasting it, she said, 'There is chalk in this flour.'

'The milk has been adulterated as well,' replied Felea. 'Someone is using the monies raised to buy adulterated food and keeping the rest of the monies left over for themselves. Why did the Officers in Charge not inform Francis or the trustee?'

'Someone is in it for himself,' said Helena cynically. 'Francis must investigate. They would not listen to us mere women!'

'You are right. Francis will intervene. He has more clout. 'Woe betide them when Francis catches them! He hates corrupt officials who distort the actions of the Emperor. The women think badly enough of our ruler without tarnishing his image even further.'

They bent to look in other sacks when a shadow loomed over them and a heavily polished black booted foot stepped in front of them.

'Well, what have we here?' asked a sardonic voice, making them look up in surprise. Staring down from his great height was Denman, a look of fury on his handsome face. His arms stretched out to them to help them up. Standing, Felea smiled disarmingly at him but he was not melted by her obvious attempts to placate him. His hand grasped around Helena's wrist and he pulled her up, not bothering to hide his anger.

'We go now my Ladies!' he said taking each of their arms in his and frog-marching them over to their horses. Two irritated women tugged him back.

'Why so heavy-handed Denman?' asked Felea 'And how the devil did you know where we were?'

'When you vanished, you were not so difficult to follow. Thomatz traced your direction. Francis knew you were up to something and left me to follow you while he was out of town. My God Felea, you must be mad to come here with the fever raging. I would not be in your shoes when Francis comes home tomorrow. He will be as mad as fire.'

They had reached the horses, but Helena stopped and refused to budge, supporting her friend's stance. 'It was well we did come Officer Denman,' she said. 'The food is adulterated and scarce. The women are selling themselves to the officers for coins to buy food. An officer is profiteering from these women's ill situation.'

'It is not for you to investigate these problems. Leave it to the authorities!'

'Oh, how many children would die before the authorities heard about it?' retorted Helena. 'We only found out about the corruption by accident when we came here. The corruption would have carried on for months and the human casualties would have risen.'

'Your bleeding hearts will get you killed,' said Denman standing his ground.

'Denman,' said Felea. He let go of them, facing them; his handsome face still clouded with anger, his brown eyes dark and challenging his Commander's wife. He would not allow her to defy him. He stood in place of her husband, his role outweighing any friendship he owed her.

To hell with her temper! Her safety was all that concerned him. He knew how Dreda would think and behave in the circumstances. He would get her out of here at top speed and face her wrath later.

Whilst in in his cups Dreda had admitted to Denman he hated her tempers but enjoyed their making up which nearly always ended up in the bedroom; he charming her, seducing her out of her ire. She did not stay angry for long, her sunny temperament warring with and surmounting her anger but she could be a frost-piece; her smouldering eyes turning to cold green pebbles when she wanted. She could bear a grudge if she felt she was treated unfairly and wisely he steered clear of upsetting her.

'At least we have a heart!' retorted Helena, his clinical detachment irritating her. He ignored the camp women's dire position and was fixated on getting them back to safety. He rounded on her curtly, snapping at her, his eyes gleaming dangerously. He looked like a big golden cat on the prowl ready to slap her with a vicious paw.

'Given your reputation I would expect this of you. Careless of your position and safety as you are but Lady Felea usually has more common sense!'

'Stay Denman!' asked Felea. He had no idea what was up here. 'I had a vision of women selling themselves to the officers for food and a girl being hurt by a man.'

Helena ground her teeth when Denman shrugged in that indifferent detached way she hated. A user of women he accepted so casually the status quo. He would think differently if instead of a poor homeless woman his sister was vulnerable to a man's abusive hands and orders.

'Women have always sold themselves for luxuries?' he demanded. 'A ribbon for their hair or a brooch or new gown. It is the way of the world. What is new?'

'An officer has sold their provisions and adulterated their food. A quarter is no of use; putrefying. They have no choice! They must sell themselves for necessities. Look at the children, weak and suffering from malnutrition. Some of the women are enceinte when their husbands are not here. More babes to feed soon!

'This must stop!' She shook him roughly by the lapels making him listen to her. He saw she was serious. Perhaps the situation was worse than was made out by the Officer in Charge. He thought he was a lightweight whose shifty eyes tried to avoid his own when he asked about the visiting ladies. He detached her fingers gently from his lapels.

'There is no need to assault me Ma'am,' he said softly but secretly liking her close proximity to him. She smelt of vanilla and roses. He wished to tangle his fingers in her golden locks and run them through her hair; to bury his head in her tangled mane and kiss her neck and shoulders, she smelt so divine; womanly and soft, even in her anger. He wanted to taste her again. She was like a narcotic. Without knowing he had become addicted to her. Damn the girl!

For the first time a woman was pulling him and trapping him in her web, quite unknowingly he realised. She pushed him away all the time, but he was experienced enough to know she recognised the chemistry between them, the sensual pull that dragged him to her. She was denying it and trying to distance herself from him. He foolishly resented it. He should be grateful she was not acknowledging the pull and should push her away and stop any intimacy growing between them.

She was too dangerous for him. He still wanted no permanent attachments, and yet he regularly dreamed of her soft body lying next to him, her locks splayed across his pillow. What would he give for her green-blue eyes to gaze on him as if her universe revolved around him, like Felea gazed at Dreda, her lover and soulmate? They had the perfect marriage; she a spirited beauty, intelligent but not clingy, an independent woman who cared for him but was wise enough not to jeopardise his position in the Imperial State.

Sighing deeply, he stood back reluctantly from Helena, denying himself her closeness. Her eyes were sparkling now like hard emeralds, the moody blue disappearing as her wrath took over her spirit.

'You need slapping into reality sometimes!' she said with force, ignoring his widening eyes.

Jesus Christ! She was really riled up. Few things wound up Helena. A quieter girl than Felea she was detached and cool to the point of iciness at times, having for years learned to keep her mouth shut and avoid the wrath of a brother who looked for reasons to slap her.

Strangely, he was one of the few men he knew who could rile her. Perhaps, that same chemistry that drew him to her also made them war with each other, he wanting to master her and she wanting to remain her own mistress. It made for an inflammable combination! He daren't not touch her intimately for once that spark was lit the flame would consume them both!

'The man who organises the provisions uses his power to abuse the woman,' she snapped. 'Felea had a vision where she saw him disable the woman by hitting her. We went to his tent and stopped him hitting her with his crop. He was aiming for her spine and would have paralysed her. Felea pointed her gun at him and said he is now confined to his quarters and another man must take his place. The girl is coming back with us. She is still bleeding and must stem her blood and tend her wounds or an infection may set in.'

Denman's temper nearly took off. *For Christ's sake! When would these women learn their lesson?* He blamed Helena for this. He knew he was thinking unfairly but without her spirited accomplice who was as adventurous as herself Felea would have left the situation until Dreda had come back. She had no other woman friend who would jeopardise her own safety to take such action or risk alienating her husband.

Helena needed her head examined after falling into the hands of the brothel keeper and nearly losing her virtue. Despite that she had risked coming to this place where a man was seen in Felea's vision molesting a woman. Whatever she might argue, she was risking being violated herself coming only accompanied by grooms and a female companion.

He knew this type of men. Like himself they saw woman as toys, playthings; uncaring for the consequences of their actions. Unlike himself, this beast was a man who hated women, enjoying power over them; wanting to hurt and defile them and enjoying making them submit to his will and endure his sadistic attentions.

He must ask Dreda to talk with Helena. She would not listen to him but Dreda must convince her of the dangers her behaviour led her to. *She needed a husband and quick to protect her from herself.*

'Where is this man?' He intended to make sure there were no repercussions from Felea's intervention. 'In that tent over there,' she pointed out. 'Felea warned him he was confined to quarters for the immediate future and Francis would move heaven and earth to protect these women from any retribution he might want to dish out. She also said he would be charged with corruption and treason should he harm them.'

'Well done Felea! Just the right thing to say in the circumstances! See, she thinks things out before she says them,' he said to Helena, hoping his barbs pierced her ego. He was sick of her snapping at him when he had come with good intentions to save them from any mishap or harm.

Felea smiled noting the mutinous look on Helena's face. Denman was blaming Helena unfairly for this episode. He was covering up his anxiety. He cared for her safety but would not show it, pretending he cared as much for the safety of his Commander's wife.

She knew he wanted to wring her friend's neck for openly defying and challenging him. They riled each other continuously, just as she had argued with Dreda before he had proposed to her. Something had to happen to bring them close to each other, to admit they held tendres for each other or they would war for ever.

Denman stalked over to the tent, his normal good humour having disappeared. That is what that girl did to him whenever they argued. He became a tyrant, barely recognising himself; he the nonchalant charmer who barely put a foot wrong. He realised it was because he had never cared enough to upset anyone. With this girl he cared too much. He would willingly upset her, to protect her under any circumstances. She was now in his blood, damn her!

Opening the tent, he saw the man lying on his bed. He assessed him quickly. From the top of his shiny gleaming boots to his snowy cravat he was full of himself, an arrogant cur who put himself before duty and these poor women.

Walking to the tent Denman had noticed the state of the camp, the cabbages putrefying! He had seen the weevils in the rice and grain. This food was ancient; the cast offs traders bought for small coin. This man had expensive tastes. His tent smelt of expensive cologne and cigars bought from the money he had swindled from the charity and the women.

The man arrogantly assessed Denman, putting his back up. Few men riled him. This lazy bastard knew he was in the shit but still stared him back. He made him want to knock his teeth down his arrogant throat. Denman wore the uniform of a senior militia officer and the man should have stood up to acknowledge a more senior officer in another branch of the Imperial service. The Militia was an independent unit but Denman although no abuser of his position still towered above him in rank and expected the respect due to his station.

'Up!' said Denman, 'I wish to talk with you!'

'Certainly!' said the man raising himself slowly and lazily.

'And call me Sir, Officer,' bit out Denman in that chilling voice that used to terrify young recruits on the training field when drills were being carried out. 'Get up before I haul you up and kick your lazy arse from here to the canteen.'

The man moved like lightning and stood up and saluted. Denman looked him over from top to toe. The officer was now beginning to understand the type of man Denman was.

'My name is Officer Denman from the State Security Bureau, third in command.' He paused for a minute to let his words sink in. 'You may have heard of me.'

The officer blenched, the colour draining from his tanned cheeks. He had heard of this man, a man not to be trifled with. He had a reputation for being as experienced in the battlefield and the militia as his friend Commander Dreda and was as hard as nails himself!

'Yes, Sir.' The last word was emphasised this time and Denman smiled. His name and rank had at last penetrated this dolt's thick skull. He now knew he was completely mired in the shit.

'If you harm any of these women in this camp or these visiting ladies you will bring my anger down on your thick skull and I am not one to be trifled with. I will send troops soon to reorganise this camp and you had better make a list of the monies you have swindled from these women and how you intend to pay them back.'

'You understand?' he thundered at him. How a quietly spoken man could sound so loud and angry puzzled and scared the officer at the same time.

'Perfectly Sir.'

'We understand each other then,' replied Denman. 'I want out of your miserable presence. Only a pathetic excuse for a man harms a woman physically. You make my skin crawl.' He strode out of the man's tent.

The women had heard their conversation and the fear in the officer's voice. They offered him drink and food, their admiration showing in their faces.

'Thank you, but no ladies, I refreshed myself on route. You need it yourself.'

He asked an officer to ride to the nearest town and buy fresh food with a purse he gave him, after retrieving Felea's sovereigns. He gave them back to Felea.

'The Emperor will want to replace the food and I am his servant. I pay his dues. He strode over to the Officer in Charge. 'I want that officer replaced and a competent man put in his place until I find someone permanent from outside who I can trust to undertake the role. I am charging you with the safety of these rebel women. If any are harmed it is your neck that will roll both figuratively and literally. The Emperor dislikes corrupt officials intensely and the hangman's noose is always ready to deal with them.'

The Officer's face turned white. 'I will personally ensure they are not harmed Sir.'

'Good,' said Denman tersely. 'We at last understand each other. Good day!' Saluting, he left the man gawping and made his way to the waiting women. Felea smiled at him. He reminded her of her husband; his decisiveness and calmness under pressure, his ability to impress on others the seriousness of his words. He was not in a good humour though. Rage emanated from him. She had never seen him so angry. What had worked him up so?'

Dreda had said Denman's temper, rarely roused, was as bad as his. Helena was one of the few people Dreda had seen make him really lose his temper, an admission he cared for her more than he would admit.

Denman approached the women. 'We move now, no arguments!' he said looking specifically at Helena. 'You heard my words. The women will be safe now. He will not gainsay my orders.'

'We need a horse for the girl,' said Helena. 'She can ride with the groom on his horse,' he said dismissively. Her wounds had been attended to and she looked fit to travel. 'What will you do with her?' He thought she would still end up on a protector's bed. The keen assessing looks she had given him had given him an idea of her character.

'Try to find her decent and honest work,' said Felea.

'I think you will be disappointed,' said Denman.

'You think all women are the same,' said Helena.

'Unfair my Lady! Just women of this ilk. Mark my words she will be in a man's bed as soon as you can click your fingers.'

'She has never been given other choices,' said Helena.

'We will see,' said Denman cynically. How often had he had his coins removed by such a woman in return for services rendered?

'Why are you in such a bad humour?' asked Helena.

'Why indeed?' he asked, rounding on her. 'You ask that! Only a doltish idiot would not understand the dangers of riding into a fever infested camp and then confronting a dangerous man who one believes has molested women in the past.' She flashed another look at him. His words stung, aimed at her.

'We were perfectly safe Denman,' argued Felea, refusing to allow him to attack her friend when she was more at fault if anyone could be blamed. He was over-reacting like Francis would, being overprotective.

'Men like that will not stop at peasant girls when they lust after a woman,' bit out Denman. 'When I rode in the camp I saw him eyeing you up. He left you alone because he saw me, a stranger coming in who might inform on him to his seniors. Your naivety is too great to be believed!'

'No man would attack the wife of the Commander of the Security Bureau Denman! The Officer in Charge is a coward and not bright, but he was watching us the whole time and was hovering outside the tent. He would not have let us come to any harm!'

Denman ruefully admitted to himself she was right. He would have told the man her identity. His own name had scared the breeches off the officer. Dreda's would have made him shit them. However, he had no intention of letting them know they were right. He intended to make them feel as guilty as possible as Dreda would have done.

'Nevertheless, he may have hurt you before the Officer could reach you. Or perhaps you wanted a bit of excitement, sample a bit of rough Ma'am?' he said looking accusingly at Helena. 'It is not the first time you have laid yourself open to scoundrels who have eyes on your body and your virtue.'

'Denman!' cried Felea outraged. Looking around her, she knew others were interested in their argument; others who could make a thing of this. To try to save their necks if they thought he did not believe their story and their group was divided.

Divide and conquer! Dreda had so often talked of winning battles and arguments this way. They had spoken so softly so no-one outside their group could hear their words but the waves of anger reverberating between Helena and Denman were clear to others to make out. She must bring this situation off the boil, to stop them picking at each other, opening old wounds.

Helena was furious, stalking toward him again and poking him in the chest. He backed off before he grabbed her hand, resisting the temptation to pull her to him for a kiss. She hissed at him. 'You think all men are like yourself and brand me a harlot! Felea, he has said before I dress and behave like a hoyden and deserve to be treated badly by men.

'You assaulted me before, kissing me without permission and threatening me with a hiding.' She barbed him with her cutting words, her beautiful soft green-blue eyes now filled with tears. His words had cut her to the quick and she could not hold back the tidal wave that was threatening to show him how betrayed she felt by his words. She spat out her words. 'You are as bad as that man in the tent! No gentleman!

Denman responded just as acidly. 'Rather melodramatic Ma'am. You belong in the theatre. An assault? Ask me and will show you an assault. If I had my way you would be over my knee, my giving you the hiding your father should have dealt you years ago. You may have turned out better; an obedient miss instead of a disobedient virago who lacks common sense.'

'That is enough, Denman! Helena, ignore him! He hates his will being gainsaid or being contradicted. It is the army man coming out in him. Francis is the same, getting on his high horse if I disobey any orders he considers important. Francis has mellowed. He no longer expects absolute obedience from me. Denman, you should find a wife. Marriage would suit you and improve you; make you more tolerant and humane.'

Denman ground his teeth in despair. These bloody women matched each other in insolence. He would leave Dreda to deal with his wife and deal with her he would as sure as the sun rose each day. He may not give her a hiding, but he would make her feel so bad she would obey him for a long while. He was a lenient husband but not where her safety was concerned.

He would argue no longer with them. He caught Helena around the waist enjoying feeling her softness and warmth. 'Up with you,' he said and tossed her into the saddle roughly, her hat knocked off her head. He picked the offending item off the ground and tossed it to her and walked to his own horse.

Damn the girl! He was actually quite proud of them, both risking their necks, as Dreda would be but if they were harmed he would never forgive himself for not guessing fast enough what they were up to. Dreda had left them in his safeguard.

A quiet and brooding group of people rode home. Conversation was stilted, and an icy façade was maintained. Felea knew she was in the wrong deceiving Dreda and felt guilty but he had treated her like a child. The girl she had rescued had commented boldly on Denman's words, giving Helena a knowing look. Perhaps Denman was right after all. She was a bold piece and wouldn't fit into a decent household if she was a gossip and malicious. She would be given a trial at first in her own household, to learn how servants should behave. Everyone deserved a second chance, but any transgression and she would be out. In her husband's household secrets had to be kept and servants had to be trustworthy.

Getting through the door, she was glad to find Dreda was not home. 'In two days' time,' said a footman. 'He has been delayed,'

'Will you let us explain it to him or will you snitch on us?' asked Felea. 'Can you be trusted to admit it to him?' asked Denman seriously.

'Sweet Jesus, Denman, we are not children! We have to tell him if he is to deal with the food adulterers.'

'I will leave it in your hands then. I will put feelers out to find out who handles the food purchases and their transportation and pass the information on to Francis.'

'Damn the man,' said Felea when he had left. 'He is too bloody loyal to his friend. It is the few morals he can muster,' she exclaimed. 'He makes me feel a bloody traitor to Francis. I just didn't want to worry him unnecessarily.'

'Well we are home safe, so he should remain calm,' hoped Helena.

Denman had no desire to exacerbate Dreda's anger with Felea and decided to set Thomatz and Hadreni on to finding out who the person was in the city who was buying the cheapest food he could lay his hands on. That officer must have some help here. The sacks had the name of a city trader although local food could have been bought fresher. Cheapness and profit had been more important to the men involved.

He was aghast by how stupidly the women had behaved. Dreda had described Felea as sometimes impetuous and fearless and careless of her safety but Denman thought she had left that behind now she was no longer a young girl and a mature bride. He could believe it of Helena. Under that cool feminine exterior was a managing female used to having her own way and running a farm as well as any man. She might look as if butter wouldn't melt in her mouth, but he knew she would not take orders easily from any man, even if it were for her own good.

She needed taking in hand before she did something that harmed herself. *She needed a strong man to manage her,* he thought, but would not apply himself to thinking who that man might be. It was too uncomfortable for him to think of a man whipping her into shape and making her mind her manners and him.

Felea was on edge. She must tell Dreda about her visit to the camp before Denman told him. He would stay quiet for only so long. He was a man's man like her husband, perhaps even less liberal than Francis, expecting his women to be obedient to his command. Mind, he had never been married.

Francis was more liberal now he was married and his respect for her had increased as she had consolidated her uneasy position in society and her status had risen. She rarely spoke out of turn now having been warned a week before her marriage that by becoming engaged to her he had endangered his position in the Imperial Court. Some people, even the Emperor had questioned his loyalty to the Imperial power and she was still considered a traitor by others.

Dreda had protected her whilst others had tried to trip her up with her innocent words and actions. Now wiser to the words and actions of the devious world she rarely spoke of politics, keeping her strong often critical opinions for Dreda and her few dear friends. She appeared the perfect society hostess, gracious and intelligent and interested in the poorer vulnerable sections of society who she helped by organising money raising events.

The daughter of members of the forward-thinking intelligentsia, she had inherited her parents reforming interests. She impressed on Dreda the need for social change. Some cynical critics accused him of being led by the nose by his pretty young wife but Dreda knew how far he could encourage the Emperor to make changes. Not even for his beautiful wife would he endanger his position and influence in the Imperial Cabinet to press for social reforms that the Emperor would reject out of hand. Social change was slow in Taylia and Felea had to accept that and accept it she did.

Finally, Dreda arrived home, first attending the Bureau as was his wont to find out if anything damaging or out of turn had happened in his absence. Felea waited for him with bated breath dreading telling him the events that had occurred. She hoped he would act reasonably. She had felt tired these last few days since the long horse ride home. A lethargy had overtaken her, and she felt hot and sick. She wondered again if she was enceinte. Counting days, she hoped not and Dreda was always so careful when he visited her bed.

Dreda had picked up some papers and read them in his carriage. *What the hell?* he thought, as his eyes moved over the pages. *Felea you have gone too far this time!* He cursed and swore. The Officer in Charge at the women's camp had been removed after a visit by his wife. It was Denman who had removed him after he arrived home with the ladies. The new Officer in charge had written to him telling him the women were now being nourished appropriately and the offending officer who had swindled the women and the charity had been arrested and was in the fort under lock and key until a court martial could be arranged.

He could only guess some of the circumstances. The new Officer in Charge also hoped his wife and her friend had arrived home safely and had not been upset by the altercation with the offending officer.

'What altercation?' asked Dreda of himself. 'Were they assaulted or injured?' Denman had been there, and it sounded as if he had guarded their safety.

Denman was not at the Bureau, so he couldn't get the facts straight before he confronted Felea although he knew she should have the right to explain her actions to him herself. He climbed out of the carriage smacking the papers against his side in anger. Felea saw him through the window and her face fell. He knew already! Denman was out of town until this evening, so he couldn't have snitched on her.

She ran to the door and waited gracefully for the footman to open it. 'Francis,' she smiled politely. 'How nice to see you back.'

'Felea,' he nodded, kissing her hand but regarding her coldly as if they were strangers. He waited, giving his cloak and coat to the footman who left quickly, sensing an atmosphere between the couple. In the servants' dining room, he drank saying, 'The cat is amongst the pigeons now. He gave her a look as if she had murdered someone. He is in the devil's own temper. I would not like to be in her shoes.'

The cook, one of Dreda's old retainers said, 'He is a cool customer but lie to him or keep secrets from him and his temper is roused. He hates deceit or subterfuge in his home. He has enough of that at work and doesn't forgive transgressors easily. I hope he will forgive our Lady. She is so young and sweet.'

'You should see her when she is in a temper with him,' said her abigail. 'Sweet? She spits fire at him with those fierce eyes. Even he stands back when she is in a murderous temper. She is a match for him any day and he loves her to distraction. He may ignore her for a while, but he will come back to her eventually. He cannot resist her and will want to be back in her bed as soon as possible.'

The footman came down. 'He has taken her in the study for a talk. You know what that means. He has something serious on his mind and she looked worried stiff.'

Dreda had led her to the study, his place for secret or serious discussions, the walls and doors being thick.

'Sit down Felea,' he said sitting himself behind his enormous desk. 'You have some explaining to do, I think. I am a lenient husband, but I dislike being deceived. You know that very well. I am disappointed in you.'

He threw the letter in her lap. 'I hear the circumstances of your visit from a stranger. Embarrassing and unnecessary, don't you think?' he said in his grave patient way, as if he was talking to a child, not his grown-up wife. Indignant, she replied, 'If you had accompanied me when I asked or provided an escort I would not have needed to go behind your back. You are as guilty as I.'

He acknowledged she was right in his treating her as a child, but he had been worried about her health. Perhaps he should have sent Denman to look at the camp as it obviously interested her very much.

'Why did you go?'

'I had a vision about women wearing inappropriate clothes and selling their bodies to the soldiers for food. They were starving but what was worse was one girl was beaten savagely and paralysed, disabled for life. I thought I might prevent worse happening in the future if I intervened.'

'To challenge an officer is totally inappropriate behaviour for a lady. You should have referred the situation to Drachman or Denman in my absence.'

'I have already been admonished by Denman,' she said. 'I do not need another tongue lashing. And poor Helena! He suggested she welcomed the inappropriate attention and behaved like a hoyden. Her eyes were filled with tears. She will not forgive him for ages.'

'I am not concerned with Helena. She is not my wife. Don't try to distract me Felea. Tell me what happened to the last detail. If I am to deal with this case efficiently and fairly I need to be accurate. I will hand it to Drachman if you have not already jeopardised the case by interfering. I hope you did not claim to be acting on my authority?' he questioned angrily.

'Give me some credit for common sense Francis,' replied Felea her temper rising.

'When you show some common sense I will,' he retorted. Ignoring his retort, she restarted her story. 'When we went there the women would not readily cooperate. They were clearly scared of someone. They said they needed to give the men their bodies in return for food. We found the food was old and a quarter was putrefying. It was adulterated as well. The children were suffering malnutrition.'

'What is this to do with the Officer who has been relieved of duty? It is a serious action Felea and must be justified.

'I cannot be seen to court martial an officer merely because she has offended my temperamental wife,' he said deliberately bluntly to worm the truth out of her.

'Treat me like a sensible person Francis. When have I asked for an officer to be removed merely because he had offended me? If I had, a large number of your officers would have been removed when they treated me as dim the first few months I started working at the Bureau translating for you.'

Dreda's eyes narrowed. He had wondered if his men had showed respect for her at all times, but she had never mentioned any transgressions. Clearly, she had ignored any rudeness or disrespect. She was more mature than he had thought. He would talk to his clerk tomorrow and Denman, and Drachman his second in charge to determine if she was being treated appropriately; deserving the same respect as any hard working, skilled person working there.

'If any of my men show disrespect you must tell me Felea.'

'Forget it Francis. You show me less respect at the moment than any of your men could. I am a little girl in your eyes,' she said wretchedly.

'The facts Felea!' demanded her husband, giving her no quarter. He intended she would wriggle as much as he could make her. He was blazing mad! The new Officer in Charge had outlined the improvements he was making in hygiene and had mentioned the deaths of women and children in the camp. It was a hot bed of fever. She had endangered her life unnecessarily.'

'We were watched by this officer. He was sinister and raped us with his eyes. Even dressed as ladies he would still have approached us inappropriately, but he saw Denman riding in and left abruptly.

'He took a terrified girl into his tent. The women told us he was the man who organised the distribution of the food. He was clearly abusing his position to receive sexual favours from the women. He had bought cheap old food and the women received so little they were forced to give their bodies to him and others. Some of the women were enceinte as a result of the attentions of the guards. The place is a mess Francis and must be sorted out.'

'It has been due to Denman's intervention. The Officer in Charge has been removed and your enemy the potential abuser is awaiting a court martial. Denman despite your criticisms took the situation very seriously.'

He waited for her to continue feeling it was going to get worse. She looked so nervous he could almost pity her if he wasn't so angry with her. This dispute must be dealt with swiftly and not allowed to tarnish their wonderful marriage, but he couldn't allow her to behave like this and endanger her own safety even if he risked raising her wrath and reducing their love life for a while. He didn't want a frost-piece in his bed but reckoned that was what was going to be there in the near future.

'I told the women what I had seen. They took me seriously saying he had hurt one girl gravely before and when another had complained about his behaviour she had disappeared from the camp never to be heard from again.'

Dreda's eyes narrowed again and his pulse in his neck quickened. The situation was worse than he had imagined. Life in the camp for the women must have been horrendous. He did not blame Felea for intervening. He would have in her place if he had a compassionate heart like hers.

'When the tent was opened the girl was whimpering, covered in cuts and bleeding. He mocked her and told her to wipe herself and bend over the chair. He hit her with her crop despite her pleas for mercy. She was scared he would break her spine, so we intervened.

'I threatened him with my pistol first and Helena drew hers as well. We both warned him he would lose his job once you heard of his criminal acts; treason and conspiracy to corrupt officers of the state I think were the actions you would take against him.'

'You should have been a lawyer Felea,' said her husband thinking how talented she was.

'I would have liked to if women had been allowed to practise in the Imperial courts,' said Felea. Her husband was unbending a little, perhaps understanding her position at last.

'We made him lie down on his face and made our escape. The girl is acting as our scullery maid at the moment.' Dreda frowned. He did not want such a girl in his house. Surely there were places she could be put in to keep her safe, the workhouse for example, until a more suitable job could be found for her.

'I want her out of my house as soon as possible Felea. She may not be trustworthy.'

'Our house Francis,' Felea said with emphasis. 'I have found her a position in another household in the country. She starts in a week's time. Is that early enough for you?'

'Indeed, but may I remind you whose name is on the lease of this house, Madam?'

Dreda had no desire to behave the domineering husband but he had to reinforce who was the head of this household if he was to protect them both. His position was now safe in court as she no longer spoke openly nor out of turn, keeping her criticisms at home, but life in their court was always precarious and he could always be stabbed in the back. His lovely wife could never comfortably engage in politics nor involve herself in army politics or discipline. She was just out of her league, the people operating in this world being more deceitful and duplicitous than her.

'Denman came over.'

'I wondered where he had been during this altercation.'

'When the man left us, he inspected another part of the camp with the Officer in Charge. He did not know we went to the tent. When we came out we inspected the food and he came over and was very nasty to us and dragged us forcibly back to the horses.'

'Good,' said, Dreda. 'At last someone acted with common sense.'

'When he had heard of our visit to the tent he visited the man himself and threatened to thrust his teeth down his throat if he hurt us or the other women. Just his name terrified the man as did yours.'

'Capital! He is a man to be feared if he is wronged or angered.'

Bastard, thought Felea. *My opinion is not important, nor my actions praised but Denman is now the hero.*

'He explained the action he and you would take against the officer. He also warned what would happen if the girl was hurt in the city and told him he must account for the monies he had swindled out of the charity.'

'All in all, he wrapped it up as I would have expected it of him. That is why he was my second-in command Felea. He knows what to say and when to intervene. He only intervenes in things that concern him.'

Felea ignored his intervention. At this moment she was ready to walk out of the house so insulted did she feel.

'Helena and he argued. He didn't want to bring the girl, but Helena said she had had no choices when he said she would revert back to whoring in the city. He insulted her, and she was very upset. He was so rude to her. He blamed her for influencing me when it was my idea to visit the camp. She accompanied me to give me moral support and help me.'

'That is all! At least you have admitted being at fault.'

'I do not admit being at fault,' flashed back Felea. 'You were an overbearing husband, so I made the journey without you or my aides. Perhaps, I found more out being with one lady than if we had gone together. Have you thought about that?'

'Damn your insolence, Felea! Do you ever listen to wise counsel?

'Certainly, I just don't listen to you all the time. You lack wisdom sometimes and cannot bother to explain your reasoning to me. You issue your dicta and expect me to obey without question.'

As angry as her now, Dreda bit out, 'You knew what I was when you married me Felea. I warned you I was not a liberal husband.'

She remembered back to his proposal and her uncertainty at the time as to whether she should marry him. 'You said you would respect me Francis but at the moment I see no respect. Perhaps we should rethink our relations. I think I might be better living on my own.'

'No chance Felea. Forget leaving me. You are mine and will stay here.'

'Very well Francis. We can live in the same house but conduct separate lives,' retorted Felea.

This was now no small dispute. This went to the heart of their marriage. Respect and the right of one partner to determine her own behaviour. Felea knew Dreda would try to prevent her leaving. Leaving him would leave him a laughing stock in the eyes of the world, something he could not tolerate. His marriage had shocked the ton when he married a rebel supporter's daughter. Their enemies had given their marriage a year before it broke up. He had no intention of fulfilling their prophecy; proving his doubters right. Marriage was for good he had told her on their wedding day. He loved her with all his heart.

She had thought he was changing, becoming more liberal, kinder and more tolerant. All her good thoughts of him were now washed away by his intolerance and humiliation of her, his lack of respect for her opinions. She went to go out. He got up and swiftly met her at the door, his hand over her hand, closing it before she could exit the room. He took her chin in his hand and pushed her back against the door.

'You must promise not to talk about this to any strangers Felea. Denman and Helena are the only ones you may discuss it with.'

'Yes Officer,' she said insolently.

'I want your word you will not leave me when I am out of town Felea.'

'What do you think I am, a sneak thief, a con-woman leaving in the middle of the night?' she countered, making him feel ashamed of himself.

'I know not what you are or what to think. I trusted you and you went behind my back. That is not the behaviour of a trustworthy wife Felea.'

'Yours is the behaviour of an autocrat, a husband whose views hark back to the last century. Would you not like to chain me to the bed or make me wear a chastity belt? Do you trust me with other men or think like Denman thinks of Helena, that I invite inappropriate remarks and regards and insulting behaviour? You are two of a kind!'

'Such melodrama Felea. The only thing I want is a compliant wife who keeps herself out of danger. A woman who looks for excitement in balls and in the bedroom, not in rebel women's camps.'

'Find such a wife then because I am not that woman, Francis. You knew what I was when you married me, a damned nuisance if I remember you calling me, who looked for trouble and it was always finding me. If you want a damned compliant wife, then look for one outside of this house and tell me when you want a divorce. I will willingly sign the papers, you Bastard.'

He would have believed her if her eyes were not filled with tears. He had hurt her when he had merely wanted to discipline and frighten her. He had been too overbearing. Only Felea could make him angry; he cared so much for her and it cut him to the quick to know he had hurt her so.

He pulled her to him, holding her so tight she could not move. 'I want not you to leave my love, nor to maintain separate households and lives within this big house. I fear you endangering your life and mine by your rash actions, the consequences you often cannot see but I can.' He pushed her face up and kissed her passionately. He kissed her eyelids after lingering on her mouth.

'I cannot argue with you Francis. I have the headache and it hurts so. I need my bed-chamber, to sleep alone tonight.'

Disappointed, he looked keenly at her. This was not a rejection by an angry spouse. She looked tired and hot. He felt her head. It was hot, and her eyes looked sleepy and feverish.

'Did you get close to the ill women my love?' he demanded, fear growing in his heart.

'Only one mother and I held her baby when she would faint from the malady.

'By Christ, Felea! We must get a physic to you. What did the women suffer from?'

'I know not Francis. I just felt sick today although I have been tired these last three days. I thought it was the hard journey.' He opened the door and called the footman. 'Madam is tired and feverish. I want a physic called and a hot bath and hot blankets and hot drinks in her bed-chamber immediately.'

'No arguments Felea,' he said picking her up in his arms and carrying her to her chamber.

'Now I have had you in my clutches for a while I have no intention of letting you be taken away by a mere fever. Who else was with you?'

'It was the scarlet fever,' said Felea thinking hard, 'and two grooms and Denman and Helena were with me. Helena is here in this house and the grooms are perfectly healthy. Denman is coming to see you in an hour. He gave me the opportunity of explaining myself to you before he grassed me up.'

'That is Denman.'

'Yes, the perfect gentleman,' said Felea sarcastically. 'Gentlemen stick together despite the rights and wrongs of the situation.'

'That is what I adore about you Felea. Your gentle humour! Acidity instead of honey on your tongue.'

'Go to the devil Francis Danitz. Your friend will meet you there. You can torment other poor women together and leave me to my dreams.'

'You will never lose me my Love.'

She just put her head on the pillow as he laid her on the bed and waited, her abigail hovering like an old woman. She fell asleep once she had reluctantly drunk a sleeping draught.

'I will watch her,' he said. 'When the physic comes bring him here straight away. It could be the scarlet fever. 'The abigail looked tearful. He snapped, 'Don't fret Woman. She is young and strong and healthy and has a will of iron.

Providing she wants to get well, he thought, *after she said she wants to leave me and I wouldn't let her. Will she want to get well if she thinks this house is a prison?*

He could have cut his tongue out for upsetting her and denying her freedom when she was ill. Even if had let her leave him he could have persuaded her to come back. She was very forgiving, his Felea; too forgiving and tolerant sometimes unlike his judgemental and bitter self. She was changing him for the better but every so often he dug his heels in like today and regretted it later when he had had time to think this words through.

'Call Lady Helena to me here and the grooms to the butler. I want chambers prepared for the grooms in the apartment. I want them isolated for a week. When Count Denman comes I want him brought straight to me. From now on this house is closed to all visitors until we are sure the fever is banished.'

He sat by the bed, holding Felea's hand until Helena entered. Wary, she sat on the chair he motioned to. She clearly expected a drubbing, but she had already had that from Denman who tended to act like an older brother. Funny that, when he clearly held a tendre for her. He was looking after in the only way permissible without declaring an interest. One day, he must come off the fence and put his money where his mouth was as the saying went.

'My wife has a fever which I suspect she caught in the camp you two visited. She thinks it could be the scarlet fever.'

Helena nodded. 'It was going around and the child she lifted up showed the symptoms.' Dreda contained his anger. It was of no use losing his temper with Helena. He needed her help.

'Do you suffer from any of the symptoms?'

'Not at all! I may escape it if I am lucky. I had it when a child and am probably immune to a second batch.'

'You were also brought up in the hinterland, eating healthy foods straight from the farm and developed stamina working on your farm. Felea was brought up more gently but with less fresh produce and may be less immune to sickness. I spoke with Felea and she told me the facts concerning your visit.' He hesitated, wondering how much he should trust this young woman. 'I intend to sit with her during her illness. She looks as if the fever will peak in the next few days. She was angry with me and threatened to leave me Helena. I forbade her to leave the house.' Helena's eyebrows rose.

'It was a great mistake,' he admitted. 'I must stay with her and persuade her that her life is worth living even if she wants to leave me after her recovery. I do not want the servants to hear her saying she wants to leave. Servants talk. During the few periods when I need to leave the room I would appreciate if you would watch over Felea for me. You need not stay near the bed. Denman will also stay with her for me. He has the constitution of an ox.'

'Of course, I will help. I am sure she didn't really want to leave you Francis. She is devoted to you. You are closer than any other married couple I know.'

'That is comforting to know but I acted the heavy-handed husband forgetting how intelligent and wise my wife is. I treated her like a child.'

He decided to tell her more about their life before the wedding. 'You do not know all the circumstances of our lives before our wedding Helena. When we became engaged some malicious people questioned my loyalty to the Emperor as Felea's father was a rebel supporter and help-mate.

'At one point my own career was threatened and Felea's welfare and security was only protected by my status as the Emperor's chief political advisor. Some people tried to trip her up into betraying herself as a rebel supporter. Once we married the rumours stopped and we are safe but visits to the camp could stir the gossip again.

'Felea's intervention was inappropriate. She should have reported the blatant breach of their duty to me. Acting on her own could have jeopardised any actions we could take against the men as it may be thought she acted on my behalf without the authority to do so.

'Denman has put the officer who attacked the girl behind bars to await a court martial. He is an official in the Emperor's pay and has the appropriate authority. I intend to nail these men Helena, but through the appropriate channels. The army loses the support of the peasants when the officers are corrupt, and we need all the goodwill we can muster. This officer also appears to be a sadist and should be stripped of any power and right to wear the Imperial uniform. He is not a man of honour.'

Helena understood his position now. She had not understood the shady world he still operated in and the dangers that lay waiting for the unaware. She still felt he was over-bearing at times and should have accompanied Felea when she asked him to, but she would not involve herself in the argument between man and wife. It was for them to sort their issues out.

'Whatever you want I will do to help you Francis,' she said. 'Let us pray Felea recovers quickly.' They heard steps on the stairs and Denman after knocking put his head around the door.

'My God, it is true then. Your butler warned me the house was full of sickness.' He looked sad and angry at the same time. 'What has she?'

'The Scarlet Fever we think. I will stay with her and nurse her if you could stay here and relieve me occasionally. Helena will also help. She seems to have escaped the malady.'

'Is that wise?' asked Denman. 'She could catch it still.'

'Unlikely! I think the contagious period is over. You look healthy?'

'Never felt better. Just tired due to travelling.'

'I have isolated the grooms in the apartment, but they seem healthy. The house is to be closed for visitors until further notice. Felea and I had words and I want to make sure I am here when she wakes up.'

'Took a tongue lashing badly, did she?' asked Denman knowing how formidable Dreda could be when angry.

'I should have waited until she was well, but I didn't know she was ill and went in heavy-handed. In case she says it out loud she wanted to leave me. That is why I will tend her in place of the servants. No gossip shall leave this house if I can help it.'

'When do you want a break?'

'You sleep for four hours whilst I take my turn here and then you can relieve me.'

'No,' said Helena. 'I will take the first watch. She is fast asleep and will barely stir. When the fever takes hold, she may need someone stronger to hold her still. You gentlemen will be more useful then.'

'A sensible suggestion,' said Dreda and they left her there.

'That girl is a Godsend,' said Dreda whilst on their way to their bed-chambers. 'No fear of sickness. Felea's abigail is less than useless, crying and believing her dead and buried already.'

He changed the subject, not wanting to think of Felea slipping away. He could not cope with losing her. 'You handled the officers at the camp appropriately and probably saved the situation.'

'You would have been proud of the way the women handled the officers. I only heard a little of it, but they remained calm and rescued that girl although she is not the innocent they think she is. She is a bold piece and will have a man's hand up her skirts quicker than fly if she gets the chance to earn some gold sovereigns.'

'Felea has a position in another household for her in a week's time. I am uneasy having such a girl in my household with my position and the papers I bring home.

'I will wake you up when I need a rest Denman. Sleep well and keep Felea in your prayers. I hope this illness will bring home the dangers she puts herself in when she fails to heed my advice.'

'She is aided and abetted by our blond friend. Before she came here Felea had no female to create trouble with,' said Denman testily.

'I think you are unfair. Felea went to the camp on her own before we were married. Helena may aid her, but my wife is quite capable of finding trouble on her own.'

He smiled ruefully. 'That is why I was attracted to her at first, her spirit. Unfortunately, when she has a vision she must follow her instincts and help whoever is in trouble. I must watch over her more carefully in future.' He stepped into his chamber and fell asleep on the bed immediately, still in his clothes. He had to sleep, or he would not be good for looking after Felea later.

Helena sat reading a book watching Felea carefully. She was gradually burning up, a good sign that the fever was building up to a peak and after two hours she became restless. Helena held her down under the sheets keeping her warm, but she fought her.

She rang the bell. Felea was surprisingly strong for such a slim little thing. 'Call Officer Dreda and ask him to relieve me please,' she asked the abigail. 'I also need fresh drinking and washing water for your mistress.'

Dreda came immediately, half dressed in breeches and shirt. He was bleary eyed but held Felea down while Helena washed her face and neck.

'Go to sleep now Helena. Denman can take the next stretch. In the morning you can take over for a few hours.' She left leaving him to his lonely watch, making sure the servants brought him some nourishing soup and bread; all he could eat whilst he was so anxious, his appetite having disappeared. Whatever else she might think of the man, he clearly loved and adored his wife and intended to try and pull her through this malady. The physic confirmed it was the fever and told them the crisis would be over in twenty-four hours.

Through the night Dreda and Denman watched over her, making sure she stayed warm despite her sweat drowning the bedclothes. The sheets were changed and by morning the fever had reached its peak. She tossed and turned in her sleep and yelled out, 'I want to leave this household Francis. I must leave.

Dreda felt his heart was breaking at these words. He cursed his insensitivity and the dangerous society they lived in. He must make amends to Felea when she recovered. The physic thought she would live having survived the night. This bout of fever was not as severe as the previous years was and she was strong. Still her heart could be affected, and she must lie still and not tax herself when the fever broke.

The fever finally broke during Helena's watch. To her relief her friend slept peacefully, shivering with the cold that now overtook her as the fever left her body. Weak and tired she no longer fought the covers, snuggling under them for warmth. Helena called for Dreda.

He rushed in. 'The fever has broke and she sleeps peacefully,' explained Helena. 'You have a good meal and sleep yourself.'

'Guard your own health!' said Dreda. I can't thank you enough for helping us at this time.'

Embarrassed she said, 'The grooms are still well as is Denman. He is sleeping like the living dead after sitting up for hours.'

'He could always sleep well even on hard earth,' explained Dreda. 'Why not ask him to take you for a ride in the park later? Fresh air will do you good and the physic says you will not spread the lurgy.'

'I may do that,' she said but reluctantly. Dreda went to Denman's chamber and entered, waking his friend up. 'I would like you to take Helena for a ride. She has been in this hotbed of infection for days and must feel cabined and confined.'

His friend yawned and pulled himself up, resting on one arm. 'I fancy a ride myself. I am aching from sitting reading books. Will she come with me? Last time we spoke for more than a few minutes she was staring daggers at me and abusing me.'

'Use your considerable charm on her instead of scolding her and she will. I want to buy her a present. Find out what she might like. You know more about the fripperies women like. You have bought enough for your paramours in your time.'

'But she is a lady, not a bird of fancy.'

'I am sure you could worm something out of her.'

'A horse actually. She mentioned a horse of her own.'

'Capital. Ask what kind she wants? I am back to my wife before she wakes up.'

Denman thought a little ride might sweeten Helena up. He had been harsh, but he thought he had been justified. He was in awe of the calm way Helena braved the sickroom and calmed Dreda down. Dreda had lost his usual insouciance as Felea had grown worse. Helena had squeezed his hand and made him relax. She was a quiet companion any man would be proud to have in his house. She had hidden depths; depths he would enjoy divining if she were not an innocent.

Dreda sat by his wife's bed. Opening sleepy eyes, she looked blearily at him and frowned, not the best way of noticing him but at least she was alive. He held her hand until she woke up properly but then she removed it remembering their argument. It was time to clear the air.

'Felea, if you need to leave this house I will not stop you. You are a mature woman and know what you want.'

Her eyes widened. He would not stop her leaving. Was he ashamed of her or scared she would bring danger to his household?

'What do you want Francis?'

'I love you and want you to stay,' he replied simply, tenderness in his eyes; that moody blue again, the colour they turned when he wanted her to make love to him.

'I must sleep Francis,' she said, wanting to avoid a confrontation with him. She felt too ill to discuss their relations with him. They would argue again. They were too different; he an old fashioned ex-army man and she an intellectual, a radical.

She turned on her side, burying her head in the pillow. Dismissed, he squeezed her hand again and called her abigail to her. She could take over the nursing now Felea didn't talk in her sleep anymore.

He went back to his chamber aware that his wife had not forgiven him. Felea would ruminate a problem and then come to a rational conclusion. She was the most rational woman he had met. When Helena had spoken with her she might behave more reasonably, his masculine mind unable to understand her reasoning. Until then he must stay calm and friendly.

He visited her every few hours, holding her up while she fed herself. She was wary of him. This was the man who de facto ruled the kingdom when the Emperor was away; a man who made decisions over the lives and deaths of others; a harsh man who rarely allowed his decisions to be questioned! And yet he was holding her like a nurse would, feeding her spoonful's of broth, gently laying her back on the pillow, soothing her still fevered brow.

She did not recognise this gentle Dreda. He had changed since she had married him, a kinder man appearing, but he had still remained the authoritarian disciplinarian, demarking boundaries within their marriage, boundaries she should not cross. His indifference to issues she considered important still angered her.

He still mocked her on occasion, making her feel small and insignificant, treating her like a child with no wisdom. He had loosened the leash a little and she had had no regrets about marrying him until their recent argument, but would he ever treat her as his equal? She thought *not*.

For four days she slept on and off with Dreda or Helena sitting beside her waiting for her to wake up. They read to her, Helena during the day and Dreda during the evenings but conversation was still stilted between the married couple.

The morning of the fifth day she rose on feeble legs and asked to sit on the balcony. Dreda was told this request and personally carried her there and swaddled her with blankets and rugs.

'That man loves that young woman to death,' said her abigail to the servants. 'He has cared for her as if she were a sick child.' She pursed her lips as if puzzled. 'She seems cold to him as if she no longer cares for him.'

'They had a devil of an argument the day he carried her to her bed. Perhaps she has not forgiven him.'

'I would forgive him,' said the chambermaid. 'He is such a kind and handsome man. I would not look twice at another man if he was in my bed.'

'She is more than a match for him,' said the butler, one of Felea's admirers. 'He was lucky to catch her. He is a moody devil and unpredictable. All of his previous women wanted his fortune. The Lady Felea had her own estates and only wanted him. A rare and honest lady!

'He was a callous selfish man before he met her, totally ruthless, uncaring about the consequences of his actions. She has changed him for the better but something he has done has annoyed her. I would not want to be in his shoes. Lady Felea is rarely angered but holds a grudge for ages when she does.'

Felea was still undecided. Dreda had given her more time, leaving the Bureau early, seeming to value her company more. He had had one fiancée who he admitted he had neglected whilst he was an army officer. She had slept with another man as a consequence. He had learnt his lesson and had paid more attention to his young wife, recognising she needed his company but the Bureau still took precedence, always. She considered sadly, he was still the Emperor's man first and foremost and husband second.

She had known this when she had married him, having lived in his villa with him and his aunt under his protection according to the Emperor's orders. He had gained her work for a few hours a day at the Bureau recognising her formidable intellect but there he was the senior officer, barely acknowledging her, his head buried in paperwork or chairing meetings.

She had made few friends in the haut ton since she had nearly been betrayed by others before their marriage. Dreda insisted on vetting any friends and often found them lacking, sycophants or bad malicious gossips. Lonely at times, she had appreciated Helena's company, recognising a kindred soul, an adventurous personality and keen intellect. Helena's interests were different from hers, less academic but they complimented each other.

Helena was still perturbed by the scenes she had seen at the camp. She wanted to help prevent young girls being induced into prostitution, but the cause was unpopular in society. Most privileged women accepted the high rate of women in prostitution in the cities and blamed the girls for their lack of morals, not the social circumstances that forced them into prostitution. Felea was an exception having nearly been violated by one of Dreda's militia officers in the past.

'An orphanage Felea, to take the girls from their families before they are sold to the brothels and give them a home and training until a position can be found. I just need the money.'

Dreda was full of blunt, too much to mention and Felea offered to support the charity if Helena should start it.

'I don't know where I will be in six months' time. If I fail to find a husband, I will be back at the farm again.'

'You will find someone or some way to stay in the city although I envy your independence. Sometimes I wish I was still single,' admitted Felea to her friend for the first time since her fever.'

'Oh Felea,' cried her friend shocked. 'You adore Francis and he you. Compared with most married couples you seem so happy and relaxed. Francis is more like a friend or soulmate to you than a husband.'

'I thought so until that episode at the camp. Now I think he is no different from the rest of the married men at court. He no longer trusts me.'

'He told me some wicked people are still trying to undermine his position and question your integrity. He said he overreacted because he was worried someone would distort what you had done and the officer in question would escape his deserts.'

'I told him I wanted to separate Helena after he admonished me. He refused to let me leave the house but later said I can if I want.'

'You would hate to leave him Felea.'

'He said he wants me to stay but it is my choice. We hardly talk now. Our intimate evenings by the fire are over. You must have noticed he stays in the Bureau now and eats elsewhere and I sit and dine with you.'

Helena noticed Dreda was at home so little now. Two weeks had passed since Felea's first day out of bed but the coolness between the couple had not diminished. In fact, the gap between them had developed into a gulf that neither could bridge.

Helena decided it was time to leave so that the couple would have their evenings to themselves and they could reconcile their differences. They might be different personalities and have different interests, but they were a perfect match and their love for each other couldn't be denied.

Denman had asked her to ride that afternoon and she wore her best sea green riding habit which drew out the green in her eyes. They were talking civilly now although she still resented his criticisms which she thought unjust.

He rode to her, leading the prettiest chestnut mare she had ever seen. No evil-tempered creature here, just the spirit of her colouring and the energy and drama of her breed. She tossed her head when she saw Helena but eyed hungrily the apple Denman placed in this new lady's hand.

'This lady is for you,' said Denman, 'a present from Dreda for helping him with Felea. He asked me to pick her out and I thought she matched your temperament; lively, spirited but generous. We thought you would prefer her to jewels.'

'Oh yes,' said Helena, 'much preferable.' She fed the animal the apple, laughing as she took it greedily. The mare took a fancy to her hat which had false fruit on it and knocked it off making Helena laugh.

'A thief as well Officer Denman. You trained her well!' She shook her head regretfully.

'I can't take it from Francis. She is too expensive.'

'Not at all. She is one of his mare's foals he breeds at his farm. Dreda and Felea would be upset if you didn't accept her.'

'Even though I encouraged her to take a risk going to the camp. I think he wished me at the devil!'

'Not at all. In fact, he thinks both of you were brave and Felea assessed the legal situation perfectly.'

'I still think he thinks we were foolish.'

'Perhaps a little as did I but we were both very proud of you. I wish there were more women like you. I heard you want to start an orphanage.' She was surprised. He usually scolded her. She felt a warm glow when he praised her. To hide her embarrassment, she explained her ideas.

'In order to prevent some girls ending up on the streets and in brothels like I nearly did. Of course, there are some who will never reform. You were right about that camp girl. She left the house after several days of hard labour and has vanished into the ether.'

'You can change the environment, but it is difficult to change a person's ingrained personality. The army and militia have shown me that.'

'Now my Lady, show me what you and this horse can do. She is nervous, so gently around the park today and one day I will invite you to my farm and you can race her against my lad.'

He lifted her onto the horse and watched her slender figure lean across the horse's neck, breathing and whispering in the animal's ear. The horse enjoyed this gentle handling and instead of rearing she responded to the gentle pressure of Helena's thighs and they flew across the parkland.

Denman knew she was letting off steam. It was early in the morning and no-one else was there. Let her gallop to her heart's content. This was the real Helena, not the perfect miss the patronesses wanted to mould. She reached the trees laughing and he caught her up.

'She is divine!'

'Like her mistress then,' said Denman, the ladies' man.

'Stop funning Officer,' she said and rode off. He noted she hated listening to compliments from him, treating him like a friend or brother. He wondered why. He helped her down and took the reins of the animal.

'I think she has had enough excitement for today,' he said, noting the animal's bright eyes and nostrils snorting.

'What will you call her?'

'I don't know.' She pursed her lips and wriggled her nose in that way he found so enchanting. 'Juniper I think. Because of her colouring.'

'Good choice. Back to the house now. How long are you staying?'

'I leave tomorrow. Francis and Felea need to be alone.'

'I worry for them,' said Denman knowing he could trust her with a confidence. 'They were the tightest couple I had ever met before her illness. Francis was devastated when he thought he was going to lose her. I think it brought it home to him how much she meant to him.

'I have never seen a man so devoted to his sick wife but Felea seems to so detached and unhappy.'

'She is not the Felea I knew before she was married. Felea was passionate and sometimes impulsive, taking risks like the Felea at the camp. Married life has calmed her, and she hardly speaks a word out of place.'

'I think she no longer wants to fit into the model nobleman's wife. She feels Dreda confines her and tries to mould her. He mocks her and patronises her as if she is a child. She resents him.'

'She was always different, an individualist. I wondered if she would fit into the rigid court life but Dreda gave her some work in his bureau and she seemed happy.'

'She hinted some of the men had disrespected her and given a rough ride. She didn't tell Dreda and the situation changed for the better, but her skin has toughened.

'I work at the Bureau and didn't notice. We men must be insensitive,' he said thinking back to some of the jokes that flew around when she started.

'I think she may want to separate from him Officer Denman.'

'I thought as much. Dreda is like a bear with a sore head at the Bureau. He is on shifting sand, not knowing how to bring her round. I have only seen him like this once when Felea was pretending indifference to him and he could not decide whether she loved him and whether he would propose to her.'

Chapter nine.

Felea was sitting in the salon when Dreda entered. As pretty as a picture, she took his breath away. For such an energetic woman she seemed content, creating an exquisite piece of embroidery, her room an oasis of tranquillity. Not for the first time did he wonder how lucky he was to have won the hand and heart of this talented, intellectual but creative woman.

He watched her silently, wondering how to reach her. Withdrawing slowly, almost imperceptibly from him, he felt her slipping away into her own world, her mind shuttered against him. A telepath, she could always close her mind to others, but he had broken down her carefully constructed barriers; breached her walls and gained her trust until they were so close he could almost hear her brain tick and second-guess her thoughts.

He had no intention of allowing this painful war of attrition to continue. He hated this sterile desert of a marriage. Frustrated after a month of celibacy, he missed Felea dreadfully, wanting her back in his life and in his bed. He needed her near, to taste her sweetness again, to smell her perfume on his sheets.

Felea felt him come in, her sensory endings dancing, unsettling her. His nearness always disturbed her; turned her world upside down. He stood behind her, placing his hands on her almost bare shoulders, his fingers gently slipping under the fine lace straps of her morning gown, stroking her skin.

He felt her tremble under his touch, not the tremble of one revolted or scared but the tremble of awareness of him as he placed his body close to her. She might pretend indifference but as he caressed her silky skin her pulse raced, and he felt her heart beat quicken as did his when he pulled her gently, closer to him.

'I have some papers for you Sweetheart,' he said moving to take his place on a chair opposite her. He placed some folded papers on her lap taking the embroidery ring away from her.

'Please read them now. You need not make a decision yet but read them you must.'

'What are they Francis?' asked Felea warily. He had stayed away from her bed; left her to her reflections, put no ungentlemanly pressure on her; allowing her the space she needed to lick her wounds and recover her energy.

'Read,' he said opening the first for her to peruse. 'It is a trust document. I promised you I would put your estates and dowry into a trust for you. It is done now. Your independence, your freedom!'

Her mouth dropped open, astounded, her pupils wide as her eyes misted over but she said nothing. Unable to stand the silence he then opened the other document.

'A small house you may wish to use in this city if you still desire to move out or you may prefer to move to our country villa if you want somewhere peaceful to contemplate your future. It is your choice. There is also an account made out in your maiden name.

Felea was confused. He was offering her a way out of this marriage as she had demanded of him. Had she embarrassed him so much he mistrusted her and no longer wanted her as his wife?

'Thank you, Francis, I will peruse these in depth. They will help me make up my mind. You have made everything so much easier for me.'

'I want not a slave wife, Felea. I want a wife who lives with me, shares my life and my bed willingly, not forced to stay because she has no other choice. I want a wife who stays because she loves me.'

He took her hand and kissed her palm holding it tight; refusing to allow her to withdraw it from his own. He had taken the biggest gamble of his life handing her the pathway to her freedom. His happiness depended on her choosing him over her financial and other freedoms.

He had thought their marriage strong enough to withstand their arguments but now he was not so sure. Would the cement that held them together crumble away or hold them fast? The wall of trust he had built had eroded but he hoped it could be restored. A perceptive man, he manipulated his fellows easily but Felea was still a closed book to him even after blissful months of marriage. He hoped he had read her mood and mind right. Dictate to Felea and she would challenge him back but offer her choices and she would take the most rational path. Her birthday was tomorrow. He wanted to make it special and his goal was for her to come back to his bed willingly.

'It is late, and you are tired.' He had felt her ribs through her thin muslin dress. She had resembled an exotic fragile butterfly, but she now felt like a bag of bones, so delicate she could break if hugged too hard. Dark shadows were under her eyes, ringing them; her face so thin her enormous eyes stood out as if they did not belong there.

'Have you eaten today?'

'Some of cook's broth. Three bowlfuls. He is determined to fatten me up.'

'You could ill afford to lose weight before your malady took hold,' said Dreda.

'I eat what I can digest. Cook is making some tempting cakes and ices tomorrow for luncheon.'

She saw Dreda's eyes light up. He had a sweet tooth and the cakes were as much for him as for her birthday. Cook always spoilt him. She had seen him neglected when he was a boy at his parent's house and always had a treat for him; sad as he changed from a sensitive generous boy to a callous hard man.

She had moved to his house when he had offered her a post and had appreciated the change in him when Lady Felea moved in. He was becoming the kind boy she knew again and with the boldness of an old retainer she had told Felea she was good for him. He was becoming human again.

Dreda carried her up the stairs. She needed no help, but he enjoyed the excuse of holding her tightly again, feeling her curves and softness. He tumbled her on the bed his eyes dancing as she hastily covered her slim silk clad limbs. His eyes focused on her, his imagination running riot as he remembered those limbs tangled around his waist as he loved her.

Felea recognised that look, the look of a man who liked what he saw. She might be a bag of bones, but she could read the lust in his eyes. No matter how much they argued she was still his woman and he wanted her.

She was just not ready for him yet. She still felt cold inside; nothing there where her heart should be. She had felt rejected by him that fateful day in the study. He had virtually accused her of behaving like a sneak thief, deliberately deceiving him and pretending to usurp the Officer in Charge's authority.

'I have an apology to make you Felea. I thought your actions could be used against me again and I overreacted. I also was worried you could have been hurt. I think you were both incredibly brave confronting that man and standing your ground.

'I wish I could use you in our legal system. You would win more cases for me than our existing counsel. You have an excellent legal brain and I was a fool not acknowledging it at the time. A dolt.'

There he had said his piece and waited for her reaction, his fingers crossed behind his back. His future depended on whether she believed him.

Felea was flabbergasted. Barely ever had she heard this stern man apologise to anyone. She knew how much this meant to him, apologising to a woman half his age who had betrayed his trust. Perhaps, this was the first step to a reconciliation; a small step but it was there at last.

'I was wrong even childish not waiting for you, but I was frightened someone might get hurt. I felt I needed to do something myself. I had been feeling trapped for a while. I knew when we faced that man we were in deep water and we got out as quickly as we could.

'My Darling, you should have told me your feelings. I would have come with you to the camp. I had no idea you felt cabined and confined. I should have known. You have had to bite your lip for so long due to the sinister acts of our enemies.'

He sat on the bed and ran his fingers over her lips. 'I can't lose you Felea, I need you so much. You can take the house but don't dismiss me from your life.' He felt her relax. He was on the right pathway to a reconciliation, but he would not push too quickly. A master strategist he knew when to retreat.

'I would like to make your birthday special tomorrow Felea. There is the theatre and a ball we might attend if you are not too tired,' he said getting up and making for the door.

'I think I would like that Francis,' said Felea pleased but sad at the same time he was leaving her alone that night. She was still bewildered by her feelings.

Dreda was happy. Tomorrow he would present to her a necklace and earrings he had bought. He would dine her and dance with her and charm her just like when they were engaged. No longer would he allow her to feel lonely. She was worth more than his job to him. She was everything to him!

The next night Felea wore a green gown which bought out the gold flecks in her green eyes. She was wearing the emeralds Dreda had given her that morning with her chocolate and rolls in bed. He was a most generous husband and she had wound her arms round his neck and hugged him. Her mood had improved over night and she wanted to accompany him to the ball.

The play was a romp which suited their mood and the ball was a crush. Dreda circulated amongst the crowds always searching for information as was his wont. He kept an eye on her, ready to take her home if she felt faint. She was holding up well.

This was what she needed more often. She was young; still not yet a matron with young children, she needed excitement in her life.

A young man in uniform approached her, admiring her with his eyes. Dreda stiffened. This new man from the Bureau clearly didn't know her identity or he wouldn't have given her what was clearly 'the eye.' When he kissed her hand naked jealously tore through Dreda. He thought he had better go to the card room before he embarrassed his wife and himself. *This marital tension must be getting to me.*

Felea had no romantic interest in the young man but she was flattered by his attention. She saw Dreda move to the card room and gave the young man her hand for a dance. 'I have not seen you at these crushes Ma'am,' he said clearly enamoured of her.

'I have lately been sick,' she said, 'but I am well now and enjoying a night out.'

'You dance delightfully Ma'am,' flattered the young man. He saw rings on her finger and looked disappointed. 'Your husband is neglecting you!'

'Not at all. He must mingle. His role extends outside of the Bureau you know. He must talk to everyone. Anyone may have information that may aid him.'

'I don't know your husband, Ma'am.'

'Officer Dreda, Officer,' she said watching the smile disappear from his face. She touched his arm as they came together in the next reel of the dance

'Don't worry! My husband expects me to dance with his officers. I know most of them, but you must be new to the Bureau.'

'I am Ma'am,' he said but made a strategic retreat as soon as the dance was finished. *Coward!* thought Felea. She much preferred Denman or Thomatz or Drachman. They were afraid of no man, not even her severe husband.

She repaired to the retiring room and sat there a moment tidying her hair. Smiling at the other women there, she was perturbed to see them look contemptuously at her. Felea's antennae rose; her instincts for danger had been honed during the last year. Her husband's reminder that their enemies still tried to undermine them rang in her ears.

Silence cut across the room. Her ears burned when she realised she had been the object of their conversation before she had come in. Then one female bolder than the rest said, 'One would think when a lady is in the city for so little time she would take more care who she is with and where she goes, especially if her husband protected her from ending up in Helmand several times.'

'A friend whose brother gambled and helped the rebels would taint one's reputation by association, wouldn't she?' said one snidely.

Felea wondered who this friend was but guessed it could only be Helena. Helena had heard rumours recently that her brother might have fenced stolen goods. She would go back to the farm to divine the truth and search for any loot stored there. She did not want the militia turning up to check her barns and then accusing her of fencing the goods herself. Her name was already tainted by the death of her brother. Dreda said he would send men to help her investigate her brother's actions if she required help.

'A lady never visits army camps without a gentleman to accompany her.'

'Some women look for trouble,' said a third putting her oar in. 'They like to associate with the 'rough'. They get thrills from doing this.'

'Most husbands would reject their wives if they found out.'

'Quite right too. It is interesting when women disappear from society for weeks isn't it? As if their husbands don't want to be seen with them.'

'Some women think their status gives them the right to act as if they are the Emperor's officers.'

'My husband would not let me use his name or status. He would give me a hiding.'

Felea recognised these women. They were wives of army officers Dreda had served with, but their men had only gained low status and the privileges associated with those. He would not entertain any of their husbands in his Bureau. These women clearly resented her and the status she had earned by being Dreda's wife. Not for the first time had she wished she had more than her translating and coding work to earn her own status.

Horrified, she realised Dreda was right. Her trip to the camp was now being discussed abroad and her motives questioned. Her name and Helena's were being dragged through the mud; all because they had gone without an officer in attendance. She had been naïve but had thought she was no longer being targeted by Dreda's enemies. She realised she had earned her own enemies now who hated her for being herself, not just for being Dreda's wife. She felt sick with despair but had an insight now as to why her husband had overreacted.

At last the women got up and tidied their dresses and left her to her melancholy thoughts. She looked up when another group of harpies appeared. These women were always the first to spread rumours around and she avoided them like the plague. She realised how lonely she had been before Helena had arrived. Helena was one of the only women she felt she could trust and she would go soon.

One harpy said maliciously, 'I would not dance with a young officer and leave my husband alone with other women.' Felea's eyes widened. She pretended to examine her reticule.

These women were the mistresses of the sly dig, the poisonous barb thrown carelessly over their shoulders.

'When a rake marries a girl just out of the school-room he tires of her easily and soon reverts back to more experienced women.' Were they referring to Dreda? He had taken a mistress after losing his memory and forgetting his engagement to herself. Could he be doing that again, rejecting her, despite his sweet words last evening?

She rose, curtseyed and left the room wishing them to a painful death. She saw her husband had disappeared and regarded the room carefully, looking for him. The long windows were open on to the terrace and she could perceive some shadows out there. Conflicted, not knowing whether she should look to see if he was there she gave in to her doubts and put her head around the window door.

She could see Dreda with a woman dressed in an elaborate and flamboyant red gown. Her heavily painted nails shone blood red and she painted her lips the same colour. He faced Felea but could not see her from where she stood.

He looked serious. The woman put her arms around his neck and pulled him close to her, drawing him to her for a kiss. Felea gasped. She was stricken with jealousy. She could have gouged the woman's eyes out. Feeling jealous was unusual for her but she now understood how Dreda had killed a man for hurting her.

She could just hear their conversation. Dreda gently and firmly took the woman by her hands and pushed her away before she could finalise the kiss.

'I am flattered but no thanks. My wife is woman enough for me and I do not advocate adultery Ma'am.'

'Why should you be honest when she flouts your authority and goes behind your back, visiting rough army men?' demanded the woman. Dreda pursed his lips. He hated confrontation and bluntness. His was the weapon of the scalpel not the axe, delicately slicing his enemy to pieces. He smiled a false smile, trying not to show his disgust of this desperate woman trying to take his wife's place.

'My wife is an honest woman. Her integrity shines out. If she deceived me, which I dispute, it was to save the life of a vulnerable woman. I would have got there too late. Officer Denman aided her, but she had dealt with the situation admirably on her own.'

'She manipulates you Francis,' said the woman contemptuously. 'You would not have had wool pulled over your eyes years ago before you had met her.'

Dreda was torn. He respected this woman in her role as one of his spies but despised her for attacking his wife. Love for his wife won over his role as Commander of the Bureau. He had to defend Felea and stop the gossip mongering.

'My dear Josephine. Your concern for me does you credit but I must warn you that if you spread rumours you will not be welcome in the city nor any other place my wife and I frequent. Take this as a gentle warning. My wife is now the most important thing in my life and I trust her.'

The woman heeded his warning. He had destroyed the life of one other woman who had threatened Felea and gossiped maliciously about her. The woman was now banished to a rural hell-hole, last heard of marrying a cit for his money. No status nor social enjoyment in the rural backwater. She would not risk Dreda's vengeance. He paid his spies well and there was always a wealthy protector amongst the officers at the Bureau to endow her with the luxuries she deserved.

Felea smiled as the women pushed past her, eyes downcast, frightened that Felea had overheard her words. She was under no illusions now. Her husband would always attract the attentions of other women and whilst in love with her he would act honourably as he had had done just then. He was no saint though, a virile man who enjoyed their bedroom activities. Withdrawing and pushing him away was asking for trouble.

Dreda was a sensitive man under his hard-outer shell. One day he might no longer accept the rejections and turn to women who would flatter him and give him what he wanted; women who sought nothing other than jewels or pretty things; the sort of women Dreda had enjoyed before their marriage.

A wise woman would recognise what she had, the good qualities Dreda brought to the marriage; the man he was gradually becoming. She Felea, would embrace his good qualities and try to ignore his worse features and making the best of their marriage in the future.

Dreda recognised her gown and called softly. 'Out here Felea please.' He took her down the lakeside walk. 'Remember when we were here last?' he asked, stopping and putting his hands on her shoulders. She remembered well.

He had accused her of being too friendly to other men and she had said he would make too severe a father for her. He had admitted he felt no fatherly feelings toward her. Mistaking his intentions, she had said she would not become his mistress and he had remarked he did not seduce innocents but to be careful; other men would not be as honourable. Several days later he proposed to her.

'Yes, I didn't understand your intentions. I thought you wanted to offer me a carte blanche.'

'I had already decided that afternoon to marry you. That is a decision I have never regretted my love. I want you to know that.'

'Nor I, Francis,' she admitted. 'You are maddening, infuriating, insufferably arrogant at times but I enjoy living with you even when you dominate and manipulate me.'

'And you are the most annoying, insolent, provoking woman I have ever had dealings with, but I have missed our spats Felea. Without you my life is boring.'

'Well Husband, perhaps you need to make my nights more exciting,' she said. 'I have missed being with you in the evenings as well.'

'At your service Ma'am, starting with tonight!'

He took her by the arm, guiding her through the crowded ballroom watching for Denman. He smiled at him and Denman recognised the smile of a happy relaxed man. His friends were as one again, their dispute over, their marriage stronger.

He envied their intimacy as Felea regarded Dreda again as if he were her world. Mayhap, one day he would find love like that if he took the chance to grab it by the neck and not let it go. He wished he could take the risk!

Chapter ten.

The trip to the camp had consolidated the women's friendship. They went to the theatre and opera with Dreda and Denman, making a foursome. Felea had watched Denman closely when he was with Helena. Dreda had told her about his determination to guard and look after her at the villa. He had hinted Denman held a tender for her but had been put off by her coldness to him.

Helena was a calm, secretive girl who kept her thoughts to herself. Felea could not tell her feelings for Denman but noted her eyes followed him across the room when she thought he was not looking. She seemed to melt into his arms when she danced with him. If asked about him she changed the subject rather too quickly for a girl who did not care for him. Felea suspected she was pretending to herself she did not hold a tender for him.

As for Denman, she thought he was circling her, boxing clever, trying to make up his mind about her. Heralding from the top drawer, a diplomatic family, he could not afford to make a mistake and bring scandal to his noble family. He must choose circumspectly, setting up other ladies as flirts and only dancing with Helena once at any ball. He was shielding her from rumour and spite. Except for his rides in the park with her in full view of the critical eye of 'polite society' he only escorted her among groups of friends and behaved irreproachably.

Helena kept Denman at a distance, treating him like the other men who gave her bouquets and complimented her. She began to relax with him and they began to behave like good firm friends. Flirting was as natural to Denman as breathing but he had made no effort to flirt with her recently.

They talked about horseflesh, a subject they were both knowledgeable about. She was surprised to hear he helped his father breed thoroughbreds at the family farm. He intimated that if he retired from the militia he would breed and train horse flesh for racing. He noted her eyes lit up and then clouded and she looked sad.

'What was on your mind?' he asked, wondering what could have made her happy and then so despondent.'

'Oh,' she said, 'nothing,' not wanting him to think she was self-pitying. Six months before she had been poor, head buried in farm work without a future but now she had opportunities if she married well, more than other women in her situation. *I should pull myself together and grow up.*

'Tell me,' he urged. He wanted to know what made this unusual girl tick. She was so secretive; she hid her feelings and motivations so deep he couldn't divine her thoughts most of the time. How he wanted to earn her trust and make her share her thoughts with him. She was the first girl he had ever wanted to sit down and talk for hours with.

'I just thought how wonderful it would be to have the freedom and money to devote oneself to the past-time one loved.'

He understood then. Her future was bleak. By his licentious gambling her brother had taken her choices away. Only by marrying could she gain the financial independence and security she required. If she did not make a good marriage she would be stuck on the farm trying to make ends meet. He had seen other woman like her end up drawn and tired, aged quickly, bearing the burden of hard work and worry. He hated the thought she could end up like that. He decided he could help her even if she had to return to the farm.

The next day he met Dreda. 'Francis would you and Felea like to come to father's farm for a short sejour?' Dreda's eyebrows raised. While he enjoyed meeting Denman's family he felt there was more to this than a social visit. 'Of course, my friend but to any particular purpose?'

'I would like to help Helena. My father would lend her a stallion if she had some mares he could serve. She is horseflesh mad and we might come to some accommodation if she was tempted by the horseflesh on father's farm.'

'Felea said she admitted she is sometimes bored. Society life is too superficial for that young girl after the busy life of managing the farm. After she saw the poor girls in that brothel she said she would also like to start an orphanage to rescue young girls before they entered such places. She just doesn't have the money to start such an affair and Felea thinks it might put off some traditional men who do not want their wives involved in such things.'

Denman admitted, 'Some men are blind to what goes on or what to ignore what is under their noses. They enjoy the women but ignore the fruits of their excesses, the children the women bear. I admit I have never given any thought to fate of the women I enjoy and the consequences.'

'Nor I,' said Dreda. 'I had little conscience until I met Felea, but she has brought home to me the consequences of the actions of men since I married her.' He changed the subject which had become uncomfortable for both of them, both being wealthy entitled nobles, licentious in their youth. 'So, if we come in a few days what is your plan?'

'To show Helena that even if she doesn't find a husband she might still have an income breeding horses.'

'But she would still live on the farm, a lonely life for such a popular girl. No chance of a family! She enjoys society life as much as other women. She just needs something to stimulate her brain like Felea.'

Dreda saw his friend frown and purse his lips. 'Perhaps she could still live in the city and lease some land on the outskirts.'

'Unlikely, unless she intends to stay with her aunt and uncle forever. No, the girl will have to find an accommodating husband who accepts his wife will train and trade horseflesh like a man or she will leave for the family farm.' He watched for

Denman's reaction to this statement. Denman shrugged his shoulders pretending indifference.

'Well I will still invite her and some others as well to stop the gossips talking about us.'

The next week he watched Helena arrive in Felea's carriage. Slim and lithe she jumped down, refusing the groom's help. She ran over and climbed on to the paddock fence, her skirts gathered around her and sat watching the stallion race around the field. She wore her golden hair in loose waves, blowing wildly around her body; elemental, melding with nature as if at home there; watching intently, totally absorbed by the stallion and his mate.

So absorbed was she, she failed to notice when he came up close and put his hands on the rail each side of her. She started and exclaimed, 'Oh, Officer Denman, I was so entranced by the animals I forgot my manners and did not notice you.'

'I am delighted you managed to come,' he said, still standing behind her, trapping her there. She leant back against him for a moment enjoying his warmth. He was solid and strong, and he smelt of the hay that was sticking out of his hair. He had been moving hay-bales for his father, his sleeves rolled up, his biceps showing; a man who enjoyed action and hard work.

She felt his chest, as hard and firm as steel. This man could play the dandy in the ball or drawing room but put him on the farm and he was in his element; a man who could not sit still for long, a man who made things happen! Like Dreda he had to keep occupied, his forceful body requiring physical work and his sharp mind requiring stimulation. She remembered what it was like to be held in those strong arms and kissed by him.

Damn the man! He was making her think like a wanton again. Despite all the men she had met in the city she had never felt such strong feelings for a man as she had for Denman. Just by looking at her he rocked her equilibrium and made her hope for things she should forget. She would be lucky if she married a kind and gentle man who could provide for her security.

She had to forget this rake, this womaniser who pursued and discarded women when he had taken what he wanted from them. She moved his arms away from her gently and turned to face him. He had that tender expression on his face again, damn him! He almost made her want to trust him.

Denman had stood there, smelling her fresh scented hair, enjoying her softness. He wanted to bury himself in that hair and kiss that delicate scented skin. She was the most desirable girl he had met. He had met more beautiful ladies than Helena but there was something different that characterised her and set her apart from other women; a tranquillity that made him want to stay with her and a vulnerability that made him want to protect her. Rested against him, she had appeared to enjoy him holding her; but then she had stiffened, and that impassive expression was back on her face as she turned toward him. She smiled but it was a false smile as if she needed to trick him into thinking she was happy.

'Officer Denman, you promised me a ride on your new mare, after I had spoken with your parents again.' She put her arm in his and he took her to his parents accepting her rebuff. His parents were delighted to meet her again. Helena fitted in with his lively family as if she was one of them, delighting everyone with her easy manners and intelligence. A horse mad family she fitted well with their conversation and lifestyle.

Denman took her for a long ride before his friends were up. Dreda was gradually weaning himself off the habitual long hours of the office but urgent matters still pricked his conscience and made him spend more time there than they wished. Long mornings in bed were a treat for them. Denman's parents indulged and spoilt them, their servants delivering them their coffee, chocolate and rolls in bed allowing them more time to themselves whilst their friends rode and exchanged pleasantries.

Denman rarely had Helena to herself. He intended to enjoy her company without having to worry about his behaviour being commented on or reported by trouble-making gossips. The groom accompanied them to maintain the proprieties, but he kept at a respectable distance enabling them to enjoy some privacy.

'Let's race to the willow at the end of the bank,' said Denman. 'The last one pays a forfeit.' Seeing her hesitate for a moment he taunted her. 'Are you game or chicken?' She laughed, unwilling ever to turn down a challenge!

'Chicken be damned!' she retorted and followed him. He raced her along the river bank giving her no quarter. She had borrowed one of his stallions. She knew she could not win this race by normal means; his stallion was bred for racing. She threw herself into the competition, her hair flowing behind her, her head forward; determined to try to win this race by other ways.

He realised it meant everything to her to ride at a fast pace again, away from the city where she must usually ride sedately to please the patronesses who dictated to society. Her icy controlled façade hid a fiery spirit untamed, waiting to be released. Denman realised like Felea this girl had hidden depths. He wanted to be the man who plundered those depths, to tame her and direct that fiery passion to satisfy his needs.

She had spurred her horse on and took a short cut through the trees; through the shallow water and up the bank again. She overtook him.

Got you! she thought as she galloped by, not looking back nor wasting a second. She wanted to prove she could ride as well as him. He knew she was a good rider, but she had not tested her skill against his.

He had stopped wondering where she had gone and then he saw her flying by. *By God, she could beat me.* Fiercely competitive like herself he pushed his horse forward, the fiery beast responding to the challenge, enjoying the chase as much as he. She was within a furlong of the willow, but she heard a thunder of hooves behind her as he came closer and his horse's neck reached past her as he passed the tree.

Damn the man. His horse was bred for this. She met him, and he got down. He lifted her off her horse but didn't let her down when she had reached the ground. He had a queer look in his eye as if he was assessing her again. He swung her around and around making her laugh with him.

He put her down. Smiling he put a hand on her shoulder and lifted her chin in his. He undid her hat and tossed it on the ground.

'And now for that forfeit.'

'We did not agree the forfeit,' she said breathlessly knowing what it could be.

'Winner decides,' he said firmly, pulling her closer and claiming her mouth. It was a tender kiss, undemanding at first. Seeing the awareness in her eyes and feeling her tremble and respond to his light caresses, he increased its intensity. His arm wrapped her against him in a kiss that seemed endless.

She finally pushed him away and said crossly, 'That was taking unfair advantage when you knew you had a stronger, faster horse.'

'You should have asked the forfeit before you took up my bet,' he said, holding her still; reluctant to let the moment past.

'I didn't expect you to act ungentlemanly,' she retorted.

'You cheated by going through the water.'

'We didn't state the boundary of the race,' she countered.

'I had to win by any means,' he said. 'I wanted that kiss.' He took her hands in his and kissed her palms. 'You are beautiful Helena.'

She tugged her hands back. 'And we must get back Officer Denman.' They heard a noise behind the trees.

'Hello there!' yelled out a hidden figure and Denman moved forward; shielding her from the newcomer's sight whilst

Helena tidied her hair and put on her hat, making herself look like the elegant cool gentlewoman again.

A man and woman rode to them. 'Gooday, Denman,' hailed the man and waited for an introduction to Helena. Denman cross he had been disturbed, put on a false smile and said smoothly, 'Lady Helena von Vagna, this reprobate is Count von Hichen and his sister Countess von Ratchen. What brings you here von Hichen?'

'We were just riding along our boundaries inspecting fences, but we saw your horse flying by the river and thought we would introduce ourselves. Are you attending the next ball?'

'No, we go back to the city. My father is showing Lady Helena some stock she might breed from on her family farm. Dreda and his wife are here also but meeting us very soon for a picnic. We went on ahead, so Lady Helena could try out the horse.'

Helena smiled at the woman. Inside she was nervous. If they had been seen kissing this pair could gossip and she could be accused of being compromised. The woman didn't seem to jump to conclusions and said, 'When next you visit the farm send your card Lady Helena. We will invite you to our soirees or balls.' She turned her horse and said, 'Come Brother we must away to the villa. Our guests are waiting.' Her brother pulled a face but left, waving to Denman and Helena.

Denman saw Helena was anxious. 'You need not worry. They saw nothing but would not make anything up. Dorothea was caught in a compromising position and that is how she is married to her Count. She will not throw stones.' Helena rounded on him.

'That is not the point. I could have been seen. You have no reputation to lose, but I do.' She climbed with difficulty on her horse, rejecting his help and galloped away, as fast as she could, leaving him standing there. For someone not caught in a compromising situation she seemed inordinately upset. He shook his head. He would never understand women.

Helena entered the villa at a run, surprising the servants. Felea could sense her agitation. She followed her friend up the stairs and knocking entered her bedroom.

'What is wrong?'

'Nothing,' her friend said and then sat down on the bed and said, 'oh it is no use hiding the truth. It is Denman. We raced our horses and he won and demanded a forfeit. I let him kiss me.

'It was not a friendly kiss Felea; it started out that way but became demanding and passionate. We were nearly seen by two friends of his and I could have been seen to have been compromised but he saw it as a jape. He was flippant. He sees life as a mere joke.'

Felea could have slapped Denman, both for embarrassing her friend and jeopardising her reputation, but also for toying with her.

'I will be a better chaperone for the next few days and make him keep his distance from you. He is dangerous Helena, not to be trusted. Normally he doesn't chase innocents, but he sees you as a challenge.'

She left her and found Dreda who had left her in the bedroom in a sunny mood that morning and was surprised to see her angry.

'What's up?' he asked wondering what he had done. 'It is nothing to do with you. It is your damned friend Denman, kissing Helena by the river. They were disturbed by his friends and she could have been compromised. He needs to keep his hands to himself.'

'I will have a word with him,' said Dreda. 'It is unlike Denman to risk compromising a virgin. He really must desire her. I wondered when he asked us here to the farm if his feelings are growing deeper than he has admitted.'

'Well if they are he needs to be honest and do something honourable about it, pay his addresses. I will not have Helena's reputation destroyed by his immature behaviour.

'I am on it,' said Dreda.

For the next two days Denman kept her at a distance and only spoke to her when the others were there. One morning though he had held her a little too long and too tight when he lifted her off her horse. As she reached terra firm he steadied her and placed a kiss on the underside of her wrist. She looked up at him and saw he was watching her with that tender look in his eyes which sent her heart fluttering. But she hid that reaction.

She steeled herself, putting a smile in her face and said quite firmly taking her hand away. 'Officer Denman, you must not flirt with me so. I do not take your flirtations seriously, but others may think otherwise. Here we are safe but in town gossips may blow your kisses out of proportion.'

Denman let her go but felt angry, conflicted. In one moment he did not want this girl to think he anticipated matrimony with her but then the next he wanted her to react to his kisses, to be in love with him. He was a total bastard. A fickle player with women. He deserved his rebuff. He led her in and left her there to sit with his mother.

Furious, he saddled his fiercest stallion. The highly-bred animal sensed his anger and tensed, waiting for his master's instructions. With a nudge of his thick strong thighs he commanded the horse to move forward and the animal obeyed, the bond between animal and man requiring no verbal instructions.

He rode his animal across the fields, jumping the highest fences, letting the lively animal have his head, his own blood pumping inside him until his adrenalin left him. He quietened the now tired animal and let it eat grass while he slid off and sat by the river, drinking from his flask until he felt relaxed enough to go home.

His feelings for this young woman were tearing him apart. Never had he felt so torn. He had thought he cared for him a little; but with that toss of the head she had said she regarded him merely as one of her flirts; no more important that the dandies who meaning nothing to her were allowed to take her hands and dance light kisses on them.

His father sat with Helena. A wise man, he had not commented on this young girl. Denman never brought his 'ladies,' to the family farm. He kept that side of his life away from his family although they knew his propensity toward liaising with light-skirts. His father was surprised when this young girl visited the farm again. Unlike Denman's usual women, this girl had common sense and didn't talk about fashions all the time. He could see what had attracted Peter to her.

He cared not for her lack of dowry. Many wealthy titled men married impecunious women whose menfolk had gambled their money away. It was the way of the world. Her character was more important.

This girl was serious, too serious perhaps for his light-hearted son, but her life had been hard. Occasionally he saw a different side of Helena, the side his son brought out, a lighter less serious side. A different life might make her a more relaxed and lively girl. If so his son was the man to do it.

He had never seen his son so contented, nor relaxed with a woman. A fiercely energetic man, he moved usually from one source of entertainment to another until he bored quickly of it. Instead, during the girl's stay Peter stayed at home listening to her sing and play and conversing or playing cards with her.

He was a changed man, content and tranquil. His father wanted that for his son. His job no longer provided him with the satisfaction he needed. He had outgrown his boyish enthusiasm for the army. He needed a different direction.

Bent, heads together over a horseflesh catalogue, these young people had argued and wrangled good-humouredly and selected their animals as if they were going to auction together. His son had found his soul-mate if only he had the good sense to recognise it. He would not interfere. Peter was not a man to be pushed or rushed. He always made his own mind up, but his father feared he might lose this girl if he did not make up his mind quickly. Women like her didn't appear very often.

Denman took his friends to the river for a picnic. He helped Dreda unload the saddlebags. Felea and Helena sat against the tree on blankets. They made a pretty picture, Helena's green-blue eyes and golden hair a foil for Felea's dark smouldering beauty.

'Beautiful,' said Dreda watching them. 'Both of them. Felea grows more beautiful by the day as she matures.'

'You are a lucky man,' said Denman feeling jealous of his friend's intimacy with his lovely wife.

'You could be lucky if you took the leap. Happiness is waiting for you.' With that enigmatic comment he went to the women and helped put out the wine and tortes and bread and fruit.

Denman followed him pensively but joined in the laughter pretending a happiness he didn't feel. To those with him he was the same jovial man without a care in the world but recently he had begun to feel lonely, incomplete, his life unfulfilled. He would have to find something to occupy himself.

The last evening, he sat with his parents and Helena. 'You know you could breed animals and make a secure income for the farm,' said Denman broaching the subject for the first time. His father said, 'I will lend you a stallion if you give me the first foal in exchange.' He knew she wouldn't accept charity readily. The foal was a salve to her pride.

'Your uncle could lend you an advance on your allowance for some mares,' suggested Denman.

'I have some small savings I could use already. I will think about it,' said Helena. 'I don't know where I will be in a few months' time.'

'That girl thinks too much,' said his father privately to his son when they were on their own. 'She is too cautious. She needs a strong man to sweep her off her feet and take charge and make some decisions for her.' His son ignored the implications of his father's comment and merely said, 'She has few choices but will make her own mind up. She is not a girl who can be pushed or bullied.'

*Like you, h*is father thought. *You have met your match at last my Son and she is twisting you in knots.*

Denman helped Helena into the carriage and kissed her hand again, ignoring her frown. 'Good luck in the city. I will see you soon.' Helena sighed and sat in the carriage and took out a book. Felea read her own journal. Later she would talk to her friend when Helena's feelings seemed less raw. Denman had withdrawn inside himself, not acknowledging his deeper feelings for Helena. She in turn was pushing him away. She felt like knocking their heads together. *Oh well, if Helena received more offers Denman might get a shock and face up to his feelings. We will have to wait and see.*

Dreda took Denman to one side one evening. Having downed one bottle of brandy Dreda thought Denman was receptive to conversation and ventured giving some advice.

'Felea is worried about Helena, Peter. She fears she is too innocent and doesn't understand the intentions of men yet. Denman looked up. A man's man, it was unusual for Dreda to discuss the romantic ways of young women. Something specific must be on his mind for him to broach such a sensitive subject with his friend.

'What men are after her then?' asked Denman pretending indifference. Dreda was not foxed by him. He had been friends too long with Peter for him to pull wool over his eyes. Denman's knuckles were white as he held his glass too tight.

'No-one in particular yet,' said Dreda and saw his friend breathe a sigh of relief. 'Felea just isn't sure she understands the rules of the game when more experienced men flirt with her. She might take their advances seriously and get hurt if the men are merely indulging in light flirtation.' Seeing the light, Denman asked, 'And what are these men supposed to do.'

'Make it clear their intentions do not include marriage.'

'I thought Helena was enjoying flirting with young men. She always has a large entourage wherever she goes. She is one of the most popular girls of the season despite her age.' He treaded carefully with his old friend. 'Felea is delightful but she does tend to behave like a mother hen with the young girls she takes under her wing.'

'She was a young girl and almost thrown to the wolves. She would not want a young girl's reputation damaged by a fast fling with an experienced man or even the rumour of such a liaison. Nor would she want her hurt by a more experienced older man.'

'I take your point Francis. No need to rub it in. You need not worry about Helena. She told me in no uncertain terms at the farm she doesn't take my flirtatious remarks seriously. My reputation has gone before me, sadly.'

Dreda was sympathetic, having also lusted after forbidden fruits when Felea was under his roof. He would not interfere in his friend's love life. It was up to Denman to decide if he wanted to pursue more than a friendship with this delightful young girl. He had to warn him off though. He had promised Felea he would protect Helena from his lecherous friend's attentions.

'I think it is now more than remarks, isn't it Peter,' said Dreda. 'You have never kissed innocents my friend but perhaps you have never been tempted so much. I know how you feel. I was the same with Felea and had to make up my mind whether it would be matrimony or avoiding contact with her.'

Peter nodded. 'I will make it even clearer my intentions are honourable but do not involve matrimony. Tell Felea I will treat her friend like a sister and leave her chaste although I admit it kills me to do so. Every time I hold her in a waltz I have the desire to take her in my bed. She becomes more desirable with every dance.'

Chapter eleven.

'Lady Helena.' She looked up from the salon where she was attempting a water-colour. Painting was not her forte, but every debutante was expected to be proficient in producing water colours, so she tried her best.

'There is a person to see you my Lady.' The footman usually a confident fellow looked uneasy and unsure of himself.

'Well I am 'at home'. Who is it?' she asked, puzzled. *Why was he prevaricating instead of showing her the visiting card and introducing the person?*

'The person is not of the quality my Lady. She is the girl Lady Felea introduced into her household and disappeared soon after.'

How the devil did he know about that? Servants must have blabbed. Even Dreda's loyal and overpaid servants clearly couldn't be trusted. Helena didn't trust the girl and wondered if she was after a post in her aunt's household. Perhaps the gentlemen she had serviced were not as gentle or as generous as she had imagined. Nevertheless, she might have some information about the men who ran the camp and embezzled money from the Emperor's coffers. She would allow her an interview but rid herself of this girl quickly after she had said her piece.

'Bring her in, Grogni.' The girl quickly entered looking around the salon in an assessing way, her sharp narrow eyes valuing the pieces of Holbein and rich drapes and carpets. Perhaps she wondered if there was a place for her in this rich household or how much her information was worth.

'How can I help you, Maria?' asked Helena coldly. After helping her and possibly saving her from severe injury, the ungrateful girl had paid them back by scarpering without giving any notice.

'It is more likely how I can help you my Lady,' answered the bold piece.

'Explain!'

She did not invite the girl to sit down but without being asked she gracefully perched on a chair. She wore the clothes of a whore who had fallen on her feet. Perhaps she had been taken in to one of the wealthier brothels and taught to speak like a gentlewoman as she attempted the cut-glass accent of a member of the quality. She clearly did not walk the streets standing on street corners opportuning the soldiers who frequented the bars. Jewels adorned her neck, peeking out from the low-necked dress which showed her ample bosom. Her hair was extravagantly curled and primped, topped by a feathered hat.

'I have information that would interest Commander Dreda.'

'Why not go directly to his household then?'

'I thought I might not be welcome and gain entry,' the girl said honestly. 'You might pass the information on to Countess von Danitz.'

'To what purpose?'

'To safeguard her husband's life! I have missives that might interest him.'

'Give them to me then,'

'I don't have them with me. My protector has them.'

Oh. So that is where the jewels and fine clothes have come from. And she intends to extort money out of me for the information. She thinks me soft!

'And your protector is?'

'It would not be wise for me to tell you my Lady. It might be assumed he was one of the conspirators wishing to harm Commander Danitz,' replied the girl craftily. *And then who would pay for your jewels and finery?* thought Helena cynically.

'If you come with me you can peruse the documents in safety.'

'Who wishes Commander Danitz dead?'

'I don't know. The documents referred to in the letters are in code. Neither my protector nor I can understand them, but the letters definitely state he is to be done away with.' Helena noticed her refined language and accent were slipping away in the girl's anxiety to persuade Helena she was telling the truth.

For some strange reason Helena believed her. She was crafty but not clever, using her beauty and amiable personality to make her way in this harsh world. She almost felt sorry for her. She wondered if she was literate or did she rely on her protector to read the letters.

Sighing, Helena thought she would have to read the letters herself. She would give the documents to Felea who 'broke' codes for the Bureau being a linguist and mathematician. Felea had taught her a little of the methods of codebreaking but she was not as proficient as her friend. She could write basic codes, but she had not the intellect to master the science behind sophisticated code-breaking.

'How, now to get the documents?' she asked herself. She was not fool enough to go on her own. This might be a way for the officers at the rebel camp to take their vengeance out on her. Dreda and Denman were out of town. After what had happened at the camp she and Felea would not go on their own again.

'I am not prepared to go with you on my own. Perhaps your protector would like to share a jail with common criminals? I can ask Officer Denman to arrest you two.'

'That officer and Commander Danitz are out of town,' said the girl contemptuously. 'Try again my Lady.'

Damn and blast! The girl has done her homework. 'There are other officers who will do my bidding.'

'Do you have time my Lady? Dare you risk the Commander's life? The men who wish him dead may already be acting out their role.'

Curse the girl! She had Helena over a barrel. Felea had said there had already been attempts on his life during the short time they had been married. Many people in the court and Cabinet wished him out of the way. His attempt to cut corruption in the army had made him many enemies who would willingly pay one of the unemployed vagrant soldiers to kill him and blame the rebels. He was under no illusions; he and Denman needed to watch their backs all the time.

Helena needed to buy time until the officers at the Bureau could help her. Officers von Thomatz and von Hadreni might be available. How could she summon them without these people knowing? They knew Denman and Dreda were out of town. They must have a source inside the Bureau or have bribed the household servants of the two men.

'Countess Von Danitz will wish to accompany me. She is a trained codebreaker. She will want to know the names of the potential assassins. She is not the sort of woman who will stand by and watch others intervene.'

'Very well. Let her come.' The girl thought this might push the price up. Everyone knew the Count was full of blunt and the passionate Countess loved her husband dearly. She would pay any price to safeguard his life. It would only delay the meeting by a few hours.

'Send her a letter immediately,' ordered the girl. Her demeanour had changed from a quiet deference to aggression, her back straight and eyes challenging Helena to disobey her will. 'I hold all the cards,' shouted out her stance.

Good, thought Helena. She wrote Felea a letter outlining the problem and the girl's demands. She invited her to join her immediately to look at the documents. She showed the letter to the girl who surprisingly could read fluently. What the girl didn't know was Helena had written a few lines in the limited code she had learnt from Felea. Felea was a good teacher and Helena thanked her good fortune she could remember enough to explain to her friend she must get in touch with the Bureau to arrange their help.

The girl took it and left to give it to her driver. Helena summoned her footman.

'Follow her discretely and find out who owns the carriage.' she told him. The girl came back and audaciously demanded coffee and cakes. Helena restrained the desire to strangle the forward creature and started to question her about her life since she had left Felea's household. Any information might help Dreda catch the criminals.

The girl was surprising garrulous now she thought she had the upper hand and told Helena where she lived. Gartiz was a district dominated by the demi-monde, who inhabited houses leased by the rich noblemen and cits to house their whores. She didn't tell Helena who her protector was. She would have to wait to find out, that is, if he didn't use an intermediary to supply to her the documents.

Felea read the letter with dismay. All the fears she had buried came back to haunt her. Dreda had admitted he had behaved recklessly and taken unnecessary risks whilst he was a young officer, betrayed by his fiancée and neglected by his indifferent father and mother.

He had not valued human life much, either his own or his enemies and had acted harshly, more harshly than was needed at times. His enemies, too numerous to be counted, had been trampled underfoot in his desperate need to prove himself by climbing up the slippery hierarchy to be the Emperor's favourite. Now the chickens were coming back to roost. His enemies were coming out of the woodwork. If the Emperor showed he was out of favour the knives would be well and truly drawn.

She needed to know who was behind this potential assassination attempt. She could guess at a few names. Dreda had taken her into his confidence so she wouldn't betray herself unwittingly to his enemies in court. She needed Thomatz's street connections and Hadreni's understanding of the minds of the

Cabinet, Army and Militia to find out who was undermining Dreda and where they operated from.

There was a secret passage leading from her husband's chamber which only two servants knew about apart from her and Dreda. She asked her husband's valet, his former batman in the army to use the passage and tunnels under the house to reach the Bureau. The letter he carried seemed innocent if it fell into the hands of her enemies but when held under water a message written in alum told the officers in the Bureau they needed to make haste and follow the three women.

He made off and she hastened to her carriage, taking the slowest route to Helena's residence. Anything to buy time for the officers. Maria was waiting, striding around the room, impatiently slapping her hands against her thighs.

'Something must have gone wrong,' she exclaimed. 'She is taking too long.'

'Not at all. The Countess always takes ages to ready herself to go out.' She got up. 'Hark, I hear a carriage.'

An imperious knocking on the door proceeded a small whirlwind rushing through the salon door. She stopped and looked the girl from top to toe, shaking her head, as if shocked at the girl's temerity. She addressed Maria directly.

'You girl, you summoned me? You have information about enemies of my husband who wish him dead?'

Maria quaked. Dreda was one of the most influential persons in this land but his wife by repute could twist him round his finger. If their plan failed this little woman could ask her for death warrant. The look Felea gave her told her she would enjoy doing it. This woman was out for blood.

'My protector has letters which refer to documents written in code which we can't decipher. The letters refer to a death plan outlined in the documents.'

'The names of the men who wrote the letters?

'I am not to tell you until you have talked with my protector.

'How much do you want?' demanded Felea bluntly.

'That is for my protector to decide.'

'How do you know he will not take the money and abandon you?'

Maria looked sick for a moment. The thought had clearly crossed her mind. She tossed her head and said defiantly, 'He will take me. He needs me.'

Fool, thought Felea. *He will dispose of you when you bore him. It is you who has made contact with us. He hides in the shadows taking the money. You are his public face, known to the servants and will hang on the gallows while he slips away.*

Helena knew by now who the carriage belonged to and the owners place of residence. 'We should go now Felea.' She held a purse up.

'Maria. This is one hundred sovereigns as down payment for taking us to your protector. It is yours for your needs only. The remainder we will negotiate with him.'

The girl's eyes lit up for a moment. This was more than she could earn in a lifetime whoring. If she pleased these women she could retire to the country; pretend to be a widow and get a husband and lead a respectable life. No whoring or fear of violence or abandonment and impoverishment in her old age. There was a way out of this life.

'I will take you to my protector. His name is Victor von Mendetz.' Felea nodded and they followed her to her carriage. Helena had told her groom to inform the Bureau as soon as they left. Felea racked her brains. She had heard the name before. As they reached the man's address she recalled with dread the man's reputation. He had served in the militia with Dreda but had been dismissed for dishonourable conduct by her husband.

Embezzlement was common in government offices and Dreda dealt with it stringently in the Bureau. The man had lost the perks of office and his pension and had taken a poorly paid job as a clerk. How could he afford to set his mistress up in style in this house? He must be in the pay of someone more powerful and richer than himself. It was the name of that man Felea wanted.

A servant opened the door a crack and peered at them with rheumy bloodshot eyes. 'Mistress Dentra. My Master awaits you.' He led them to the salon where a man sat reading some papers. He got up and bowed and clicked his heels as if coming to attention.

'Countess von Danitz, I am honoured to meet you at last.' He took her hand and kissed it lingeringly. She was the most attractive piece of ass he had seen in years. He lusted after her, jealous Dreda had won the prize for himself. It was one more reason he hated Dreda. Dreda had everything he desired and was out of his reach. Perhaps it was not too late.

He might get the money and Dreda's woman if he played his cards right. He could take her somewhere far away with the money and Dreda wouldn't know of the plot to kill him until it was too late. He would be dead. Maria could be disposed of easily. Many whores were found in the river every year, their usefulness outlived, and their knowledge of their protectors' secret lives too dangerous to let them live.

His sponsor was a rich man and would pay richly for Dreda's death. He had been plotting his downfall for years in court with no success. It was not for nothing Dreda was referred to as the Vulcan by his enemies. He gave nothing away and had few friends who would not leak secrets. Only by marrying the rebel's daughter had he nearly made a false move, but she was now a favourite of the Empress and his position more secure. Impatient, his sponsor had given up trying to libel his enemy with the mark of the traitor and had decided harsher means were required to usurp Dreda's position and power. He had desired Felea as his mistress when Dreda was gone but Felea's property was now in trust, a recent act of madness by Dreda.

Only a fool would give a woman financial freedom. Felea would be independent on the death of her husband; not forced to find a second husband or protector as his sponsor had hoped after Dreda's entailed estates went to his male successor. He Mendentz, would not care what the law said about a woman's estates. To the devil with the law. He would take her by force with him and subdue her until she accepted her role as his whore in a land too far away for her to leave his household.

Felea bowed but took her hand away and stood a distance from him. His kiss felt like that of a snake, dry and papery. He was older than Dreda and loose living had made him fat and ruddy cheeked. His jowls were full, the sign of a heavy drinker and he smelt of stale tobacco. She wanted to retch. She felt sorry for Maria having to bed this man at his whim.

'Where are the letters and documents you promised to show me?' He laughed. This little woman was daring to demand he do her will. The vixen needed to be shown her place. Dreda had been seduced and bewitched by her. Public report held she could twist him around her little finger. He had become soft in his dealings with the rebels, encouraging the Emperor to waste good money on schools and hospitals to turn the youths away from the rebel cause. She needed a real man to tame her and if his luck was in he was just that man. A slap or two would change her tune and make her respect a man's wishes.

'Later Countess. First, we toast your coming here. Some Madeira perhaps?' He intended to drag every last minute out, to show her who held the winning card and make her compliant to his will. Helena intervened, directing his line of fire away from Felea.

'Sir, thank you for your hospitality but it is too early for alcoholic beverages. Some tea perhaps.' She held out her hand for him to kiss curtseying deeply. Perhaps this one was more amenable to a man's touch. He had heard rumours her brother had been a traitor and she had needed of a man with a deep purse. He rang for tea.

'Sit ladies.' He took the documents he had been perusing and divided the letter and documents between the two women while Maria nervously looked on. She had noticed his keen interest in Felea and the way he had mentally undressed Helena. She clearly felt insecure and unsafe.

Good God, thought Helena. It was worse than she had imagined. His sponsor, for he was clearly being paid, wanted him to arrange for a group of men to wait for Dreda in an inn and arrange for his meal to be poisoned. The landlord was primed and bribed. The men were the insurance if the poison failed to do its job. A sabre and pistol would then suffice to finish the task. She did not recognize the name of the sponsor von Herzen, but she passed the letter to Felea who gasped.

'The murderous bastard. He has been trying to destroy Francis for years,' she told Helena. 'He tried to black Francis's and my reputation before we married.'

'Sir, may we have the document to peruse?'

'How much is it worth?' he asked.

'Name your price!' She cared not how much it cost if Dreda's life could be saved. Anyhow, Dreda would send his hounds after them and hunt every last one down and hang them for their temerity.

'Twenty thousand sovereigns.'

'When and where?' Felea demanded, wanting this over and done with.

'Tomorrow, at a destination I decide. You and Lady Helena can be the couriers. You stay tonight at your house and then come back to me. If the militia are informed you will be my insurance. I intend to leave safely with the money.' He gave her the coded document. She took out a small pen and made notes in a book she carried with her.

'Not all the information is here. The name and address of the hostelry is missing.' she exclaimed exasperated. He was playing with her.

'You surely did not expect me to supply all the information without any money passing first.' Helena noticed Maria did not mention the hundred sovereigns she had already been given and laid claim to. If she was Maria, she would be out of this household in a flash and on a coach to a city far away where her protector could not trace her.

To Felea he ordered, 'Bring back the sovereigns tomorrow and I will give you the second document.'

'It is too short a time to get the money,' protested Helena.

'You will do it.'

Felea took out writing paper from the valise she carried. She wrote a letter of authority to her bank manager and gave it to the man to deliver to the manager's houses.

Thank God Francis made me a separate account in my name. He was a most generous husband and she had enough to pay the man. She knew the manager who was a good friend of Dreda and managed the Bureau's finances. He would ensure the monies were transferred to Helena tomorrow morning.

The two women left quickly. Felea thought of the man who could be her nemesis and destroy everything she loved and valued. Financially she was secure, but she knew her physical safety and security and position in court still depended on Dreda's status. She might be popular with the Imperial family but Dreda had protected her from the vile insinuations about her allegedly traitorous leanings before they were married. Dreda had described the court as a viper's nest, the courtiers speaking with forked tongues and turning on the unwary if they found a weakness or vulnerability they could attack.

Felea had felt the man's eyes scan her body as they went down the stars. She felt denuded. She knew by now her message should have reached the Bureau and was not surprised to find Josh von Hadreni sitting in her armchair in her bed-chamber when she arrived home.

'Felea, at last!' he said, getting up and putting his hands on her shoulders, looking carefully into her face.

'Are you unharmed?

'Yes, for the moment but I don't trust Mendentz. He was eyeing me as if I was a potential whore. I think he wants the monies but will still betray Francis. We go back tomorrow with the monies. We must take him alive and use harsh measures to find out where Francis will be attacked.'

'I had intelligence about a potential attack weeks ago. We have two locations. Hope they are not red herrings. Our best officers will be there in four days' time waiting for the assassins. Dreda and Denman have been warned to be on their guard.'

'I will go back tomorrow with the monies.'

'I will already be there in the garden with officers to take these men. Try to sleep now. You need your wits about you to defeat this man.'

The next morning, they went to the bank. The Manager opened the vaults himself. The urgency of the request worried him.

'Countess, if you require my aid or advice please make a rendezvous with me at your convenience.'

'Thank you kindly, Sir. I may need more money at short notice in the future.'

He kissed her hand. 'If you or Lady Helena are in trouble, please don't hesitate to contact me.' They bowed and left, not wanting to prolong the conversation with the helpful but nosy man. Dreda would hate his business being discussed in public and Felea respected his privacy. They rushed to Mendentz's house with the monies.

He was there waiting for them with another man. Maria was nowhere to be seen. *If she had any common sense she would have done a bunk,* thought Felea.

'The monies?' he demanded.

'The document?' she answered just as imperiously.

'We could relieve you of your monies without giving you the documents.' he warned.

Where was the fun in that? He was toying with her; playing her as she if were a puppet on a string.

She turned as if she were to go. 'Do you want the monies, or shall I go and inform the Bureau?' It was the biggest bluff she had made in her life. Dreda's security depended on her carrying it off. Mendentz could have stopped her leaving at any time but he had just enjoyed teasing her. He decided tormenting her was less important than gaining the monies and securing his comfortable retirement.

'Stay Countess, I was just jesting.' He took the valise from her and weighed the sovereigns. 'Capital.' He gave her the document for all the good it would do her. It was genuine, but she was not going to leave his residence in time to save Dreda. She would be imprisoned here until the deed was done and then accompany him with or without her agreement to his new home.

Lady Helena might also be taken to be his friend's new companion, otherwise she might fall accidentally into the river with Maria. Maria had vanished last night, but his accomplices were searching for her. Little did he know, but Hadreni had bribed the cook to give her a message and she had gone to a place of safety. She would be a useful source of information about her protector's friends and colleagues if she were guarded.

Helena perused the document. It seemed genuine. The hostelry was one he often stayed in. The owner had recently sold out, but it was comfortable and positioned conveniently so it had been kept on their schedule. It was the last stop on his journey home and within easy reach of the Bureau. She wondered why he was letting her have this information and guessed he would not let her go. She was to be a hostage or worse. He might have designs on her body from the way he had been mentally undressing her.

'Now I have the information I will leave,' she said but he held her arm in a tight painful grasp until she gasped and grimaced.

'Not yet, Countess. You didn't believe we would just let you go, did you?' Helena had pulled two pistols out of her reticule and hidden them the folds of her riding skirt. She aimed one at his head. Two paces away from him, she could not miss even if she was a lousy shot. Mendentz went for his own gun but Helena with the other gun shot it out of his hand. He dropped it rubbing his bleeding hand and put his hands up in defeat.

Felea had pulled herself away from Mendentz's weakened grasp and pulled her own pistol out of her pocket.

'How many more men are in this house?'

'Only one more in the kitchen.' *That means at least two.*

'Whistle to Hadreni,' she ordered Helena who opened the window and produced a very unladylike whistle which sent Hadreni and his officers to the back window which was open and easily entered. They sneaked to the kitchen where they found a burly chef. He was clearly ex-army and jabbed at them with his carving knife but Hadreni sliced his arm with his sabre and disabled him.

'Where are the others,' he snarled, threatening to poke the man's sore wound with his sword.

The man went puce. 'Both are in the cellar.' They tied him to a chair and descended the stairs to the cellar. The men were packing bottles into a trunk ready for their journey out of the state.

'Caught then,' said Hadreni satisfied and bolted the door on them and walked up stairs to the salon. Helena and Felea had the men sitting on chairs.

'Well met my ladies,' said Hadreni. 'You did our job for us. Dreda will be delighted.' His officers manacled the men and took them away.

'If Francis doesn't curse me for intervening,' said Felea, knowing her over anxious husband too well.

'You had no other alternative and took the best precautions. We informed Dreda by birds what was happening, and he is taking another faster route to be in the city tonight.'

'This is the document containing the location of the potential assassination, but it may be a red herring,' said Felea, still anxious about Dreda's safety.

'The threat of hot irons will loosen Mendentz's tongue and that of his men. I know them. They are not loyal and will spill the beans if threatened with torture. He was a coward and couldn't face pain in the army which is why he didn't get promotion. A more liver-hearted officer I have yet to meet.'

'Thank goodness for that. He may tell us information we need. Helena and I will go back to the Bureau and make a statement. Thank you, Josh, and pass my thanks on to your officers. Francis will be delighted with your intervention.' He kissed her hand, delighted he could give good news to his boss. Felea was the heroine of all the officers in the Bureau. She was like a sister and aunt to the officers and they would have been devastated by her loss.

Dreda rode home that night at full pelt. As usual his lovely wife had surpassed herself, showing courage and intelligence. She had shown maturity, gaining help from Hadreni, learning from her former errors. It made all his doubts about their marriage fade away. He loved her to death and wanted to praise her and share her bed again as soon as possible.

He walked in. She looked nervous and he pulled her to him and kissed her anxieties away. 'You behaved appropriately this time Felea. I am proud of you and wish you could work as an officer on my staff. We must thank Helena as well. That girl should not be left to stifle on a farm. I must try to introduce her to more eligible men.'

They went to be happy and relaxed. The location was not a red herring. The conspirators were part of a small gang of ex-soldiers who would kill for a large purse. They were not part of any political group. They were just driven by greed. Mendentz admitted who his sponsor was. Von Herzen was stripped of his cabinet office and his titles and executed. He had too many powerful friends in the Cabinet and to leave him in exile could enable him to pay others a contract to kill Dreda or even the Emperor in revenge. This time his gamble had not paid off!

Chapter twelve.

Helena and Felea were discussing Helena's opportunities. Helena had had some offers from some older men wanting a young wife after their own had died. They could ignore the lack of fortune if the lady in question was beautiful and would grace their tables. She was also good with children they had heard and had good health. Helena cursed them and asked Felea if she looked like a brood mare.

'I am surprised they don't want to inspect my teeth,' she complained.

'I was the same. The Emperor had men lined up for me who were thrice my age. Bad teeth, poor breath and as boring as hell! It didn't matter providing I could cement a good alliance for this state and I nearly went down that road when Francis lost his memory. I knew I had made a mistake and was too stubborn to admit it but thankfully Francis took matters into his own hands and made me escape with him.

'The other offers are from men in trade Felea. They want to marry a woman with a noble lineage and don't need any dowry.'

'Do you like any of them?' asked Felea. She wanted her friend to find someone she at least liked. After marrying for love Felea thought everybody should have the chance to be as happy as she was but she was pragmatic. Helena might have to accept someone she was conformation with and could make her content, if not as happy as she was with her Francis. Her husband was not an easy man to know and live with but recently he was relaxing and trusting her now and giving her more freedom to make her own decisions.

'Most of them are double my age but there are a few younger sons whose fathers want them to marry a good name. She wrinkled her nose and brow.

'Most are rather tame and lack character. They seem to lack something. I don't know what. I don't know what I am looking for.

Felea smiled, guessing what they lacked; experience of life gained the hard way in battle. Dreda and Denman were examples of men who lived by their wits, meeting challenges head on, their rawness and edges rubbed away by authority and serving others than themselves. They exuded power and determination, something that only came with maturity and the hard knocks of life.

They were held in respect by many, even Denman who pretended to move through life without any cares. When the crunch came he cast off his easy-going nature and applied himself to any task with thoroughness and focus. That is what made him such a good Colonel in the army and a high-ranking militia officer in the Bureau.

'I noticed a new man, an older bachelor who was talking with you last night.'

'You mean Count Jacobson? He has taken me to the park in his carriage and to the opera.'

'Isn't he a bit old for you?'

'We share the same interests, horse breeding and art and music and books. It might work, Felea.'

'Give it some time then.' Their mutual interests might meld them together in a good partnership and affection might develop over time. Felea thought privately that Helena needed someone younger who would match her energy and drive. Helena agreed and tried to look favourably on this man although he was nearly double her age.

Helena felt cold inside. Flashes of that kiss in the prison and the feelings it had engendered haunted her, but she thrust them to the back of her mind and called herself a sentimental fool. He might make her shiver and her heart beat faster, but Denman was a rake, a womaniser. He gave her attention because she was the latest new woman in the field and it was fashionable to flirt with and be seen with her. A new girl would be the favourite next year, and he would desert her for pastures new.Many men offered to take her riding and lend her their horses and carriages when they realised how proficient she was. She and Denman started to ride very early in the morning again when no-one would criticise her for riding at full gallop, her hair being lashed by the wind. In her top hat and veil, she was disguised, and the few onlookers marvelled at her prowess on the horse. Denman who was used to trotting sedately with many young ladies had to ride well to catch her up.

He enjoyed watching her enjoy herself when no-one was there to criticise her. She could be herself, confident, humorous and show another wilder side of her nature to him. Scrutinising her, he noticed how her riding habit clung to her slender but fully formed figure. He had always liked very buxom ladies; a good handful, he had described them to Dreda, but now he began to appreciate her ethereal figure, her tiny waist. He always enjoyed helping her on to her horse, his hands holding on to her a little longer than necessary.

He wondered what it would be like feel that satin skin uncovered, to run his fingertips over her neck and down her back, to kiss her until she was wild with passion. He suspected once a man had removed that cool, ice maiden mask he would discover a passionate lover, a wanton in the bedroom.

Dreda had hinted when he was in his cups that Felea was a delicate, sophisticated hostess in the salon but played the harlot in the bedroom, confident of her sexuality, making him a happy man. When he had raised Helena's ire he had seen a different side of her; her calm indifference replaced by passion and warmth. *The man who made her love him and introduced her to lovemaking would be rewarded well,* he thought.

He shook himself and told himself she saw him merely as a friend. There was definitely an attraction there between them, but he would expect that between any two good looking people. She held him continually at a distance, almost treating him like a brother or for God's sake like an uncle.

At times he wanted to make her notice him, but he remembered how he had nearly lost control the second time when he had had her up against a wall. He had to accept he was not the man for her. She was not the sort of girl a man took to mistress, not like the other women he associated and slept with.

He was not the marrying kind. A womaniser of the worse kind, he had never remained faithful to a woman for more than two months. He had never two timed a woman but when he tired of her he merely told her in his charming way their affair had come to an end and allowed her to drift out of his life. He knew Helena saw him as a charming but lightweight rogue who took what was on offer from any woman who liked him without caring for the consequences.

They had been riding one morning when he turned the conversation for the first time to personal matters. 'I saw you with Count Jacobson last night. He seems to have stayed longer than usual on his visit from Austria. I thought he had to oversee his estates.''I think he has put in a steward.' Denman raised his eyebrow at that, for the man was dedicated to his estate and breeding horseflesh and only paid short visits to his relatives.

'He is very knowledgeable about his animals. Did you see the chestnuts he drives? He bred them himself.'

'Yes, he took me out in the carriage to show how they moved.' She thought, *he would not let me drive it though*. He had said she would not be able to control them. She would have liked to have tried and thought the Count was rather old fashioned in his attitude to women.

Denman decided he would let her drive his carriage, even with his fierce black stallions. He could always intervene if there were problems and she clearly had a way with animals.'When is the Count leaving?''His mother and he are going back in a month's

time and they have asked me to go with them to look at the farm.'
She had not said it to make him jealous, but a knot tied itself in
Denman's stomach. The odds were shortening on this man being
'the one'. He said quietly, 'I think he is the wrong man for you. He
is too staid, but you must make up your own mind.'

'He is better than the rest of the men who have offered
for me,' she retorted. 'At least he has most of his teeth and his
breath doesn't smell like most of my older suitors. The rest are
young boys who are forced by their families to offer me. I have
few choices left to me,' she replied acerbically. Denman
acknowledged to himself she was right, but he couldn't bear to
see this spirited girl shrivelling in a loveless marriage with that
rigid bore.

She changed the subject to the virtues of certain breeds
of horses. 'I would have liked to have bred some piebald on my
farm,' she said wistfully and shook herself, knowing it was a
forlorn hope now. She could not be mistress of her own destiny
given the financial state of her farm.'If you bought a couple of
thoroughbred mares you know my father would lend you a stallion
to start you off in the business of breeding.' She considered this
offer reflected the generous and kind men he and his father were,
but she couldn't accept it. She couldn't guarantee where she
would be in six months' time. Her future was uncertain.

He saw her eying his stallion up and asked his groom to
put a lady's saddle on it. She was astonished but got up on it
quickly and set off round the park handling it sensitively. She
commanded it, even when it tried to rear. Then a bird flew in front
of it and it careered and galloped off. Denman knew how
headstrong it was and followed her in seconds on another horse.
She could not stop it.

She managed to avoid the trees but then the animal was
headed for a high wall which could kill them both.Cursing himself,
Denman caught it up, grabbed the reins and tugged it round just
as it was rearing and starting to try to jump the wall. She fell from

her saddle, but he grabbed her by the collar and pulled her in front of him saving her and the horse's neck. She was shaken and her hair was windswept, but she was safe. The possibility of losing her hit Denman hard and he held her tighter than was necessary on the way back to her horse. She wriggled free and got down as quickly as possible and thanked him. As he lifted her down she felt how strong and muscular his arms and chest were. His arms must have been amazingly strong to have turned around that headstrong horse. He in turn felt how slender and soft she was and how much more feminine than she had appeared on her farm.Her aunt was furious. Helena looked as if she had been dragged through a hedge backwards, covered in dust, hair wild. She asked to see Denman alone and demanded an explanation.

'What were you doing risking my niece's life and damaging her reputation?''That is an over-exaggeration. I was able to catch her within minutes and normally the animal is as safe as houses in the hands of such a skilled rider. She had a groom and female servant chaperoning her.''And looked a hoyden! I would have thought you of all people would know she has to try to enhance her reputation as a cultured young lady. There is enough talk of when you were in her farm. We have tried to hide the fact her brother was shot by a servant. Someone found out she had been staying in the hotel in a room paid for by Dreda and you had booked her in and they are putting two and two together.

'That is why we may send her to Austria with the Count's mother. She has a reputation for being a tartar about manners and behaviour and it would look good if she approved of her.'

Denman didn't appreciate her scolding him although there was some truth in what she had said and replied tartly, 'I hope she isn't being palmed off on to that bore. He would stifle her within a week.'

'I should remind you that Helena hasn't got many choices with a lack of fortune. You hang around her too often. That makes other men fear you are interested and they are put off. If you haven't got serious intentions toward her then back off young man. You are only damaging her chances and her reputation.'

Clearly, she was expecting him to tell her what his intentions were, but he did not know himself. For a moment he had felt sick when he thought she might get seriously hurt by a fall. He had that urge to protect her yet again, to hold her and prevent her from harm. He must be getting senile. He had never had any desire to protect a woman from hurt before.

He thought of her again and their relations, casting their conversation over in his mind. During that ride she had treated him like a friend and although he thought she liked him she was delighted to get off his horse and out of his arms. It was only when they danced that she seemed to melt into his arms and they became as one.

He did not want to harm her reputation, so he stopped the horse rides and only went out with her in the company of Dreda and Felea. Helena, thoroughly scolded by her aunt was told that Denman when challenged appeared to be happy to back off and showed no serious intentions toward her. He was his usual casual, flippant uncommitted self, a dangerous man to young women and to be avoided.

Thoroughly demoralised, Helena agreed despondently to her aunt's wishes to go to Austria with the Count. Denman annoyed her, but no other man could stimulate her intellectually or make her laugh as much. If she could not have him then the Count might do. She must make the best of a bad situation.

She had little dowry and without money she could not develop her mother's farm. Only poverty and hard work lay before her unless she could find a wealthy husband. She hated being a noble woman. At least a girl born into poorer circumstances might have learned a trade and could earn her own income and become independent even if she had to work hard and support herself.

The day for leaving came. Denman hoped she would not be an engaged when she returned but he could not stop her going.

She spent ten long days getting to Austria, but the farm was in a beautiful valley surrounded by lakes and trees.

His mother had been frosty but polite during the journey. At dinner she met the Count's stepfather, the Duke and the Count and the family talked horseflesh the whole evening. The Count promised to show her the horses the next morning. She sat by the lake that evening and remembered another evening sitting by a pond.

Next morning, she was allowed to visit the stud farm. The most beautiful animals kicked the dust up and lunged at the grooms, but they were already sold at a great price. She expressed an interest in breeding horses; she had bred cows most successfully, but both the old man and his son looked surprised that she showed any interest in becoming a professional breeder of horses.

'Breeding cows and managing a farm was in your former days when you were forced to earn a living. Hardly a way for a respectable girl to spend her time! You should be painting and dancing and bringing up children,' said the old man.

He asked her to play for them that evening and for the first time she gained their approval although they did not like the idea of her performing at public concerts. For the next four weeks she spent her days on the farm, reading, painting and performing music. The Count took her to the nearest town for the theatre and concerts, but it was a long trip and he said he didn't do it often.

Helena began to see her life would be spent as a rural matron looking after children, quietly reading and engaging in the arts as the Count's mother did. She could not even help manage the farm as it was well organised. Furthermore, his mother gave her lectures in what a married noblewoman would be expected to wear and how she should behave. Helena was too forward, too informal with the men at court and dressed too seductively; she would have to raise her necklines.

Helena thought if she heard the words, 'This is how we do it here,' once more she would scream and wanted to slap the condescending old woman who thought because she had lost her money she was now inferior in class to her.

The crunch came when she was taken to a ball at a neighbouring villa and had listened to the Countess in the retiring room discussing how they had ignored her family's bad reputation and were giving her a trial to see if she would suit. She would have to change her clothes and manners and talk less to the farm hands and servants, but she might suit her son if she could adapt and behave less like a woman from the demi-monde.

Helena was red in the face when she left the retiring room but ladylike she kept her temper. She intended to tell the Count that she and he would not suit. He had left her alone most days and she foresaw a boring and lonely marriage. Felea had told her that Dreda's mother had been neglected by an aloof and disinterested husband and had been very unhappy and had strayed to another man. The Count also had not let her ride anything but a sleepy old nag.

She had wanted to ride wild in the countryside on one of his chestnuts, her hair streaming in the wind like she had done with another man a fortnight ago; a man who had let her be true to herself, not a missish well behaved caricature. She missed Denman, she admitted to herself. She missed his teasing, his challenges to ride faster, to beat him in a race. She even missed his criticisms of her, knowing they were well meant and designed to protect her from malicious gossips. She had begun to accustom herself to his presence every day, even when he was his most irritating and domineering self.

She suffered another ten days in the carriage with the mother but with a sigh of relief she ran into her aunt's house. When she threw her hat into the air her aunt thought it meant an engagement was in the offing. She was disappointed but not surprised when her niece said she would reject the offer. The

Count had hinted that he would propose when he came in a week's time and had interpreted her quiet politeness as a potential acceptance.

To Denman she merely described the farm as beautiful and the horses as magnificent. She seemed flat when she mentioned them. The day of reckoning came. The Count arrived and made his offer to her aunt and then to her.

'Thank you for your kind offer but we would not suit.'

He was stupefied. 'How dare you, an almost penniless chit of a girl with an appalling reputation and a family scandal to boot, dare to reject me?'

She tried to remain calm and told him that she was honoured by his proposal, but she was too modern a woman to fit into his and his mother's expectation of behaviour of a Countess.

He was then furious and spat out, 'Everyone is expecting the marriage. It will provide a good alliance between two families with a long lineage and will please the Emperor and the Grand Duke, a good political alliance.'

When she repeated and reinforced her rejection he held her arm and hurt it as he turned her to face him. There was no affection in his expression, merely pique and resentment and disgust.

'You hoyden, you are just a flirt and a tease, a whore who took me in. My mother warned me about you, but I didn't believe her.'

Helena tried to shake him off and snapped back angrily in a most unladylike manner, 'I don't give a damn about your mother, your reputation and I don't give a stuff about your fortune. I want to be my own mistress, not a missish wife waiting for you to come home and give me a homily about what I should wear and how I should behave.'

Getting into the swing of it now she continued. 'And I don't want to be bored silly by the same things repeated over the breakfast table by a man who is only interested in his damn horses. You and your family are some of the most ignorant pompous asses I have yet to meet. You read books but have only a superficial understanding of them and your appreciation of good music is nil.'

Neither of them had hear the door open or saw Denman step quietly in. He had heard the raised voices and thought she might need some help. His raised his eyebrows when he saw she was in a right royal rage, her eyes blazing and cheeks red. This was not an intimidated young girl but a virago on the warpath ready to sharpen her teeth on the man who had the affront to insult her.

Hearing what she said he clapped her and said, 'Bravo! You have only said what a lot of people have thought for a long time.' Both parties to the argument rounded on him. 'Who told you to interfere?' she said, 'I can handle this myself.'

The Count said, 'This is a private matter between the lady and me,' and so saying he tugged her in the direction of a room leading off the morning room. He got one step away and his hand was roughly shaken off the girl and held in an iron grip.

'Lady! I thought you called her a hoyden and a whore. Now apologise or I will break your arm, or would you prefer a duel?' He twisted the man's arm until he was bending. He was the type of man who bullied women but is generally a coward. He feared a duel with Denman who was regarded as a master fencer and crack shot. He muttered an apology.

Denman not satisfied said, 'Sorry I didn't hear that,' making the man say it louder and grovel even further and he then let him go. 'And let me warn you that if you or your mischief making mother dares to harm this girl's reputation I will come after you both and you will rue it. I don't make idle threats.'

When he had gone Helena turned to him. Yet again he had saved her from an unpleasant situation and she was beholden to him. She hated this feeling that she owed him something, but courtesy required that she thank him.

She said simply. 'I am deeply grateful for you dealing with him. I knew he was pompous, but I didn't think he would react like that. You saw him for the man he was.'

'It is sometimes easier for a man to recognise the qualities or demerits of another man than a woman and vice versa.' He took her hand in his, but she tried to pull it away. The Count had only said what Denman had said, 'She had behaved like a whore!' Twice she had been insulted now.

He knew she hated being beholden to him, but he had something to say to her. Grasping her hand even more tightly he kissed the under part of her wrist. 'I owe you an apology Ma'am. You have never behaved nor dressed like a whore. It was my anxiety speaking; I feared you would be hurt and I would lose you to that pimp.'

She did not know how to answer him; he was looking at her with an expression in his eyes she could not read nor understand. Smiling and not wishing to discomfort her any longer he said, 'We had better explain these circumstances to your aunt. She must know how to fend off inquiries about your relations with this man.'

Her aunt was shocked but agreed to pretend in society that they had agreed they would not suit. What would Helena do now? The season was almost over and if there were no offers she was willing to accept she must soon go home. Helena said she would look at the other offers more seriously.

Denman listened to this with sympathy. All his life he had made his own choices and would hate to have been cornered into accepting an offer of marriage with someone he had only lukewarm feelings for. He remembered the time Dreda lost his memory and felt he was being forced into an engagement with Felea, a woman he had little knowledge of. Only poor women usually had to work, the rest becoming mothers or if unmarried, usually living with their relatives as poor relations or becoming domestic serfs.

She looked again at the new and recent offers made to her through her uncle. None of them appealed to her at all. She told Felea sorrowfully that if the farm didn't need money she would stay there and be her own mistress. Her aunt seeing that she was a free spirit told her uncle she would tell her niece to reject them all and go home. Helena would feel trapped and be unhappy like a caged bird in such a marriage.

Her uncle now decided to make her a dowry. He had wanted her suitors to make her an offer for herself, not for money. They had to accept her despite the scandal of her brother gambling the fortune away. Being reminded of this by a husband would not a happy marriage make. He would give her the dowry now to turn the fortunes of the farm round. He had gone to see it and was impressed by the way she was slowly changing the family fortunes. He allowed her to return home.

She got into the carriage and sat against the squabs, trying to relax. The journey was uneventful with no 'mad' militiaman rushing to her aid this time. She loved the feeling of the open spaces and nature after the confines of the farm in Austria. Here it was not so grand, but she felt alive.

This was home not the grandeur of a Count's palatial villa but the warmth of family and faithful retainers. Helena's mother was fading, her heart wearing out. She was spending more time in bed and had taken on another woman to chaperone her daughter in the event of her death. Helena had total control of the household now. She hoped her mother would survive one more Christmas, but it was a bleak hope. Soon she would fade away and Helena would feel totally alone. In the city when she was with her friends she also felt relaxed because their manners and lifestyle were more liberal than most and she didn't feel she had to conform to their set of expectations; they matched her own.

She worked two months more on the farm but the hardship in the region was breaking more hearts. Her family had once been one of the wealthiest in the region; but the area was poor, the harvest having failed for four successive years. Even the strongest and richest landlords were suffering lower incomes and were squeezing the tenants dry with their increased rents. More families were being evicted from their small patches of land and the children were in the workhouses until they could be farmed off to masters, some of whom abused and barely fed them.

Helena had used some of her own out-buildings to sleep some of the evicted families and had fed the families out of her own farm produce, but her yields were weak this year and her income was lower. The farm needed every acre to pay the debts her brother had incurred. She had nearly paid them all off without borrowing from banks or money lenders, but the farm could only break even this year. She had to turn two families away, her heart breaking but she owed a duty to her servants and tenants who relied on her.

She sat in her study her head in hands thinking of alternative plans to raise money. Perhaps she needed to use her tiny reserve to buy some mares and take up Denman's kind offer. Pride was no use if her family and farm had no future. She would write to him and accept his father's offer before her savings were used to pay off debts.

Denman received her letter and smiled in relief. At last Helena was using her head and not letting pride stand in the way. His father had told him to make more advances to the young girl.

'Would she accept a partnership if he remained a silent partner?'

'Unlikely Father. I think she has too much pride to accept any help from you and proprieties would not allow a bachelor to offer her money. Gossips would make mincemeat out of her if they heard.'

'She needs to marry a tolerant husband who shares her interests,' said his father. Denman smiled but did not reply. He would write back and repeat his previous offer.

Helena came back from her marketing. Prices for commodities were rising again reducing her income. Despondent, she still awaited a reply from Denman. Was he upset with her rebuffs and would he refuse to help her. She thought *not*. He was not a childish or vindictive man. She needed to act soon, or she would have to sell some stock and her yields would fall the next year. Financial worries played on her mind, casting a cloud over her normally happy personality.

She went sadly to the paddock and was taken aback by the sight of a stallion and four mares careering around it. The stallion was enjoying the company of the ladies who teased and flirted with him.

She had to find out where the horses had come from. From behind her came a, 'Good evening, they are handsome, aren't they?' It was Denman. She had suspected he was the source of the gift of these animals. Torn between anger and pleasure she demanded, 'I was prepared to accept the stallion but not the mares. Where have they come from and how do we take them back.'

'Whoa! The mares are a gift from your uncle as part of your dowry; you knew he was going to give you something. Better than jewels eh? The stallion is on temporary loan from my father. He doesn't need any more foals for a few months, so it was just eating him out of house and home for a while.

'You should be able to sell one or two foals and then breed more each year. After a few years you could have good breeding stock and have your own stallion as you have done with your cattle. Your uncle has bought you more of those as well and more vines and olive trees. He is also sending some of his own men to repair the house for you and improve the water supply.'

She was so relieved and happy after all the snide and catty remarks she had suffered and the rumours she had heard, that some people had exercised so much kindness toward her.

These animals and plants would secure her future; she could be her own mistress again.

She wiped some tears from the corner of her eyes and put out her hand and thanked him from the bottom of her heart. Seeing her so happy made him feel full and content. It had not cost him much to ask this small favour of his father. She was not a gold digger; just a few horses and hard work would keep her happy, so unlike the other women he had known. They went into the villa and over dinner she decided what names the horses could be called. He disagreed with her, saying the names were flowery.

'You are still too much an army man, wanting the dramatic. These beautiful ladies grace the fields like lilies. What is the stallion's name?'

'Power.'

'Again, a masculine name. I bet you named him.'

'Yes, you are right. I didn't want any namby-pamby name for him.

No, she thought, *there is nothing namby-pamby about you, or anything that belongs to you.* He was a man through and through, tough as steel but there were hints of sensitivity deep under the surface of that manly exterior. He could fight one minute but be caring the next.

They sat by the pool together enjoying the spring evening. He experienced a feeling of contentment he had never felt before. He wanted to take her hand again, but she deliberately sat a foot away from him, aloof. There was a gulf between them, a gulf he had caused when he had abused her, called her a whore.

She had forgiven him, but he still felt her hurt. He wanted to bridge the gulf between them but for once he was at a loss for words. He had apologised but it hadn't been enough. He had destroyed the delicate trust that had been growing between them and he felt it was too late to start again.

'I am starting back early tomorrow but your aunt and uncle would like to come here in about a month's time. Your uncle will be delighted with the progress you have made on this farm. He said you were a good farm manager and he is proud of you.'

'They have been wonderful. They left my family alone in the past because they were so ashamed of my brother and worried his reputation would damage their daughters' 'come outs'. I didn't know they had met him in the city at a soiree. He was as usual drunk and abused most of the guests. He insulted me behind my back saying I was a whore looking for a man who would provide me with a fortune.'

'They said once the girls were out and settled they would have sent for me and my mother and provided us with a home.'

'They are good people, the salt of the earth,' agreed Denman, understanding their position. He had judged them lacking in the past. He got up. 'I must retire if I am to start early tomorrow.' He took her hand and kissed it again, noting the shiver that went through her at his touch.

He left her by the pool, drifting her hand in the water, an ethereal fairy like figure, a sad expression on her face. He wanted to rid her of her sadness but moved quickly into the house, ignoring his feelings for her. She seemed to be aroused by him as any beautiful girl would be by the attentions of a handsome man but that is as far as it went. She still treated him as a friend, a friend for whom she had affection but just a friend.

She wondered why he was leaving so quickly and why he had given her so much help. He was leaving because he did not want to damage her reputation. Chaperones or not, a man visiting a girl living as her own mistress could cause tongues to wag and he had business to finish at his father's home.

Helena sat for hours in the moonlight remembering that last kiss on her wrist. He seemed to like her company and had tenderly kissed her hand, but he usually treated her like a niece or daughter. He was forever dictating to her, guiding her; warning her she should behave like this or not like that, like a guardian.

Only twice had he behaved like a lover when he had kissed her in the prison and after their race by the river bank.

She had felt the tingle go through her body and her pulse race when he had kissed her, but she had not given him any encouragement, thinking he, a flirt and confirmed rake, was toying with her. He was a heartbreaker, a womaniser and she felt if she gave her heart to him he would break it. She preferred to withdraw from him, to contain her feelings although she felt cold and dead inside.

Chapter thirteen.

Denman arrived back in the city after making a short visit with his family. Even his lively happy family couldn't dispel the gloom that surrounded him. He threw himself into work with a vengeance and attended all the balls, smiling and pretending all was well. He could not pull wool over Felea's eyes. She saw the despondency and sadness in his eyes when he thought no-one was watching and his smile dropped. Amongst all the gaiety he was lonely, a man who lacked direction.

Helena sent letters to Denman outlining her plans. The covering of the four mares was effective, they were to bear young. With her savings she had been able to buy more livestock, not wanting to rely on the harvest. The poor rains yielded enough grass to feed cattle but not to maintain grain for the starving peasants who were revolting against the high taxes imposed by the Emperor.

She bought some goats and gave their young to some of the families for milk and cheese. More families were starving and leaving for the already overcrowded cities. The parents often died of the fever and the children were sent back to the villages to rely on the poor law. If she had money she would build an orphanage where the young would be looked after appropriately with warm clothing and good food.

Denman read these sad tales in her letters and sent a donation for the families which she gratefully received. He also felt her own fears and hardship and wanted to take the burden off her shoulders. He worried that she was getting too involved again, helping the peasants and rebel families as Felea had done.

Felea had been investigated by Dreda before their marriage and had nearly lost her head in a noose when someone betrayed her. He wrote suggesting she asked Felea for funds. Felea raised money through charities for the rebel families and could give aid without blackening her reputation. She sent monies and advice for her friend, but Denman still feared Helena might endanger herself. She did not know how suspicious minds worked in the city.

Dreda summoned Denman to his office. He threw a packet at him. 'Read it, it concerns Helena.' Denman tore the paper out of the packet. He felt cold like a stone.

Sweet Jesus. *What had that girl got herself into this time?* She attracted trouble constantly. Dreda watched him assimilate the information quickly.

'Her brother was at fault, not her,' he said at length.

'No matter,' warned Dreda. 'Others who are quick to apportion blame, accuse her, as he used their farm to hide the goods while waiting to fence them. I have had to put off Officer Yemetz who wanted to search her farm and arrest her. He believes she is implicated. There was a letter intercepted from a man called Grehi which said he was to visit Angelo's sister and share the loot her brother left her. He indicated Angelo acted as intermediary between the arms sellers and the rebels and Helena would aid him.

'Despite the fact that she was on trial for murdering her brother?' asked Denman incredulously.

'Indeed, to us it seems idiotic, but he put it to me she wanted her brother dead in order to take over the operation and gain the rewards herself. He sees her as a clever managing female who has the brains of the family instead of her malingering weak brother.'

'He is right about the managing female. She hardly ever listens to a word of advice and goes her own way,' said Denman exasperated.

'She took your advice about the stallion,' contradicted Dreda mildly.

'Only when she was on her uppers and feared her farm would be damaged if she didn't magic up some income sharpish.

She is a contrary girl and would turn a man grey if he tried to manage her. No wonder she hasn't caught a husband yet.

'I thought she had given up trying.'

'Formally yes, but Felea still tries to hook unsuspecting men for her when Helena comes for her balls.'

'She would make a wonderful hostess for any man,' said Dreda. 'If I weren't a happily married man I might try for her myself.'

The look he received from his friend would have shrivelled a lesser man. 'I only joke my friend,' said his tormentor. 'Everyone knows she has eyes only for you when she is in town.' He watched his friend for his reaction. Like Felea, he was tired of Denman pretending indifference to Helena. His friend was miserable but would not do anything to remedy his situation.

'I think you are sadly mistaken. I am a friend or more like a man in place of a brother she goes to for help and then discards.'

'You once called me a coward when I refused to acknowledge my feelings for Felea but are you any better? When the girl is in town you shadow her, but do not tell her how deep your feelings are for her.'

'If I thought my feelings were reciprocated I might risk telling her I hold a tendre for her, but I am sure I would be rebuffed.'

He changed the subject. He was sick of mooning about. A good fight would shake some sense into him. He was going soft spending too much time in the Bureau.

'Are you warning Helena about a possible investigation of her interest and a potential search of the farm?'

'I think she is in danger from other sources. Her brother may have left some criminally obtained goods on the farm. We know he was engaged in robberies and the goods have not yet been regained. His fellows may also be after them. Hadreni's sources think his friends are in her region again and may pay her a visit.' He mentioned a few names Hadreni had given him.

Denman's blood ran cold. These men did not take prisoners. They left villages burnt out behind them. They were cold-blooded killers and would torture to gain the information they required. One of them, more sadistic than another had also violated the young girls in the village, enjoying their families watching them suffer their fate. It was not enough to rob. He had to inspire fear into his victims, ensuring their compliance with his activities in the future.

A supplier of arms and goods to the rebels, the villagers knew he had the rebel chiefs on his side and could call on rebel troops to enforce his commands. His men had terrorised one region and had been moving nearer to Helena's locality for greater spoils before Angelo had died.

Angelo's title had given them status and creditability in the region. No-one suspected the friend of a noble even if that noble drank and gambled his future away. He was a merely a dissolute member of the rural nobility who wasted his future like many young men.

'What should we do?'

'You must visit Helena and warn her of the danger. She will listen to you if you bring a letter from me. She must appear whiter than white and dissuade her enemies in the city from poisoning minds. She might wish to visit Felea for a while.'

'Why me?'

'Who else cares for her as much as you do? Good God Man, face up to your feelings. You would rush to her if she was in danger even if I didn't ask you to.' Ignoring this comment Denman said, 'Her mother is dying. It is unlikely she will leave her and there is no-one to manage the farm.'

'If her mother dies I can send my agent to look after the farm temporarily. If these men are as dangerous as they appear, preserving the security of the state is worth forgoing my agent's services for a while.'

'Very well, I'll go if you choose to write the letter for me. I don't want her to think it is my idea or she could reject our fears.' He was conflicted. One minute he wanted to meet that woman again and another he wanted her out of his life. She haunted him every night, in his dreams. He had tried to forget about her, but her image stubbornly woke him up at night when he dreamt of holding her in his arms and making passionate love to her.

Chapter fourteen.

Denman arrived without warning, feeling it was safer that way. He could sortie her farm first without anyone knowing and find out if anything was there that was suspicious. Despite the letter Dreda had shown him he still did not believe she was involved in the rebel uprisings. No, she would be a toy of more wicked devious fellows. Her servants could have used her land without her involvement and there was still the treasure her brother had stowed away someplace. It was a conundrum he needed to solve.

He quietly searched the out-buildings, thoroughly inspecting the huts and stables and byres deserted when the new house had been built to accommodate a larger family. He was rifling about in boxes which looked as if they might contain rifles.

His heart was in his mouth. He worried not for himself but for Helena. She could be implicated in this if she wasn't careful. Moreover, those men might try to beat the truth out of her if they wanted knowledge of where her brother had hidden his loot. She was in trouble whichever way one looked at the situation. A slim vulnerable fragile girl, she was at the mercy of those brutes.

He opened the chest and pulled a rifle out of the hay. It was as he thought. Newly ironed, this rifle was the type used by the rebels. She was up to her neck in trouble. If Yemetz had found these she would have been in gaol faster than she could blink.

He heard a noise and moved like lightning, his pistol in one hand and his sword in the other. Someone was watching and listening at the door. Denman reacted automatically. He opened the door so quickly a slim boy-like figure fell through, stumbling against him as he wrapped one arm around his neck, painfully choking him, while his other arm disabled the figure, pinning his arm behind his back.

'Stay still or I will break your neck,' warned Denman then loosened his hold as he recognised the body he held imprisoned.

There was no thick muscle or sinew; only softness and a perfumed skin and voluptuous breasts disguised in manly clothes crushed against him.

The figure gasped for breath and coughed as he released his grip. She looked up recognising her captor.

'Was that really necessary Officer Denman? Nearly strangling me! If you had wanted to use my barn, I would have opened it for you myself.'

'I am sorry I do not know my own strength, but you have some explaining to do my girl.' He pushed her to the chest and pulled out a rifle. 'What do you know of these?'

'It is the first time I have laid eyes on them,' replied Helena, fear in her eyes. 'Someone must have put them there and thought we didn't use these buildings. I allowed some evicted families to use these and wanted to know if they are watertight in case we use them again.'

'They are rebel army issue, brand new and ready for use,' said Denman harshly. He did not want to frighten her, but she needed to know how serious her position was. 'I will inform Dreda immediately. He will want to lay a trap to catch those who deposited them here.

'I don't know anyone who works with the rebels,' said Helena. 'I will go back to the villa and ask my servants if they have seen anyone acting suspiciously.'

'Call them in to be interviewed by me in your study in an hour's time,' said Denman. They are less likely to lie to me.'

Looking at him she thought, *he is right*. He wore the look of an uncompromising militiaman again; no warmth exuding from him; only discipline and efficiency; the armour of a man dedicated to his office and his Emperor.

'Why are you here Officer Denman? 'Am I under suspicion?' she asked. His manner was so cold she thought he wasn't telling her everything, treating her like a child again.

Felea said Dreda had done the same under the guise of protecting her and it had maddened her as well. 'Read this please,' said Denman now they had arrived at the villa and she could sit down. 'A drink,' he asked taking the decanter and offering her a brandy.

'Please,' she said her nerves jangling now. He poured it out and sat opposite her. 'You need to know one of the officers thinks your brother was implicated in supplying arms and goods to the rebel forces.'

'He may be right,' she said. 'I have heard rumours to that affect and I am looking through his papers he hid in the house. How does that concern me?'

'It concerns you because the Officer thinks you were implicated and may have wanted your brother dead, so you can take over the operation and get the blunt.'

'Me?' she said stunned.

'He thinks you are a managing female and brighter than your brother was. He is right on both accounts but,' as she opened her mouth to castigate him he said, 'don't get on to your high horse.'

Her eyes sparkled angrily. First a murderess and now her head could be in a noose for aiding rebels. For some inexplicable reason it was important to her that he believed her.

'I don't believe you supplied the rebels with any arms although I think you would aid the rebel orphans even if you risked your foolish neck.'

'I am grateful you don't think I am a traitor Officer,' she said acidly, 'even if I am a managing female.'

'Take that as a compliment Ma'am,' said Denman, 'but if others know your skills and attributes you could be in danger. I will ask Officer Dreda to send some officers to guard you and look for the loot your brother hid here.'

He got up and walked around the table to her. He took her chin in his hand and forced her to look up to him. What was he after? Her heart beat nervously as he speared her eyes with his own. A stern expression was on his face, but it warmed as he smiled at her.

'Be careful Ma'am. You are not quite up to snuff yet. You should marry and get a husband to take care of you!'

She twisted her head from his grasp and irritated asked, 'Do you have any suggestions for a groom Officer? I am afraid names are rather lacking at the moment. I have a small dowry due to my uncle's generosity and a farm that barely makes ends meet. I have to use the dowry to invest capital to modernise the farm, so we can guarantee to eat in the future. The harvest failed again this year.'

She waited for this information to sink in and then continued. 'I am two and twenty, not an ape leader yet but not in my first blush or youth; nearly on the shelf. My brother was a gambler and drinker who not content with gambling and drinking our fortune away also helped the rebels. Now I am the sister of a traitor. Not a good catch for any husband, do you think?'

When he hesitated she said, 'No, I thought not,' answering her own question. 'You have no names to give me and I am not a good catch. I think I will just stay here and do the best I can but thank Officer Dreda. I appreciate any help he can give me and if I hear anything about the rebels I will send him news immediately.'

Denman could hear her bitterness. He had no intention of rubbing in her misfortune, but it was best she understood her position. If she came back to the city she would find a husband eventually. God forbid, it would not come to the point where she would have to sell herself to one of the rough-mannered elderly cits who came to the city to buy a wife.

She deserved better than that, but he couldn't think of anyone he knew who would suit her other than himself and she would reject him out of hand. She snapped at him even when he came to help her. He rubbed her up the wrong way all the time. It was better to let the little sharp-tongued vixen cook herself in her own juice.

They interviewed the servants. Only one young girl seemed uneasy. Her brother had disappeared from the village and no-one knew his whereabouts. Denman said he would trace the young man and he helped lock up the rifles where no-one without keys to the outbuildings could access them. The sooner he got back to the city and organised a party to guard the girl the better. He had sent messages by birds and Dreda would know the state of affairs before he arrived back. He had only to say goodbye to Helena and then get on his way.

Helena insisted he stayed for luncheon. A meagre repast of soup, bread, cheese and fruit was put before them. He could see they were sharing their bounty from the harvest with their tenants. Her hands were calloused through hard work. She had lost weight she could ill afford to lose, and he guessed she was working on the land again. She had less servants than before and she had admitted she had not replaced the ones who had left for the better life in the city.

How he wished he could take the burdens from her but any suggestion of him helping her would be turned away. She was a damned independent chit who needed taming by a strong husband. The same thought kept turning in his mind over and over again. He could not rid himself of it. She should not waste and shrivel up in this lonely God-forsaken place. She was made for a family and the bright lights of the city.

'Would you consider a silent partner on this farm? You would retain management but gain finance. Other families have gained investment and prospered.'

'Who would this silent partner be?'

'I could ask around.'

She guessed his intentions. 'Thank you, Officer Denman but I think it might be difficult for the partner to avoid interfering in my decisions.'

'Think about it,' he said knowing she had guessed he would be the partner. *Damn her, she was too sharp.* 'You need the capital until the foals are born and this way you would retain all but one of the foals.'

'I will think about it,' she said but stubborn, she would refuse to take his help. He would interfere and dominate.

Denman exasperated, got up putting his napkin down hurriedly.

'I must make haste Ma'am and inform Officer Dreda of my findings. He will want me to discuss further strategy for this region as it is a hotbed of rebel activity.'

She got up and gave her hand to him. 'Take care Officer! This is dangerous bandit territory. I would not want you to be harmed after you have ridden so far to save me from the noose and the bandits.'

'It was my pleasure Ma'am,' he said lingering over her hand as he kissed it, smelling her sweet perfume. He could not contain his exasperation any longer. 'I just wished you weren't so damned independent. It will be the death of you one day!'

Her eyes flashed angrily. She rejected his implied criticism, throwing her own challenge back at him; a challenge he could not ignore. He took her by the shoulders, his gentlemanly instincts warring with his macho desire to brand her, to tame her, to make her his woman.

Oh, to hell with being a gentleman! He pulled her to him, pushing her chin up and making her look into his eyes and focus on him and only him. She looked mesmerised, like a rabbit caught in the gaze of a stronger predator but those angry eyes widened and softened showing an awareness of him as he moved his face slowly down to hers, his glaring eyes impaling her. His angry gaze changed to tenderness as he held her tightly around her waist. Bending quickly as if he swooped on her, he engaged her in a passionate suffocating kiss.

Her breath felt as if it were squeezed out of her as he subsumed her to his will. For the moment of the kiss she felt she had no will of her own, so forcefully did he make her submit to him. He took no prisoners, this man; imprinting his personality and his demands on her.

Then just as quickly he pushed her away, making her almost stumble, as if he was angry with himself for forgetting he was a gentleman.

'My apologies Ma'am, I forgot myself. Be careful. Not all men will turn away from temptation. You need a husband to protect you!'

As if he wanted to escape, he hurriedly gathered his things and stalked out the room, his cloak swishing behind him like an angry cat, leaving her shocked and bewildered. Behind that easy-going nonchalant facade was a will of iron, a naked strength and virility, only contained by immense self-control and his desire to remain a gentleman.

He was dangerous, a man who would take what he wanted with no regrets when his self-control was relinquished, and his desire released. He could only offer her a fling or a longer carte blanche, neither of which her self-respect would allow her to accept. She must keep him aloof or lose her heart and her freedom and self-esteem. She felt despondent. A lonely life of spinsterhood lay ahead of her. Denman had spoilt all other men for her!

Chapter fifteen

Felea knew Helena secretly admired and adored Denman despite her description of him as an odious, provoking, interfering man. Amused, Felea remembered she had used identical words cursing Dreda before she became engaged whilst wanting him to admit his love for her. Denman had virtually admitted to Dreda he held a tendre for Helena, but he thought she treated him like a good friend or worse like a kindly interfering uncle or brother.

They needed someone to push them together, thought Felea, her kind heart wanting them to admit their love for each other and be content in each other's company. But how? Fate jumped in before she could act on her words.

That morning she was sitting in the bower and her head swam. A vision came into her mind of a tall girl asking for help. Concentrating her mind, she pulled another idea out of her head. It was Helena in trouble. She ran to her butler. 'I need a groom to take a message to my husband at the Bureau, urgently!'

Dreda was not surprised to hear she had had a vision. A message had arrived from Helena asking him to send some officers to help her. Denman had already left. He had made haste as soon as he had heard she was in danger. He had had no need to be asked.

Helena read Dreda's reply. Going through her late brother's affects she had found a map and letter which indicated he had hidden sovereigns and jewellery on her farm. Her field hands had noted some strangers around the boundaries of her land. Questions had been asked about how many men were on the farm and she feared someone was going to search it for the goods.

She knew her brother had been a sot and a bully but now the evidence proved he was linked with criminal activities and had sold the rebels arms and horses. She had been racked with guilt after his death, blaming herself for not looking after her little brother well enough but now realism had set in and she no longer felt any guilt toward him because of his demise.

She brought her men in from the land. 'What are the chances of us being able to defend the villa from aggressors? Five or six men have been seen in the town asking about us.'

One new field hand, now appointed stable-lad, touched his cap and said, 'We only have three young strong men my Lady. The rest are willing but are of little use against fierce bandits.'

Taking a deep breath, she said, 'I have sent a message to Officer Dreda asking for help. Pray the birds get there in time for him to send aid. In the meantime, we must ready to barricade the house. Get enough food in to support us in case they trap us here. I asked in the town, but no-one will lend us men.

She sat in her study and wrote out a letter. Her hand writing was close enough to her late brothers to fool a stranger and she copied the map placing the treasure in a different place. It might persuade the bandits to look elsewhere until help could arrive.'

She put her head between her hands. At times like this all she could think of was Denman. His image kept coming into her head. *Damn the man!* She remembered him coming into her kitchen and threatening her brother if he tried to harm her; his lazy manner hiding the fierce fighter beneath his easy-going exterior. If he came she would feel safer than if any other man arrived. Despite her rejections and insults he would always act the gentleman and act as her saviour, her knight in shining armour.

She feared he might not come this time. They had not parted on good terms and despite that last kiss there was a coolness between them as if he merely wanted to be a good friend. She wished she had his broad shoulder to lean on. Despite her skill with a gun she and a few brave young men and kind older men could not take on skilled fighters. For once she felt out of her depth and needed a more skilled fighter to help her.

She spent the next few days hiding any valuables and shuttering the windows and bringing in food. She had no illusions about the men she faced. These were not the drunks and vagabonds her brother had usually mixed with. The letters she had read showed these were hard-bitten professional criminals used to fencing their jewels and other ill-gotten gains through a variety of means and looking for more opportunities to purloin valuables.

The description of one man, a town-dweller, matched the man who would have given false evidence about her. He had disappeared before Dreda could indict him for perjury after Lucia had admitted her guilt. Helena's blood ran cold at the idea of meeting him again.

His cold eyes had focused on her without blinking and the hatred coming out his mouth when he accused her of killing her brother had made her back away so stark was the intensity of his bitterness. He would make a bad enemy. She also saw in him a dislike of women. A misogynist, he would want to tame a spirited disobedient girl with his fists. She prayed to God Dreda would send his men in time.

Chapter sixteen.

The time Helena dreaded had arrived. A group of men rode up the drive to the villa, their horses and clothes suggesting they were not locals. Helena went out to meet them with her groom, both of them armed to the teeth.

'Stay there, strangers!' she hailed them. 'What business do you have here?'

'This is a fine way to show hospitality to your brother's friends,' said a man she didn't recognise.

'Regretfully my brother is dead Sir. There is therefore no reason for you to be here if you had planned to visit him.'

She didn't like the look of him and the way he stripped her with his eyes. 'State your business,' she said, her shotgun still aimed at his heart.

'We heard your brother had died and merely wanted to offer you our condolences,' another said lifting his hat in respect. 'Thank you kindly, Sir. I appreciate your sentiments,' she said staring him out and waited for him to continue.

'And we hoped to take advantage of your hospitality for tonight.'

'I am sorry to appear churlish gentlemen but there is a malady taking over this villa and I would not want you to fall prey to it when you must have a long journey to make to your homes.'

'Oh, we will happily take the risk my dear, 'said the first man getting off his horse and walking toward her, ready to take the gun out of her arm. She stepped back and aimed it again at his chest.

'I repeat; this house is unsafe! Look at the red cross on the door.' The cross painted with pig's blood was indeed marking the house out as a house of the plague which was cutting swathes through the country, destroying the inhabitants of villages. Helena had reddened and roughened her complexion in order to make herself look ill. It was to no avail!

'I repeat we will take the risk,' the man said. 'Please let us pass,' he asked softly, but there was a menace in the quiet undertones she could not miss.' He moved forward but her groom removed the safety catch and shot two bullets at his feet, sending dust in his eyes and causing him to jump back quickly and curse him.

'My Lady said you are not welcome in her home,' said Johann, his shotgun now aimed at the man's eyes.

The man backed off coughing, spitting out phlegm and dust. He said, 'Very well we will be back in a few days when the illness should have passed its crisis. You will welcome us then.' He raised his hat and mounted, turning his horse and leading his friends away, not looking back.

'Over my dead body,' muttered Helena. 'Thank you, Johann. We may have bought a day's grace, but they will be back soon. We must prepare for a fight.'

'Yes, my Lady. I wish some of the other families would have helped us.'

'I didn't expect anything from them after they turned their shoulders to me when my fiancé jilted me. We are on our own just like before,' admitted Helena despondently.

They waited two more days, the men taking turns to stay up through the night. The following day eight horsemen arrived. It was worse than she expected. They had no chance against this number in a gun fight.

'Indoors and fasten the doors and windows,' she said, running to the door herself. She had sent the older workers and the infirm to one of their few friends to hide. Those in the house were able-bodied and healthy if not all young. At least the scoundrels had not brought cannons. Most of all she feared fire; if they tried to burn them out with oil they might bring any straw they could find in the stables. They would not stand a chance inside if these men set their villa alight.

'God speed Dreda's Officers,' she prayed. Her message had been sent four days before and the city was only two day's rides from this farm. She had faith in Dreda; he was renowned for his fast decision-making and efficiency. His men might still come in time.

The eight men set up camp in front of the villa. The leader sent his men to cover all of the doors to the villa. *Like rats caught in a trap,* thought Helena nervously, wondering if she should have kept her men outside; but what if they had been picked off one by one in the grounds of the villa?

The gun fire started an hour later, and her men responded, driving them back. Then the invaders started throwing lit torches at the roofs, some of which was made of wood and reeds.

'Oh my God,' said Helena fearing the worst. When the roofs started smouldering and lit up in flames the belching smoke penetrated through the ceiling making the inhabitants cough their hearts out.

Helena knew she was defeated. She pulled the heavy chair from across the door and yelled out, 'I am coming out!' She waited for the gunfire to cease and then walked out, hands in the air throwing her gun before her. She waited silently for the leader to come to her. Her heart pounding, she gasped and choked, her lungs nearly suffocated by the smoke. Fear gripped her as she waited her fate.

She didn't need to wait long. Out of the smoke he appeared, a ghastly smile on his face, smug and conceited, enjoying the fear and distaste he read on her face. Walking toward her he took her chin in his hand and kissed her full on her lips watching for her reaction. She felt revolted; his breath stale and full of tobacco and alcohol, a man who clearly did not much care about personal hygiene.

She shook her head away from his grasp, but he grabbed her wrist and said, 'No Missy. It is time you learnt obedience from a man!'

Pushing her forward into the villa he gave the order to quench the flames. At least the villa will be saved. She tried not to think what was to become of her. This type of man didn't take a woman's disobedience lightly.

Pushed down into an armchair in the salon she sat quietly, waiting to hear her fate. The man sat on a chair in front of her.

'What will happen to my men?'

'They will be in the stables providing they do not create trouble,' he answered, as if they were of little import.

Relieved they were to be kept safe she waited for his next move. They could have the damned maps providing her people remained safe. Dreda's men would hound them until they found them. She was sure of that! He would have hangman's nooses prepared for them!

'Your brother left papers. I want them now!'

'What papers are they?' she asked, an innocent expression on her face. A slap resounding around the room, leaving her head spinning, was his answer.

'Don't play with me girl! Where are they?' He took her by the throat and began to quietly throttle her until she gasped and coughed. The room was going black and she passed out. Woken up by a glass of water thrown over her face, she spluttered and gagged and felt her neck which was already swelling with the bruises he had inflicted. Her hair had been torn out of its plait and fell straggling around her shoulders. She felt a bedraggled hag; a creature with no mind nor spirit, to be toyed with by these cruel men.

'Where are the papers?' he demanded.

Having recovered her speech, she muttered sarcastically, 'Well as you ask so nicely, follow me and I will show you them.' She nearly dodged the blow aimed at her head. Her head singing, she decided persistent insolence was too painful. She would act more contrite in future. She led them to the desk in the study and pointed to a pile of papers lying on it.

He pushed her out of the way into a chair and she sank into it gratefully, her neck now so swollen it made it difficult for her to speak. She felt sick and her head spun like a domino. She found it difficult to hold her head up, it hurt so much, but she faced him, trying to stop her hands trembling. She wasn't going to show her fear to this despicable scum.

He perused the map frowning but at length he nodded and said to his friends, 'It seems to be what we are looking for. Tomorrow this girl will take us to the spot.' He turned to her and demanded, 'We want food now!'

'I will show you to some chambers. The rest of you will have to sleep in the stables. Dinner will be served in half an hour. We have eaten already. I must go to the kitchens. We have no female servants here at the moment and I must help prepare the food.' He let her go but sent a man with her.

She stood in the kitchen, watching out of the window, thinking how she could delay these men until Dreda's men arrived. She could drug their wine but when they woke up they would be so angry they might hurt her people in revenge for their treatment. No, she would wait until they went to find the treasure. She feared the man's reaction when he realised he was on a wild goose chase. Grehi, she had heard the other men refer to him by that name, would enjoy hurting and disciplining her.

Dinner was a noisy affair, the men drinking copious flagons of wine and one of them pulling her onto his lap, fondling her breast and noisily nuzzling her neck. She tugged herself away and ran into the kitchen shaking, remembering the other time when a man had tried to grab her. She had felt safe then knowing Denman would never let a man hurt her.

She now admitted to herself he was the man she most wanted to be here. A little voice in her head told her she loved him. Despite his irritating tendency to dominate and criticise her waywardness he had rescued her and safeguarded her. She had loved him since he had hugged her after her brother had been shot.

She called herself a fool. When and if he married he would marry a wealthy titled woman who had no skeletons in her family cupboard; a lady-like creature who would not act like a hoyden or dress like a whore to escape from prison. His family reputation was too important for him to marry such a one as her.

She called to the men, 'Leave the plates there. I will collect them early in the morning when I get up. I would like to go to bed.' Grehi shouted his assent and she ran up the stairs and locked her room. She put a chair against the handle for extra security. It held the handle still and tight if someone tried to open it. She didn't feel safe amongst those men. They would want to tumble her if she remained with them.

Chapter seventeen.

After a fitful night's sleep, she got up at dawn and cleaned the dining room and kitchen. The men didn't stir until nine, the effects of the wine overwhelming their desire to get up early and find the treasure. *Soon Dreda's men must come,* she thought, hanging on to that wild hope.

Grehi gave orders to his men to saddle the horses after they had broken their fast and he led her to her mare and lifted her onto the saddle allowing his hands to slowly cover her waist and thighs and her hips. They rested on her buttocks and the glare he received did nothing to stop his hands wandering over her even more.

'Later you will be asking for me to touch you. When our business is over here you can warm my bed,' he explained, his cold grey eyes warming with lust.

'When hell freezes over,' muttered Helena to herself but suffered his hands groping and stroking her until she moved the horse away from him. He mounted his own horse, giving her a look which boded trouble for her in the future. She led them up the mountain track to the old chapel where her brother had supposedly buried the treasure.

She deliberately took them a long route but eventually they reached the chapel and her heart sank. Two days before, Johann had opened up a cavity behind a wall and deposited some bags with pasted jewels and some of her sovereigns. She feared the value of the treasure might not be enough to convince Grehi it was the genuine article but at least they had tried.

Grehi found the cavity and opened the bag. He frowned. 'There is not much here of value except the jewels.' Stalling for time Helena suggested, 'Perhaps Angelo hid the goods in several places. He said we were vulnerable to bandits and he feared being raided.'

'Did he have any other places he hid papers?'

'There is an old safe he used in the attic. You could look there. I have had no reason to look there for papers.'

'Come Girl,' said Grehi pulling her with him. 'Back to the attics. We have wasted time here already.'

Helena took them by the same route. The men barely gave her time to dismount before she was dragged to the attics.

'Which one?' asked Grehi.

'The left,' she said and showed him where the safe was.

'Right my dear, the combination please!' he snarled. She stood on tiptoe and opened it and stood away. She had a desire to run away so scared was she of the look he gave her; a malevolent evil look that bode ill for her if he didn't find what he was looking for.

'No papers of use here,' he said spitting the words out with disgust. 'Where else can we look?'

'I have no idea,' she said stepping out of his range should he take his bad temper out on her.

'You had better think fast.'

He pushed her downstairs and sat her in the kitchen. Thoughtfully he watched her and then said, 'Get the groom. She knows something she isn't telling us. She might be more cooperative if she thinks her man will be harmed.'

'There is no need to do anything to my men,' said Helena knowing the game was up. Getting up she lifted up a tea caddy, unlocked it and gave him the map and the letter. His response was to hit her across the face from ear to ear until her head spun and her lip bled.

'A wild goose chase! You sent us on a bloody wild goose chase! You bitch. Your brother was right about you!'

'Get the horses saddled again. You Girl, will take me this time and afterwards I will enjoy taming you!'

This time Helena took him a faster route to the new destination, a small copse. She pointed to the tree the treasure was buried under.

'You dig there!' she said.

Grehi pushed her out of the way and dug the hole himself. After an hour of cursing and sweating like a pig he uncovered the bag and opening it said, 'Yes, it is what I need. Let's get back.'

Back at the villa he put the bag on the kitchen table after inspecting it closely. 'Now for dinner and a celebration. Your best wine. Get it! And then you can provide me with some entertainment.' She shivered knowing his sort of entertainment would be best served in the bed-chamber.

She would have to take the risk and drug his wine and hope Dreda's men would come before he recovered. She administered the drug and waited for the results.

After dinner the men sat in the salon steadily getting more foxed. Grehi called Helena to sit beside him and slid his arm round her, opening the high buttoned dress she was wearing like a suit of armour, shielding her against his ardour.

She tried not to stiffen and show her repulsion for him, but he could read it in her eyes. He laughed a mirthless laugh and said, 'I will teach you soon to like and respect me my girl!' Helena didn't answer knowing defiance would make him want her more. He yawned and said,

'The ride must have tired me. Don't worry I won't disappoint you in the sack my Lady!'

He pulled her up and led her up the stairs to his chamber. Closing the door, he said, 'Strip very slowly. Let's see how a high-born whore looks like!' He lay down on the bed having undone his shirt and pulled off his breeches.

Helena's mind whirled as she tried to think how to get herself out of this horrific position. She heard a noise from a distance and her heart leapt. It sounded like horsemen. But they were still too far away to help her. She had to help herself. He looked sleepy. Could she make him wait a little longer?

She reached for her hooks on her dress and pretended to fumble with them. 'Damn the things,' she said. 'I need my abigail, but I sent her away.'

'Let me,' said Grehi getting off the bed in haste. Pulling her to him he tried opening the hooks, but they were made for dexterous small female fingers and he made a mess of the business.

Impatiently he said, 'Undo them quickly or I will cut the bodice off you.' Helena took him at his word and this time opened them more skilfully, slipping her bodice slowly off her shoulders until they were bare, and the garment fell around her waist.

Grehi took a deep breath, overwhelmed by her loveliness and then growled, 'The rest. Take them off quickly!'

Helena's body felt ice cold as despair overwhelmed her. She had long given up the idea of marrying for love but the thought of losing her virginity to this sordid uncouth degenerate man made her want to throw herself out of the window and end it all. Even the brothel now seemed preferable to this fate.

She undressed, taking everything off except her chemise, a delicate lace affair; one of the few luxuries she allowed herself.

'Over here.' She sat on the uncovered bed with him. He pulled her to him and her natural reactions took over and she tried to fight him off, but he held her by one shoulder in a vice like grip.

'We no longer need your help to find the treasure. Your servants will be dead, one by one, the longer you resist! It is your choice!' He stared at her with eyes that were as cold as a fish on a costermonger's slab. 'Your choice!' he repeated. 'How loyal are you to your staff?'

They were like family to her although she believed she was only delaying the inevitable. She and all her servants would be dead when these men left. They would not leave anyone who would tell tales.

'I choose their lives,' she replied proudly and started to pull off her chemise when the door crashed open and Denman strode in.

Taking in the scene his eyes hardened. Helena shivered, and her blood ran cold when she saw his facial expression. She had never seen such fury in any man's eyes before. This was a new man in front of her, a vengeful man!

Jaw hardened, his eyes narrowed; he had the look of a man who wanted retribution. He smiled, a smile which not quite reach his eyes. He would enjoy dishing this man what he dealt out to a much weaker girl who could not fight back.

'Out!' he said to Helena. 'I will handle this scum!' He threw her dress to her and before Grehi could reach for his gun and sword he had his own sword at his foe's throat. Helena grabbed her dress and slipped out of the room where she met Thomatz and another officer she was unfamiliar with.

'My servants?' she cried, holding the dress against herself. The officers, gentlemen, looked away and Thomatz opened a bed-chamber door for her and ushered her in.

'All your servants are safe and uninjured. We have the other bandits shut like rats in a trap in the stable. Dress and come down to the salon when you feel able Ma'am.'

Hadreni went to Denman who had Grehi by the throat, throttling the breath out of him. He had never seen so much anger blazing out of Denman's eyes, a murderous expression cloaking his face. Grehi had a black eye and a cut lip and was bent over double.

'Leave him now,' ordered Hadreni. 'He is worth more alive than dead to Dreda.'

'Thank your lucky stars my Commander wants you alive,' said Denman shaking him like a rat. 'I would have enjoyed killing you slowly!' He walked out leaving the man for Hadreni to manacle.

Knocking on the door, he waited anxiously for Helena to let him in. White in face and bearing Grehi's cuts and bruises, she looked otherwise unscathed. He asked the question he feared to ask.

'Were we in time?' She coloured and replied, 'Yes thank God. My virtue is still secure.' He nodded, relief washing over him. 'I will meet you downstairs Ma'am when you feel ready to come down.'

'Wait!' she asked. 'Is Grehi still alive?'

'Just! But he will be feeling uncomfortable for a while,' he said maliciously. She saw his hands were bruised and bloody and when

Grehi was dragged from his room the man had broken teeth and a livid bruise around his neck. He walked bent, almost crouched, as if his stomach was paining him. His eyes met Denman and he seemed to shrink. He was patently terrified of the officer.

Helena was glad Denman had not killed the man in cold blood although she had wanted him to suffer for the way he had treated her and her servants. She still was not sure she liked this ruthless Denman. He felt her withdraw again. She clearly wanted away from him. How could he reach this girl? She rebuffed him at every turn. When he had bloody rescued her yet again, instead of launching herself into his arms as he wanted and thanking him, she had showed her distaste for him.

Leaving her before his emotions could overwhelm him he ran downstairs. A tide of anger had risen engulfing him, pushing rational thought away. If that man had violated her even the threat of Dreda's wrath would not have stopped him killing him.

He might say to himself he was only her rescuer but the idea of another man taking her maidenhead chilled him to the bone. He was insanely jealous of any man who wanted to take her to his bed. She was his and only his and it was his right to take her innocence. She might only see him as a friend but in his own mind she was his woman.

A flash of reality hit him. He realised he had loved her since she had played the music for him at her farm. No other woman could reach him like this feisty, managing girl did. Wise beyond her years and brave and loyal to those who loved and served her she had won his heart without even trying. The tragedy was he knew not how to win her love.

He was certain she liked him and was attracted to him. She could not deny herself when he kissed her, and her responses were the most passionate kisses he had enjoyed with a girl. He knew if he could take her to his bed he would make sure she didn't want to ever leave it.

She could not deny the chemistry that flowed between them, making him feel alive when she was with him in his arms. But it was not enough. He wanted more than physical chemistry. He wanted her spirit, her love. Without that his love would be slowly extinguished like a flame without life giving oxygen as he suffered the disappointment of living without Helena's love.

Despondent, he met his colleagues down in the salon where they now relaxed with a glass of fine brandy.

'Well!' said Hadreni having heard of Denman's infatuation with this tall blond. 'When are we to hear the wedding bells?' A scowl came over Denman's face. 'What do you mean by that remark?' he asked in his most scathing voice.

'I thought you would pop the question now the lady sees you as her knight in shining armour,' said his irreverent friend.

'The lady in question views me only as a friend,' said Denman wanting to change the subject.

'Oh, I might try for her myself then,' replied Hadreni egging the pudding. He had never seen his easy-going friend so wound up by a woman.

'If you value your teeth I would keep your lecherous hands off her,' snapped Denman, his brown eyes turning cold and dark; no warmth in them. 'She is innocent still and too good for the likes of you.'

'Just good friends eh!' mocked Hadreni.

'Stow it, Hadreni,' snarled his friend and walked out the room to smoke a cheroot.

'He has been bitten badly,' remarked Hadreni.

'I could almost feel sorry for him,' said Thomatz. 'The great lover brought to his feet by a girl nearly half his age. He is scared she doesn't return his feelings. Too scared to propose to her.'

'Is she immune to the great Denman charm?' asked Hadreni astonished. He had never known Denman fail to win a woman over in the past.

'Not at all! All the Bureau men and Felea think she is half in love with him but she denies it as does he his feelings. She doesn't think she is good enough for him given her family reputation.'

'Perhaps they need a push.' Hadreni teased Denman unmercifully but he had suffered a miserable affair himself and wouldn't wish that agony on anyone. He had found his own lady was merely toying with him wanting a younger man for fun.

He was frequently blue-devilled himself and didn't want to be reminded of his lack-lustre love life. He never entered serious relationships with women now, only using them to satisfy his sexual needs. Women were dangerous and best kept at an emotional distance. He would hold off the teasing. He wanted Denman to be happy.

'Felea may intervene. Denman has been so miserable lately, a shadow of his normal self. She may talk to the young girl and find out how strong her feelings are toward him.'

'Here's to a happy resolution,' said Hadreni emptying his glass.

Denman came back calm and relaxed after time on his own. 'And what about you my friend,' he asked Hadreni. 'Any particular lady on your horizon? Will we hear an announcement soon?' he tormented. He immediately regretted his words when Hadreni's eyes narrowed and a shutter came down on his face. It was as if a black cloud had descended over him and engulfed him. His friend had suffered the megrims for the last few years after leaving his regiment.

'You know after Liza there will be no permanent lady in my life. I have enough willing women to suffice me in other ways.'

'What will you do after this mission?' asked Denman, changing the subject to a less sensitive subject, recognising his friend was still sore about his former lady. All Hadreni's friends had been devastated when he had left the army in disgrace.

'Go back to the family farm I guess,' shrugged Hadreni 'and help my father. My brother is still too young and carefree to take on the responsibility of the farm. I wish he would bloody grow up faster. He is much more suited to a rural life than I am.'

'You will be wasted there,' said Denman. 'You will be bored stiff in a month. You are born to lead Man. The army suited you down to the ground but as you can't go back surely the militia is better than nothing.'

'Dreda said that he may want me to develop an intelligence unit in the Bureau. Ordinary militia work is too slow for me but that might work. I will wait to see if he creates the unit.'

Denman wanted to shake his friend out of his depressive malaise and make him enjoy life again. He was too intelligent to manage a farm and needed stimulation. The army would have taken him back despite the scandal he had left behind him, but he refused to entertain the idea.

Denman spoke harshly. 'Well, stop burying yourself at your farm. Licking your wounds for ever won't help. There are many decent girls out there if you look for them instead of sticking with your bits of fluff.'

'Stubble it Denman! You are the last man who should give romantic advice. That girl in the kitchen makes doe eyes at you and all you do is back off.'

Hadreni stalked out of the room, angry because his friend had spoken the truth. He was full of self-pity and his life lacked direction. His army career was ruined; he could no longer trust himself to keep his temper and make the right decisions. He hated the idea of going back to his father's villa. The old man was a domestic tyrant and disliked his elder son. They rubbed each other up the wrong way and Hadreni felt suffocated there.

His trust fund gave him financial independence from his father, but he had nowhere else to go except his lodgings in town. He had had his fill of idle pursuits like gambling and horse racing after a busy fulfilling army career which had stretched him to the limits. He was a man who needed to keep busy, to embrace something which would keep his sharp mind absorbed. He was blue-devilled and bored.

He knew there were good women in society. Dreda had found Felea and this new girl of Denman he laughingly called a friend was of the same kidney; honest, forthright and passionate. He just was not prepared to take the risk and be hurt again. He would stick to his expensive birds of fancy who knew what he was offering and accepted no long-term commitment. He would go back to the farm the next day after reporting to Dreda.

Helena sent her groom to her only friend in the locality asking for her servants to be sent back. She took over the kitchen and presented a meal fit for a king to her rescuers. She liked to work to forget her woes.

All Denman had done was to ask her if she was still a virgin. He was cool and distant to her although she could not forget the look of anger in his eyes when he had held Grehi by the throat. That was not ordinary anger. It was the wrath of a man goaded beyond endurance by the other's actions. She could almost believe he was jealous of the man trying to take her virtue but then he had not even held or comforted her and had just walked away.

How she had wanted to rest her head on his shoulder and be held in those strong arms, to feel secure for once. For years she had been the de facto head of the family, taking on the responsibilities of a woman much older than her years. She enjoyed her responsibilities but had been fighting adversity for years. The failed harvest had made her draw on her reserves of money and she worried for the future. She felt tired and just for once she wanted someone occasionally to take the burdens off her shoulders, a man as strong, resilient and reliable like Denman.

She had acted coolly herself, feeling she must keep him at a distance after that last passionate kiss. She had felt him withdraw from her; the easy relationship that had developed between them having dissipated and the kind gentle man having been replaced by a cold detached militia officer who only cared for her safety.

She felt like hitting him herself. Cool to the point of detachment herself, she wondered why Denman of all men could raise her to anger.

Denman came in bringing a deer and two rabbits he had shot. In the hills, absorbed, hunting, his internal rage had calmed down. No longer did he want to spit Grehi and watch him die painfully. He must try to remain detached and calm around Helena. He had tried to avoid her, but it was easier said than done. He had this overwhelming desire to hug her and promise her she would be safe and secure in the future.

He would look after her but what if she said she no longer needed him now the danger was over. She had not given him any reason to think she preferred him over her other rescuers. He thought gloomily, *she only wanted me while I was of use to her in my capacity as militia officer.*

'Wonderful!' she cried. 'We were going to be on short rations with all these extra bodies to feed.' He noted she had gained her colour back and was laughing and smiling, the former mischievous Helena restored again. Now in control over her little empire she was relaxed, but he was taut as a stretched rope, ready to break if pulled too far.

It was all he could do to prevent himself pulling her into his arms and kissing her senseless, he wanted her so much. He stood his back to the door watching her, unwilling to leave. She felt uneasy. He looked as if he wanted to say something, but he merely stared at her, deathly silent, the opposite of his usual jovial talkative self.

Wanting to break the uncomfortable silence she asked, 'Has Officer Dreda a new mission for you when you get back to the city?' He appreciated her opening up the neutral subject, the atmosphere in the kitchen remaining heavy and oppressive. There was too much history between them, too many painful memories and insults to be ignored. He wished he could take back the rash words he had uttered. Helena was not one to bear grudges, but she was sensitive, and he had hurt her badly.

'There are always new problems to be solved and it is more interesting recently since one rebel leader was killed but a stronger more resourceful person has taken his place.'

'More dangerous as well?' she asked. He watched her keenly. Did he see alarm in her eyes? Did she care for him a little?

'No worse than before. Dreda has strengthened his militia force with ex-army men who are more experienced than ever before.'

'Good!' she stated emphatically. 'I would hate to see you lose your life unnecessarily.'

Encouraged, he came forward a little and put his hands on her shoulders. 'No more than I would like to see you injured Ma'am. I would hate to see you lose your life unnecessarily. You could work for us if you were a man. You anticipated what could go wrong and delayed those men to give us time to get here. Your strategy and implementation of your plan was masterful, only surmounted by your bravery and loyalty to your people. My officers salute your bravery Ma'am!'

She coloured and said, 'Thank you Officer but I only did what I thought necessary at the time. Officer Dreda had helped me when I was in trouble and I wanted to net those bandits as a thank you to him.

'We have ridden the area of a scourge now thankfully. He will be deeply grateful to you and there should be a substantial reward.'

He knew what she was going to say and putting a finger on her lips he prevented her from answering. 'I know you don't want it, but you need it as well as your uncle's dowry. Swallow your pride Ma'am. You could do much good with the money. Build a school for instance for the local children or an orphanage.'

She had mentioned these in the past and nodded. He was a caring, gentle man who would take ruthless decisions when necessary but despite his privileged background she had heard he still helped the widows and orphans of the rebels he had fought. He bore no grudges against the rebels' women.

She allowed herself one-minute resting close to him, her eyes gazing into his, wanting to prolong that moment for ever but then she mentally shook herself. She was not his. He would want to marry a woman with an untainted reputation who could bring wealth and status to his family not the sister of an alleged criminal.

She pulled herself gently away from him, turning to the window, not seeing the disappointment cloud his face. 'I had better gut these animals and get them roasting for our feast this evening.' He stood back, bowed and left the room feeling gutted himself. He took his stallion out for another ride, to dissipate his frustration and make himself fit for human company that evening.

Over dinner she discussed her position with the officers. 'You should be safe here, but we will leave two officers.' said Hadreni. 'They are junior officers, but army trained and good fighters in the event of more trouble.'

'What of Grehi?'

'My intelligence suggests he is involved in many illegal schemes,' explained Hadreni.

'Officer Hadreni used to be an intelligence officer in the army,' stated Thomatz 'and helps Officer Dreda if there is a particularly complex situation which needs detailed information.'

'And Officer Thomatz here used to be a military policeman and scout and has antennae everywhere. He digs out information for me.'

'Officer Dreda has many talented men working for him,' commented Helena.

'He recruits his men from ex-army men he worked with or are recommended by officers he knows well.'

'And what of you Officer Denman?' she asked, focusing her attention on him. He had sat quietly during the meal his silence being noticed by all. He merely shrugged. 'I help Officer Dreda run the office and solve some of the complex cases when an experienced officer is required.'

'Don't be modest Denman,' said Thomatz. 'Denman was a colonel in the army alongside Dreda. Dreda was the strategist and Denman the expert implementer. They worked with Hadreni here and demolished the rebel army's uprisings time and time again. He smiled. 'Officer Dreda describes Denman here as his right-hand man, a man he cannot do without when trouble surfaces. He said he could rise further in the organisation if he wished. Under this cavalier exterior is a sharp brain Ma'am.'

'Thank you for outlining my virtues,' said Denman embarrassed. 'I am retiring to bed. I promised I would visit my parents on my way back tomorrow. It will mean a detour and a long journey. Goodnight Gentlemen and my Lady.' He rose and went out for his last cheroot. He then went to bed, falling asleep immediately having ridden for two days and then fought his way into the villa and up to the bed-chamber.

He left early, only going into the kitchen to shake the hand of Helena and wish her well.

'God speed Officer Denman. I hope you find your family well.

'I am sure I will. Look after yourself Ma'am,' he said and turned on his heel and left, not wanting to read the expression on her face as she was left standing alone there in the kitchen.

Helena took the milk jug she was holding and threw it at the wall. All her frustration and misery were expressed in that violent action. She was angry at herself and at Denman. Neither would trust each other and say what they really felt.

She understood Denman's character now. Underneath that easy-going jovial manner was a private man who rarely discussed his feelings with all but Dreda and his parents. To the outside world he seemed supremely confident, but this outer shell hid a sensitive caring man who would not show his true feelings for fear of getting hurt. She was not the woman who could break down that barrier and make him trust a woman with his heart. She must forget him for ever.

Chapter eighteen.

His parents greeted him fondly as usual, but they knew something was amiss. He seemed to have itchy feet, to be moody, snappy; unable to relax. His father, sick of the tension, finally challenged him to tell him what was on his mind. He knew his son and had felt he had been preoccupied with something or someone for a while now.

'Have the stallions mounted the mares yet?

'Yes, the mares are in foal. Helena adored the stallion and asked me to thank you again.

'Do you intend to see her again?'

'I doubt she will be going to the city for a long while.'

'So, you will have to go to see her.'

'Apart from going to bring the stallion back there will be no need for me to go there.'

'Bring her here then, your mother and I would like to meet her again. We liked her when we met her before. She was unpretentious and intelligent; unlike the vacuous featherheads you usually have on your arm.'

'There is no reason to bring her here.'

Exasperated, his father lost his patience with his eldest son. 'What are your intentions toward this young girl? City rumour would have had you married off months ago but then you neglected her until a certain Count presented himself as competition against you. You have helped her become independent and done more for her than you have ever done for a woman before. But you pretend she is nothing to you. Do you love her?'

Denman was taken aback at this attack. His father, a smooth, polished ex-diplomat was rarely this direct. His mother would have intervened if she felt he was too harsh and overbearing but she agreed with him this time; his son was for once indecisive and prevaricating. She was curious to hear his answer.

Backed into a corner, Denman finally sighed and said, 'Yes, I love her dearly, but I don't know if she wants to marry anyone, particularly me. She likes my company. I think she finds me attractive, but I have no idea if she wishes to marry me.

'She has often told me to back off and keep out of her affairs. She is too independent and now has to choose whether she wants to remain her own mistress.'

'How can you she chose if you do not tell her and offer for her? Invite her to Thomas's birthday party. Ask her! It is the only way you will find out.

Her son was non-committal. His mother wanted to shake him. He was usually decisive and could be stubborn, brave and reckless. It was unusual for him to be so uncertain. This girl must have really rocked his confidence.

As a mother she wanted her son to be happy, but he had lived an easy, charmed life and it would do him good to live with a woman who didn't fall at his feet and challenged him occasionally. This girl might keep him on his toes and fulfil him. She put him on the spot the next morning. He agreed she could invite Helena to the party, but he would not say whether he would propose. She had to be satisfied with that.

The invitation astounded Helena. His mother had made it clear it was not a grand do, a simple country affair, no new gowns were needed. Only the family and a few friends would be there. Dreda and Felea would be invited so she would not feel alone. With mixed feelings she wrote back saying she would go. She arrived in the evening tired and soon went to bed.

Felea and Dreda had already arrived. Denman wanted moral support. He felt he was being coerced into proposing by his parents. He was only reluctant to make an offer because he feared a rejection. Helena was a closed book and such a contrary girl.

Approached when in the wrong mood she might reject him out of hand without considering his offer.

Dreda understood his position having been unsure of Felea's love before he proposed. Man, to man, he said he had never seen his friend so unsettled, so restless and so flat as recently. He believed there was a natural connection between this girl and his friend. Denman had been so happy in the city when they went to the theatre. At balls they danced together as if they were made for each other.

Felea went on the attack with Helena, trying to find out how she really felt about Denman. Denman really needed to know if it was worth proposing or his confidence would be shattered. Helena was her trusted confidante and she would find out if she really wanted to be independent and remain unmarried or if she had used that as an excuse to ward off Denman when he was trying to force her to betray Lucia.

Helena started on the topic of the horses and Felea found out how kind and generous she thought Denman was.

'I don't know how I can repay him for the help he has given me with the stallion.'

'Denman doesn't want to be paid back. He is as rich as Croesus and his father frequently lends his stallions to others when his mares are in foal. He likes helping people.'

'He has helped me so often. He always seems to be there when I need him. I am ashamed to have put him to so much trouble. He must think I am a nuisance; I am ashamed I had to lie to him. He has never forgiven me for the lies I told him.'

'He doesn't think anything of the sort. He told Francis he understood why you lied to him and thought you were accurate in your description of the Count and his family.'

Felea was not entirely satisfied with Helena's attitude toward Denman. It was more of affection for a brother or cousin than a lover. Denman was not the sort of man who would want a milk and water miss who would marry him for gratitude. He would want her total love, passion and commitment.

She changed the subject and talked about the Count. Helena said how angry he had made her, calling her names and whereas Denman let her ride his stallion the Count would not even let her near his horses and said stockbreeding was not a job for a woman.

Denman could be insufferably bossy, but he did not belittle women and he respected a woman's achievements. He could not tolerate slackers like her late brother. Denman was clearly high in her estimation but whether she loved him Felea couldn't tell.

Felea decided to be brave. Very few people knew her whole story, but she told it to Helena warts and all.

'My father was a traitor who helped decode messages for the rebels. I helped him not knowing how heavily he was embroiled in the rebel cause until it was too late. My family was investigated by Francis and I bolted, trying to reach my father who had escaped. Francis chased me and saved me from being violated by one of his officers. I lived under his protection and he fell in love with me despite mistrusting women. He proposed to me but then he was injured and could not remember the proposal and his love for me.

'I was so hurt I decided to leave the city and I became engaged to another man who Francis later found to be an enemy of the state. He recovered his memory and acted as guard when I journeyed to my nuptials. He didn't want me to marry my fiancé and told me he would make me unhappy, but I would not admit my mistake.

'In the event, he kidnapped me and brought me back to the city. I thought he had given the order to massacre some rebels and rebuffed him when he said he still wanted me in his bed. I also refused to be seen by him as an object of pity when the Emperor called me a spoiled dove, no longer innocent.

'I told Francis I would not tolerate a man who made a duty marriage to please the Emperor. Luckily, he persuaded me that he had suffered from shock and now loved me as intensely as before the explosion which caused him to suffer loss of memory.

'He is a hard and difficult man to live with but is changing for the better and makes me happy. I nearly lost him because when he hurt me I pushed him away instead of waiting for him to recover his memory and understand his own emotions.'

Helena would never betray her friend's confession to others. She understood what Felea was hinting at. She had acted coldly toward Denman, partly because she was ashamed of lying to him and partly out of fear of rejection after being jilted publicly by her fiancé. She had loved her fiancé, a very immature young love but her heart had been broken when he told her father he would not marry beneath him into a scandal rocked family. She had sworn never to get close to a man again or let one dominate her.

That was why she had lashed verbally out at the Count after he had called her such cruel and untrue names. The interview with the Count had brought back the memory of all the insults she had suffered from her fiancé's mother.

'If you love Denman and I think you do you must show it to him. He is confused as to your feelings but has been so miserable since you left town. He was always so light-hearted, but he is a changed man, as if the light has gone out of his life.'

Helena took a deep breath and explained the thing worrying her. 'Felea, Denman comes from the top drawer, a diplomatic family. How could they accept the impoverished sister of a drunkard, a gambler, a libertine and now an alleged criminal? They would think I was dragging his family's name through the dirt, staining them.'

'Nonsense,' said Felea. 'You have met his parents. His sister married a merchant, no member of the haut ton. They like the person not the title. Denman is not a snob, and neither are they. He said they liked you and wanted to meet you again. Think about it!'

A master strategist like her husband she then turned the subject to dresses and how long Helena's hair had grown. A thoroughly feminine argument about the merits of silk or taffeta ensued and both women were happy at the progress of the evening.

Dreda caught Denman that evening and told him Felea had spoken with Helena. 'Felea thinks she loves you but her position is more complicated than we thought. She feels she is not good enough to marry into your family with her tarnished family reputation.'

'What nonsense!' remonstrated Denman.

'Don't snap my head off. I am only the messenger. She has had shoulders turned against her at court because of her brother's reputation. Her fiancé jilted her. You must reassure her you are not worried about status. She thinks you would only ask her to be your mistress. You could only offer her a carte blanche. Marriage would be too good for her family.'

'What absolute balderdash! I cannot believe what I am hearing?'

'Remember she is still a young girl who has been jilted by one fiancé and insulted by both men and women. She may have grown up fast, but I bet she read those gothic novels when she was a romantically inclined young girl. You know the sort where the older son has to marry for status and rejects the poorer girl who marries another for security.'

'I will have to persuade her there can be a happy ending then,' said Denman understanding Helena a little better now. He would think his strategy out.

The party was the next evening. Twenty people were there including Denman's younger brother on leave from the army. He noticed Helena and made a bee line for her. A younger version of his elder brother he charmed her and claimed the first dance.

A fast country dance was executed until they were breathless. He returned to his elder brother claiming she was one of the most charming and intelligent women he had met. Denman agreed and said, 'Unfortunately she is not available to you. You would not suit. She is too industrious for you and too independent. She would rule you in a second.'

'How would you know?'

'I have sparred with her and lost on several occasions. She has fooled me, and I am a senior ex-army officer, not a raw subaltern.'

His brother's arrogance made him laugh and he thought he would try his luck with this new girl. He asked her for the first waltz and laughing they twirled around until the world spun round.

He then took her out to the garden pool and showed her the garden and the river which flowed at the end. A perfect gentleman, when it was cold he gave her his coat and they stood on the bridge watching the river flowing in the moonlight. They were rudely interrupted by his brother.

Denman put his hand on his brother's shoulder. Thomas turned around, surprised at this firm and not so friendly grip which was so fierce he could feel it biting through his uniform. He raised his brows at Denman inquiringly.

'Thomas please take this young lady indoors immediately. She doesn't want to appear compromised.'

Turning to Helena he said, 'Your exit with my brother has been noted by others Ma'am. Come in now if you want to avoid a scandal.' He stalked back to the villa and waited at the door for them, not saying another word. His face told another story. Dark with anger he could barely contain his rage.

He was maddened further by his brother's nonchalant manner. Thomas walked Helena casually in without haste now, frowning at his elder brother's bad humour. His cavalier attitude enraged Denman further.

He exploded! 'This girl has had her reputation besmirched enough without adding fuel to the fire,' he raged at his brother. 'And you should know better,' he snapped at Helena.

'Oh, come on, old fellow, it is only a country party! Who will tell about an innocent walk by the river? You over-exaggerate. Don't be melodramatic.'

Denman, knowing he was making a drama out of nothing, became even angrier. He wanted to talk to Helena privately.

'I think you had better leave Thomas. This lady and I need to speak further!'

Thomas looked at Denman and Helena, deciding this tussle was more about his brother's possessiveness over Helena than a mere walk by the river. He would make a poor third in this discussion.

'If you are sure you wish me to leave you, Ma'am,' he said to Helena, ignoring his brother seething there.

'I am perfectly safe with your brother,' said Helena and turned to Denman to face the music.

Once reassured Helena was comfortable with his brother Thomas left, amazed at his brother's prudishness. Denman had never discussed morality with him before and his past reputation did not bear looking into.

When his brother left Denman let rip. 'You do not care for your reputation despite my efforts to protect you in the past. You are not at home, a country bumpkin. You are expected to behave like a lady in my parents' home. I am here tonight but I will not always be available to protect you. A man could easily take advantage of you if you go into the garden alone with him. This hoydenish behaviour can't be tolerated if you wish to be called a lady!'

She replied quietly, 'I know I am not good enough to be here with your family. I will leave tomorrow and not taint your family with my presence any longer!'

She turned away from him, but he stood in her path demanding, 'What nonsense is this about, you not being good enough to socialise with my family. You are as good as them and your behaviour at the farm showed you are brave and loyal.'

'But I behave like a hoyden and don't care for my reputation. Your words Officer!'

'I think you are naïve and allow men to become too intimate with you. You encourage them to be too friendly and will attract the wrong kind. Young ladies should remain modest and discourage the attentions of young men.'

It was the final straw. She had had enough of this moralising. She tore him off a strip.

'Who are you, a known womaniser who flaunts your mistresses in full view of society to give me lesson in morality?'

Hands on hips, she gave him an assessment of his character. 'You are a hypocrite, a bully and have too much time on your hands. Why do you have to constantly interfere in my business? I was not seducing your brother; I thought him a gentleman, unlike you, who kissed me when I was vulnerable.' She flung these words at him, eyes flashing, shaking with rage.

In his heart Denman knew her words were partially true, and he was jealous of Thomas's time with her, but it did not make him act any more rationally. Pent up frustration led him to grab her by the shoulders and when she tried to slap him he could not control his rage any longer. He held her by the elbows and said, 'You will listen to me, you disobedient girl. I am much older than you and know the danger you put yourself in.'

She countered with 'You are not my father and why you want to master me I don't know. I wouldn't want you for a father, you would be too prudish.'

'Your father?' He looked dumbstruck.

'Yes, you are always so severe and tell me off all the time as if you would be my guardian or my master. I treat my servants less dictatorially than you do me.'

Everything now fell into place for Denman. He now saw himself as she saw him, not in the role of frustrated rescuer and lover but as a severe militiaman, moraliser and older man who wanted to dominate her, like the Count. His jealously had made him act out of character. Felea with Helena's permission had hinted that Helena had appreciated he was more generous and kind than the Count, but she hated the way he ordered her around. It was time to show her he was not a domineering old man.

'I don't want to be your father or guardian and never did. I was put in a position of moral responsibility after your brother died and I had a conflict of interest. I could not tell you how I felt. You have not treated me as anything other than a kind friend, in fact like an elder brother. If I have been severe it was because I was protecting, you. I thought at times you were attracted to me, but you only showed me gratitude.

I assure you I have no fatherly feelings toward you at all. Rather the opposite. I have been wanting to make love to you since the first day I saw you. You are right I am a womaniser, but I have never seduced an innocent girl. I have some morals left! He took her face in his hands and looked tenderly into her eyes and kissed her gently on the lips.

'You are the most desirable girl I have ever met. I had never suffered jealousy until I saw you surrounded every evening by men queuing up to dance with you and you never gave me any encouragement. Then your aunt told me to back off as I was too interested and was compromising you. I would destroy your chances of a marriage.'

This honesty took her aback. He was baring his soul to her, but he still had not said he loved her. He clearly lusted for her. She had been right when she thought he had held her deliberately too close when dancing and when she was on his horse. She was determined now to find out if he really loved her. She knew she loved him but wanted him to commit himself. Did he want a mistress or a wife?

She had to tread carefully. She didn't want to lose him. She remembered Felea's advice about being honest with this particular man about her feelings.

'You gave me attention and took me to the theatre and I was so happy, but you treated me like Felea, a friend and when you backed away I thought you wanted no commitment. We were at cross-purposes due to other peoples' interference. Years ago, I was jilted by my fiancé and I have always been of wary of men who could betray me.' She smiled tenderly up at him, with green-blue eyes he could drown in.

'I have always shied away from commitment but no longer, I now know what I want, you!' he said. Letting go her face he took her into his arms to kiss her properly, but she still wasn't sure.

'What do you want of me? Tell me!' she demanded.

'I love you and I want you to become my wife.'

Getting the answer, she had been waiting for she entwined her arms around his neck and kissed him back passionately as the kiss deepened. For the first time in years she felt totally secure and loved.

Content, Denman look forward to his future. He was as interested in horse breeding as she and could mix that with helping her run the family farm and a job in the militia in the city. With his family fortune, he could inject capital into the stock needed to build up a good blood line and return her uncle's money. When the stud farm became too big for her to manage alone he would leave the militia.

He put this to Helena and she agreed. It was if a burden had been taken off their shoulders and their future was settled.

The end.

About this author.

This author studied history and politics and then business and law. She became a law and economics lecturer in Higher Education and later left to start her own tutoring agency. She has since run a guesthouse and lives with her husband and two crazy Birman cats in a restored cottage near to a canal in Knowle in England. Many of the novels derive from the cases she read during her teaching career.

She enjoys Zumba and yoga. She loves art and illustrates her own book covers. Her current passion is making succulent and cacti bowls for her gazebo where she likes to write in the summer.

She also writes romantic suspense and crime novels under the name of Toni Bolton and books for children under the name of Dawn Bolton.

Dawn loves communicating with readers. To be sent her newsletter please use the contact details below.

Contact Dawn Bolton on Facebook.

Alexie Bolton's Facebook page

dawnbolton@Twitter2

Dawn Bolton. Email
kixley@btinternet.com

Books by this author.

Historical novels by Alexie Bolton.

The Spymaster's Redeemer. Book 1, Dreda's Men, available on Amazon and Kindle

Crime and romantic Suspense novels by Toni Bolton.

Escape From fear. Book one of the 'Men of Valour, Women of steel series, available on Amazon and Kindle.

Whisper Softly or You're Dead. Available February on Amazon and Kindle.

'A blinding flash.' In the anthology, 'Hey you, I think I love you'. Cree Nations and Liberty Parker. Available on Amazon and Kindle.